RACING HEART

CW01391579

Also by Darci St. John

Crash into Me

RACING HEART

DARCI ST. JOHN

Bedford Square
Publishers

First published in the UK in 2025 by Bedford Square Publishers Ltd,
London, UK

bedfordsquarepublishers.co.uk
@bedsqpublishers

© Darci St. John, 2025

The right of Darci St. John to be identified as the author of this work has been
asserted in accordance with the Copyright, Designs and Patents Act 1988. All
rights reserved. No part of this book may be reproduced, stored in or introduced
into a retrieval system, or transmitted, in any form or by any means (electronic,
mechanical, photocopying, recording or otherwise) without the written
permission of the publishers.

Any person who does any unauthorised act in relation to this publication
may be liable to criminal prosecution and civil claims for damages.
A CIP catalogue record for this book is available from the British Library.
This is a work of fiction. Names, characters, places, and incidents either
are the product of the author's imagination or are used fictitiously,
and any resemblance to actual persons, living or dead, businesses,
companies, events or locales is entirely coincidental.

ISBN
978-1-83501-192-8 (Paperback)
978-1-83501-193-5 (eBook)

2 4 6 8 10 9 7 5 3 1

The manufacturer's authorised representative in the EU for
product safety is Easy Access System Europe, Mustamäe tee 50, 10621 Tallinn,
Estonia
gpsr.requests@easproject.com

Typeset by Palimpsest Book Production Limited, Falkirk, Stirlingshire

Printed in Great Britain by CPI Group (UK) Ltd, Croydon CR0 4YY

MIX
Paper | Supporting
responsible forestry
FSC
www.fsc.org
FSC® C013604

For my mother, Barbara Gean, the original Barb.
I miss you every day.

Chapter 1

Jordan Rubie had been itching to get out of town, to go somewhere. Anywhere. But even after traveling some 3,000 miles, he was still at loose ends – not to mention, bored.

So. Damn. Bored.

For most of his adult life, Jordan had spent nine months of the year circling the globe as a race car driver in the World Apex Grand Prix Motorsport Series. But a dramatic crash the summer before had ended his career, along with the only over-scheduled life he'd ever known.

His twin sister's wedding in Scotland had given him the perfect reason to pull out his passport again. On a whim, he'd decided to head across the pond early and stay at another race car driver's cottage in North Wales. Except he hadn't anticipated the only real change being the scenery – although he had to admit, Snowdon's distant mountain peaks provided a slightly better backdrop than the pine trees surrounding his private lake in southeast Michigan.

But other than that, he was still alone – and lost. Apparently, without a racetrack teeming with other cars to follow, he lacked direction. Which might explain why he'd rarely stood at the top of the podium, if he was in the mood to ponder his mediocre-at-best driving career.

He was not.

Since arriving in the village of Abersoch, Jordan had done little more than rotate between his friend Wyn's cottage and a bright turquoise beach hut and a blanket on the sand. Each day, the beach had emptied quickly as the dinner hour neared, almost as if the sun turned into a massive clock that signaled it was time to go home. And everyone obeyed, packing up beach tents and toys and dragging sand-covered kids toward the car park.

Today was turning out to be more of the same. Within minutes of the sun's usual magic trick, all that remained was a flock of seagulls, a mom coaxing her small son out of the Irish Sea, and him, a 34-year-old man sneaking sips from a flask and trying far too hard to relax.

That is until, out of the corner of his eye, Jordan glimpsed a woman walking down the beach. Even from a distance, she was far more interesting than the kid screaming bloody murder from the water, especially since she appeared to be making a beeline for his beach towel. He turned around, expecting to see someone standing behind him, but found nothing but more sand and the line of brightly colored beach huts.

After another nip of Scotch whisky, he squinted into the late afternoon sun. She would hardly be the first woman to appear out of nowhere with a bone to pick with him, but he didn't recognise her. Brunettes had never been his first choice, back in the day when he'd had his fair share of fangirls clamoring to climb into his bed. She was also shorter than the women he typically went for, not that height was a limiting factor if the mood was right.

The woman stumbled in the thick sand but managed to right herself and continue on her collision course.

'Hey, there,' Jordan called out as she drew closer.

No response.

Her face was becoming clearer as she neared, but not any more familiar — and it was one he would've remembered, Scotch or no Scotch. With a button nose and full rosy lips, she was the type of girl who was pretty whether she was made up and dressed to the nines, lounging around in sweatpants or, even better, wearing nothing at all.

Of course, there was a chance she was a racing fan. Apex drivers didn't enjoy the luxury of anonymity in this part of the world like in the United States, even washed-up guys like him. But her wrinkled gray dress and wedge sandals didn't scream fangirl, and she seemed to be looking through him more than at him.

She also didn't appear to be dressed for the part of a person operating in an official capacity. Still, to be safe, Jordan tucked his flask out of sight before waving and shouting, 'Hello?!'

If anything, that only caused her to pick up speed.

'Hi!' he said, his deep voice lifting on an extended 'i' as he realised she was definitely on course to crash right into

3

him. If there was something he knew too much about, it was crashes.

It wasn't until she was almost in his personal space that he heard the mumbling. At first, he couldn't catch what she was saying, but when he did, there was no unhearing the string of curse words. The woman was swearing like a pirate who'd managed to stub his toe on his own wooden leg.

Jordan waved both arms to catch her attention, but she didn't slow down, or stop. She didn't seem to register he was there at all − even when she tripped over his legs and landed sprawled across his lap. The seconds that ticked by with her face planted in the sand were more than enough time for him to reflect on how it had been more months than he cared to count since he'd felt the weight of a woman on top of him.

And now, one had literally fallen into his lap.

Chapter 2

Pearl Carrington rolled onto her back, squinted at the sun, and reviewed four things she knew to be true.

One: She'd flown halfway across the world to the north of Wales at the drop of a hat, only to learn that her aunt's supposed 'emergency surgery' was a breast augmentation.

Two: Said aunt was actually her mother, and the person Pearl had called Mom her entire life was her aunt. To Pearl's surprise, they had both been waiting for her when she'd arrived rumpled at her aunt's house in Abersoch. Why the two decided to drop this bombshell on her right there and then, not to mention 34 years after the fact, was as unclear as her walk across the beach. But that could also be due to the nearly lethal mix of red wine and brandy they'd plied her with before revealing her seriously messed up origin story.

Three: She may be a little tipsy. Okay, a lot tipsy – not to mention exhausted. She'd left Chicago more hours ago than she cared to count and had endured multiple flight delays and a trip across the England-Wales border in a rental car only a smidge larger than a roller skate.

Four, and perhaps most important at the moment: The sand on this beach was lumpy, and moving. There was a solid chance that, in her current state, she'd tripped and fallen into quicksand.

She should scream or grab a nearby tree branch. Or scream. Only Pearl's mouth refused to work, and she was on a beach in Wales. There wasn't even a palm tree for hundreds of miles, at least.

Don't panic.

Although her knowledge of quicksand was limited to what she'd learned from cartoons and movies, panicking only made things worse.

She needed a fifth point – and quick.

Five, five, five. She bit her lip and tasted sand. *Please, please, let there be a five.*

Then, out of nowhere, a hand reached toward her, and Pearl grabbed it.

Chapter 3

An awkward amount of time elapsed before the mystery woman allowed Jordan to pull her up to a seated position, still on his lap.

'Are you okay?' he asked.

She seemed fine, aside from the rapid-fire blinking aimed his way that suggested he'd been the one to stumble and somehow end up underneath her – which, now that he had a close-up look at those rosy lips, he wouldn't have minded.

Her hand came up to shield her eyes. 'Where the hell did you come from?'

Jordan stifled a laugh at the adorably perplexed look on her face. 'Nowhere. Well, not really nowhere. Detroit, originally. But most recently, this very spot.'

'Really? Me, too.' She squinted at him. 'The Detroit part, at least, although I live in Chicago now. Also, apparently, this spot as well.'

'What are the odds of that?' He extended his hand. 'Jordan.'

'Pearl.'

Her American English was music to Jordan's ears after days of trying to decipher the thick Welsh accent. Between that and the unexpected yet much-welcomed skin-to-skin contact, his fingers stayed wrapped around hers. They were so soft and warm that he didn't want to let go.

Her gaze drifted to their clasped hands. 'Mind if I have that back now?'

'Sorry about that,' said Jordan, quickly yet reluctantly releasing his grip. 'I'm traveling alone, and my social skills are clearly suffering from a lack of people to talk to that I can understand. I'm not a nutter or anything, I swear.'

She arched an eyebrow at him as she slid off his lap and onto the beach towel next to him. 'Picking up the local lingo, I see.'

The day before, Jordan had overheard two boys yelling 'nutter' and splashing each other while laughing hysterically. Apparently, she wasn't new to the area.

After a once-over that had him wanting to flex something, Pearl shrugged.

'I'll tell you what, I'll give you the benefit of the doubt since there isn't a chance you could top the crazy I've already seen today.' Pointing at the flask, which had come uncovered when she tripped over him, she added, 'May I?'

'Thanks, I guess?' He picked up the silver flask and dangled it in front of her. 'In return, I'll give you the benefit of the doubt, too.'

'You may want to think twice about that – nutter definitely runs in my family,' she said. 'But so far, I'm in the clear.'

As he searched her face for any sign she was joking, Pearl grabbed the silver bottle and gave it a once-over, tracing the engraved numerals one and nine with her finger. Jordan held his breath, waiting for her to ask about the significance of the number 19 as she unscrewed the cap, but she only tipped back.

An impressive gulp led to a sudden coughing fit. 'You might've told me it was whisky,' she gasped.

'It's Scottish,' he said, forcing his gaze from her heaving chest. 'Smooth, right?'

'About as smooth as my entrance a few minutes ago,' she laughed.

As Pearl took a second, far more reserved sip, Jordan snuck a glance at his surprise towel-mate. Her hair was the darkest of browns, with hints of rich mahogany when the sun hit it just right. Her eyes seemed to reflect the color of the sea where it met the mountains on the distant horizon, but more subtly than his own baby blues.

They whiled away the afternoon's last gasp by passing the flask back and forth, watching together as the boy continued to splash and ignore his mother's empty threats. But to their surprise, and apparently the kid's, the mom finally marched in up to her waist and grabbed her son. Once back on the shore, he howled as she wrapped them both in rainbow-striped towels and then carried him under one arm like a surfboard from the beach.

Beside him, Pearl ran her hands up and down her bare arms. Jordan fought a sudden urge to wrap an arm around her shoulders and pull her close.

Whoa. Slow down, man.

'Again, not a nutter, but I have a sweatshirt in my beach hut that you're welcome to borrow,' he said.

Her wide-eyed look matched the one people had given him all week when he climbed the wooden steps to number four. Apparently, the beach huts were famous for being some of the priciest real estate in the area by square footage. But after spending a few days in and out of the small single room on stilts at the edge of the sand, he still hadn't figured out what the big deal was.

'Do you seriously own one of those?' she asked. 'What are you, some sort of millionaire boy genius?'

'Boy? I'll have you know I'm 34.' Jordan seized the moment he'd missed earlier to flex a bicep and further prove his manhood. 'And I'm sorry to disappoint you, but it belongs to a friend.'

Her eyes stayed glued to his upper arm for a beat before shifting to his face. 'Does that mean you're not a genius either?'

'Not even close.'

Once Jordan was on his feet, he helped Pearl to hers and then gave the beach towel a quick shake. He was relieved that she hadn't asked about the millionaire part – that actually was true.

When they'd climbed the stairs to the bright turquoise hut, he hung the towel over the back of a wicker chair on the deck before showing her through the open double doors. Wyn's wife, Alys, had obviously had a heavy hand in decorating the tiny space, which consisted of four wooden walls, a changing room with a compostable toilet, and a small yet efficient kitchen with no running water. A bright nautical theme attempted to compensate for the lack of windows.

'I'd give you a tour but, this is it,' Jordan said.

Pearl turned a full circle and took in the single room. 'I'm...'

'Underwhelmed?' he offered.

'Disappointed. I've been obsessed with these beach huts since my first trip to Abersoch.' She pulled the sweatshirt he tossed her over her head, kicked off her sandals, and flopped onto the sofa. 'Ah, well, at least it's on brand for this trip.'

Jordan added this breadcrumb to the other she'd dropped on the beach about her crazy day. 'In that case, would you care for sparkling water, wine, or something stronger?' he asked.

'Definitely stronger,' Pearl said. 'But just so you're aware, I arrived only a few hours ago, so apologies in advance if jet lag slams into me and takes me out.'

Yet another breadcrumb. 'Noted,' he said.

Jordan dug into the stockpile of supplies he'd bought his first day. He poured a bag of cheddar and onion 'crisps' into a bowl shaped like an anchor and set it on the marine rope-edged coffee table in front of the sofa. Accidentally asking for chips — the term for french fries on this side of the pond — was a can of worms he'd wished he hadn't opened at the market. The shopkeeper had explained to him like he was a child that they didn't have a fryer on site, but there was a good chippy around the corner.

'My apologies, but no running water means no ice,' Jordan said, mixing them each a lukewarm gin and tonic and handing hers over before sitting down in the chair across from the sofa with his own.

Pearl grabbed a handful of chips. 'I'll admit that they have better chip flavors over here but God forbid you ask for chips instead of crisps. They put the soda versus pop debate to shame.'

Picturing a thought bubble floating over his head, he smiled into his glass.

'So, what are you?' Pearl asked.

He looked up. 'Pardon? What am I what?'

She stopped shoving chips in her mouth and stared at him. 'Pop or soda?'

'Oh. Team soda. Definitely.'

Her eyebrow arched. 'Incorrect.'

'How can I be wrong on a word choice?' he asked. 'Also, to be fair, I've spent a fair amount of my life traveling outside of the Midwest. You can't exactly ask for pop in a place like Singapore. They'd think you were—'

'A nutter?' Her giggle bounced off the walls of the beach hut, and she covered her mouth with one hand while waving the other in his direction. Tears ran down her cheeks before she was able to speak. 'Sorry, gin tends to have a weird effect on me. Consider yourself warned.'

'Noted again,' he said.

'We should probably address the elephant in the room and admit that we don't have a future together.' At his perplexed look, she added, 'I mean, soda? C'mon. No way I could live with hearing that every day for the rest of my life.'

'If it helps any, I hardly drink the stuff anymore,' he said. 'I promise to keep your suffering to a minimum.'

The thought of losing his only companion in months left a small pit in his stomach. Although idle chitchat had never been his forte – his dad had put him through media training to learn how to be succinct without sounding surly – he was enjoying this random conversation with Pearl.

Or he was until she interrupted his thoughts with the last question he wanted to answer: 'So, what do you do, Jordan?'

He'd expected to be asked this at some point, of course. Hell, he'd even leaned into his media training and rehearsed what he might say in front of a mirror so he wasn't caught off guard. But he hadn't anticipated it coming up in a situation like this, when he preferred the person not know his story or have a clue about the guy he'd once been. That guy was no prince.

'I'm in between jobs right now,' he said. 'I was in the, uh, family business for my entire career. But when my dad passed away last year, he left everything, lock, stock, and barrel, to my twin sister. Let's just say that things fell apart pretty quickly after that.'

Because of him.

'He didn't leave you anything?'

'Actually, that was misleading – at least, the lock, stock,

13

and barrel part. He did, but there were strings attached.' Judging by the confused look on Pearl's face, his explanation wasn't making things any clearer. 'It's all been taken care of now. You could definitely say that I got my due.'

In spades.

'And your mom?'

He shook his head. 'Cancer.'

'I'm sorry,' she said.

'It was a long time ago.' So long that he'd now had far more years without her than he had with her. 'But thank you.'

Pearl went quiet, as if her mind had suddenly drifted out of the beach hut's still-open door and was carried away in the breeze. Just as quickly, she was back on the sofa in the beach hut and her eyes locked with his. Although he would've sworn they were the lightest blue outside, under this light, they were a pale gray. He didn't know people could even have gray eyes.

Their gaze held as she stood up and motioned toward his empty glass. He handed it to her, then watched her walk to the counter and mix them fresh drinks with a generous pour.

'I assume that caused some bad blood between you and your sister,' Pearl said once she sat back down. 'Her getting the family business.'

As if he needed reminding. He took a sip, immediately grateful he'd bought the best gin the shop had in stock. Pearl's concoction was far more G than T.

'What's that saying about time healing all wounds? Not completely accurate in this case but they were stitched up

14

and healed decently. The scar should fade over time.' He hoped. 'Mia's getting married this weekend in Scotland, actually. That's why I'm here in the UK.'

'Are you Scottish? Or is her fiancé?'

'No, and no. Luca, her fiancé, is Italian, but my family is a mix of nationalities at this point,' he said. 'Mia has a thing for all things Scottish so decided to have a destination wedding at a castle in the Highlands.'

When he'd received his invitation in the mail, Jordan had realised that he couldn't miss his sister's wedding. Not only did he want to be there, but also his parents would haunt him forever if he skipped watching his twin getting married.

'And here I thought I had the market cornered on family drama.' She drained her glass and, with a loud hiccup that made them both laugh, held it out for a refill. 'Your turn.'

Jordan decided reversing her ratio of gin to tonic was probably best for both of them this round. He stared at the tonic-heavy glasses for a few seconds in his hands before turning around and handing Pearl hers. If the woman thought that what he'd shared qualified as family drama, she was sadly mistaken. Try crashing into your teammate mid-race, a guy who just so happens to be the love of your sister's life, nearly killing him and you and destroying your racing career.

Pearl hiccuped again. 'I mean, I found out a couple of hours ago that my aunt was really the teen mom who gave birth to me, and my grandparents forced their twin daughters to switch places. Do I win?'

Okay, maybe she did get it.

He gulped down a sip. 'Yes, although I'm not sure there's a prize for that.'

'I should hope not,' she said. 'Although it might take the sting out of being in such a crappy contest.'

'Agreed,' Jordan said. 'So, who spilled? The aunt who used to be your mom or the aunt who is your mom?'

'The one who is,' Pearl said. 'You might say she has a flair for the dramatic. They were both there, though.'

He smiled. 'That solves the mystery of why you're here with me when you've just arrived.'

As Jordan poured increasingly weaker drinks, Pearl spilled the kind of tale typically reserved for tabloids and clickbait – two things he knew far too much about.

'You never suspected?' he asked.

She took a healthy sip, not even noticing that he'd switched to 100 per cent tonic for the last round. 'Nope, I never even had a clue. I mean, why would I?'

'What about your birth certificate? Who's listed as your mom?'

'Di, the one who raised me. She and Top are identical, so they simply swapped identities when the hospital asked for the information. They used to brag about how they switched places all the time when they were kids. Wait' – she hiccuped again – 'are you and your sister identical?'

'Uh, no.' He shook his head slowly, wondering if Pearl had skipped a science class or two at some point or, more likely, had spiked her own drink when he wasn't looking. 'We're fraternal, but we do look alike. At least, we have the same blonde hair and blue eyes.'

Hands down, Pearl's story was the most ridiculous one Jordan had ever heard by a mile. Suddenly, driving up the ass-end of his future brother-in-law's car almost seemed rational.

'Do you want to know the worst part, Jordan? Top was my role model. My hero. She always swooped in to save the day when Di messed things up. But she wasn't a hero. She was an arsonist who returned to the scene of the crime with a Dixie cup of water, a fresh pack of matches, and a gallon jug of lighter fluid.'

Jordan leaned toward her. 'Look, I'm not defending her. But haven't you ever done something that you regretted? Really regretted? Something that seemed impossible to fix? I mean, you have to start somewhere, and unfortunately, there's rarely a perfect place to begin.'

When Pearl didn't respond, he added, 'What they did was clearly wrong, but maybe they're trying to make things right.'

'I don't think it's possible to make this right.' Pearl's voice cracked as tears began to stream down her face.

Without thinking twice, Jordan moved from his chair, planted himself next to Pearl on the sofa, and set her empty glass on the table. Once he draped an arm across her shoulders, she nestled her head into the crook of his neck and cried. He tugged her closer while she alternately edged toward him until he was full-on holding her.

It had been a long time since he'd comforted someone.

One hand glided over her hair; the other, her back. 'It's okay. Everything's going to be fine. I promise.'

Her head lifted off his shoulder with a sniff. 'You should know that I'd normally deliver a sound lecture on empty promises. But in a weird way on a very weird day, a stranger in another land telling me everything is going to be okay is exactly what I need to hear.'

'You? Lecture? I have a hard time believing that.'

'You'd be surprised,' she said, using the sleeve of his T-shirt to wipe away her tears.

As Jordan considered whether to shift back to the chair, Pearl lifted her face to his. The look she gave him said she wanted to be kissed and, given her roller coaster of a day, probably needed to be.

Maybe as much as he did.

But before he took the literal plunge, Jordan took something else. A deep breath. Blurting out that he was a temperamental race car driver without a ride seemed awkward, but if this was going where he thought it might, where he hoped it would, afterward he'd feel like as much of a jerk as most racing fans considered him to be.

Just say it.

'Pearl, you should probably know that I'm—'

'Married?'

He shook his head. 'God, no.'

'A serial killer?'

'Nope. Although I feel compelled to point out that a serial killer would probably lie about that.'

She giggled. 'I'd be able to tell. I mean, it takes one to know one, right?'

He laughed along with her. Before he could say anything else, her lips touched his.

Pearl tasted like pine from the lingering gin, and he was instantly transported to the woods of northern Michigan, his favorite place in the world. It made him want to freeze that moment, with her, on this sofa, in this beach hut, and make it last.

Only the guy who'd spent most of the past decade assuming he didn't have a conscience had apparently grown one. He lifted his face away an inch and tried once more. 'Pearl, do you—'

'Want you to stop talking? Honestly, Jordan? Yes.'

And so he did, because maybe it was better for her not to know he'd made a colossal cock-up that almost cost him everything.

Chapter 4

Pearl stirred to the sound of someone clearing their throat in the daintiest way possible. When she managed to pry open her eyes, they focused on the bodice of a breezy summer frock adorned with tiny violets. Only one person born within the last century would traipse around in a dress like that – Lady Topaz Langford, her aunt-turned-mother.

'Did we time travel?' a deep voice breathed into her ear.

That's the moment when Pearl realised she wasn't at home in Chicago, tucked into the luxury linens she'd spent too many weeks researching, and that the waves that had soothed her sleep all night were the Irish Sea and not her white noise machine. No, she was crammed onto the world's smallest sofa, playing the part of little spoon to the guy she'd bumped into on the beach and then spilled her life story to.

She nearly jumped out of her skin. Her mostly bare skin, which had a very muscular arm draped across it.

'From this day forward, you may all call me Shirley Holmes,' Top said. 'I followed the clues right to the door.'

To Pearl's chagrin, a second voice chimed in. 'Shirley Holmes, my ass. There was one clue, and it was the door, which was wide open, by the way.'

Oh, good, Diamond Carrington, her mother-turned-aunt was lurking on the scene, too.

The chest behind her shook in silent laughter.

'Well, congratulations to you both, I guess.' Pearl pulled up the blanket Jordan must've draped over them in the middle of the night, covering her lacy black bralette but, in the process, exposing more of Jordan. 'I ran into him on the beach' – literally – 'and he offered me a tour of his beach hut.'

Next to Top, Di appeared with a face full of makeup more suitable for a night out clubbing than a morning search-and-rescue party. 'Apparently.'

Pearl couldn't imagine what was keeping Jordan from running and screaming away from the three of them. Even though she'd implied that her family was quirky when she'd spilled the big family secret, nothing could've prepared him for waking up to this.

'Jordan, meet the family jewels,' she sighed.

'Likewise,' Di said with an appraising gaze.

Jordan rearranged the blanket on top of them and then tucked Pearl's body deeper into his. 'Ah, yes, Diamond and Topaz, I believe Pearl said. Hello, it's a pleasure to meet you both.'

Di winked. 'Oh, the pleasure is all ours. Trust me. And you can call us Di and Top. Everybody does.'

'If you're going to just stand there leering, you can leave.' Pearl burrowed even closer to Jordan. 'On second thought, please just leave.'

'I agree,' Top said. 'We'll wait outside while you bid your gentleman fare-thee-well, and then we'll go home and break our fast with a nice long chat.'

When her back stiffened, Jordan found her hand and laced her fingers with his. Her other hand snuck out from under the towels and shooed away their uninvited guests.

'Go ahead without me,' Pearl said. 'I'll meet you there.'

When the sisters didn't budge, Jordan squeezed her hand. 'I'll see that she gets home safe,' he said. 'I promise.'

The two women hovering over them nodded. The fact that a promise from a nearly naked stranger was enough to satisfy them of Pearl's safety proved that neither of them were fit to mother anybody.

'We'll expect her home within the hour,' Di called over her shoulder as they walked out. 'Don't think I won't hunt you down and skin you alive if she's not.'

Okay, maybe one of them was.

When the door shut, Jordan howled, his forehead resting on the back of her neck, puffs of his breath tickling her spine.

'What's so funny?' As if she needed to ask.

'Seriously?' His entire body shook behind her as laughter overtook him again. 'After what you told me last night, I didn't know what to expect, but trust me, that wasn't it.'

'Would you have believed me? I mean, it's kind of one of those things you have to see with your own eyes.'

'That may be the truest statement I've ever heard in my whole entire life,' he said, his fingers lightly brushing her arm. 'So, what's their deal anyway? And does it run in the family?'

'God, I hope not,' she said, then paused before answering his first question. Years of explaining the jewel sisters hadn't made it any easier. Pearl had learned the hard way that there really was no explanation for Di and Top being, well, Di and Top.

'If you're thinking midlife crisis, the answer is a surprising no, although they are about to turn the big five-o,' she said. 'Di manages a department store makeup counter. She says it's important for her to try out new products and looks.'

'I get that,' he said. 'But is she required to wear all of the products at the same time?'

Maybe Pearl should've been offended on Di's behalf, but since there was more than an ounce of validity to his question, she let it slide. At this point, she probably wouldn't recognise Di without one of her many faces on.

'And the other one?' Jordan asked, still rubbing her arm.

'Top's a historical romance author. She got into "method writing" years ago to help find her voice as a lady of the nineteenth-century aristocracy. Let's just say the timing couldn't have been worse for Anthropologie to come out with a line of Regency-inspired dresses.'

'She bought them out, I assume?'

'You would assume correctly. Di and I even got them for Christmas that year.' Pearl laughed, remembering the look

23

she and Di had exchanged when they unwrapped the long, flowing dresses they'd wanted to stuff back into their boxes immediately. 'I can't believe I'm telling you this, but she made us have a family photo taken.'

His hand paused, his fingers resting on the back of her hand. 'What would it take to get a look at that picture? Seriously, name your price.'

'Tempting but... no.' She giggled.

Looking back, someone should've intervened during Top's first foray into method writing, but her explanation had made perfect sense at the time. Why wouldn't the author of Regency romance novels inhabit the world of her characters? There didn't seem to be any harm in her wearing long dresses or her hair in a bun. It's not like she'd started using a chamber pot.

But then her aunt had gone and fallen madly in love with an aging earl. While doing research, Top had contacted a few members of the nobility on a whim, and Lord Charles Langford had replied and they became pen pals of sorts. Apparently, he'd assumed the sweet woman he'd been corresponding with wrote about swooning, promenades, and stolen kisses, not corset erotica. When they finally met in person, she'd been overjoyed to find herself face to face with an eccentric silver fox and not the fuddy-duddy she'd anticipated. Likewise, he hadn't been at all disappointed to discover a lovely lady who enjoyed afternoon tea with a side of kink. Within a few months, Top had married into the aristocracy. 'The earl,' as Di and Pearl called Charles — even though Top had suggested they refer to him as 'My Lord' — became the unexpected fourth member of the Carrington family.

But only 15 years later, Top was widowed, and wealthy. And fully committed to maintaining a lifestyle befitting a woman of her station in the days of yore as if it still were.

In other words, all was now lost.

'So, she's actually a countess?'

Pearl nodded. 'Believe it or not, yes.'

'What does that make you?' Jordan asked.

'Considering she's now a dowager countess, nothing but a fool,' Pearl said.

Jordan shifted to give her space to roll onto her back, then propped himself up on his elbow. A beach towel slipped in the process, revealing a sculpted chest that would give a Greek god a run for his money.

'I believe the term you're looking for is court jester,' he said with a wink. 'And you're no such thing.'

'I'm glad you think so,' Pearl said. 'And I'm sorry. I'm sure when you were on the beach yesterday, you never imagined that this is what the tide would bring in.'

'True, but you have no reason to apologise. Even with the surprise wake-up call, I'm not sorry you stumbled upon me. It was the best night of my vacation so far.'

Pearl felt heat rush to her face at his mention of the night before. 'I'll have to take your word for it since things are a little fuzzy after we,' she hesitated, 'kissed.'

Fuzzy was an understatement. At the moment, her memories were floating around the beach hut like dandelion fluff after a large puff. If only she could catch enough of them to explain her current state of undress.

Pearl had thought her days of one-night stands were finished – not that they'd ever really started. Her one and only had taken place her junior year in college after too many lemon drop shots at a Halloween party. The next morning, she hadn't been able to get out of there fast enough, even knowing she'd have to do the walk of shame home dressed as a bumblebee. Millie, her best friend and former college roommate turned coworker and current roommate, still brought it up every October.

Jordan's pout transformed into a sly smile. 'Yes, we kissed, and then, as you'd warned me, jet lag kicked in. You were out within seconds of taking off my shirt – in the middle of a kiss, actually.'

Considering what she could see of Jordan above the beach towel, Pearl could hardly believe that was true. Stupid jet lag. Stupid gin. Stupid everything.

'I've decided not to take that personally,' he added.

'You shouldn't,' she said. 'Jet lag and alcohol are apparently a lethal combination.'

'About that,' he said. 'We were mostly drinking tonic starting with the third round.'

'The fact that I didn't even notice shows what a wise decision that was on your part,' she said. 'And also the power of jet lag. So, my dress?'

He pointed at the pale gray heap on the floor. 'Also you. About an hour after you fell asleep, you got up and stripped off my sweatshirt and your dress. I don't think you were anywhere near conscious at that point.'

'So, nothing happened?'

'Besides the kissing? No. Scout's honor.'

'Oh, were you a Boy Scout?'

Jordan nodded. 'I'll have you know that you just spent the night with a pinewood derby champion.' When she arched an eyebrow at him, he added, 'But not in the biblical sense.'

For the first time in her life, Pearl exhaled an actual sigh of relief. Considering the events of the last 24 hours, it would also likely be her last.

As if he could read her mind, Jordan's hand found hers again. 'If you're not ready to deal with them, don't. You're welcome to stay here as long as you'd like. I have a cottage all to myself, too.'

As tempting as his offer was on many levels, Pearl was already miles out of her comfort zone. Not that she felt uncomfortable at the current moment. Quite the opposite, in fact.

'Jordan, you're sweet, but trust me when I say I'm not going to deal with that situation until I'm good and ready.'

'Sweet?' He blinked a few times in confusion, as if she'd spoken gibberish.

'Fine, very sweet.'

Pearl boldly lifted herself up and planted a quick peck on his lips. Or at least that's what she'd intended. His fingers sunk into her hair, keeping her mouth pressed to his. This was a man who knew how to kiss.

'Are you sure I can't convince you?' he asked, his lips moving against hers as they formed the whispered words.

Even though there was a solid chance he could, especially if he kissed her like that again, Pearl shook her head. 'One thing you should know about Di – she isn't one for idle threats. She may not be back in an hour, but she will reappear if I don't show up.'

That was all it took for Jordan to leap up and toss her the dress she'd left Chicago in another lifetime ago.

'Give me two minutes,' he said, grabbing a tote bag from the corner and heading into the changing room.

Pearl was clothed and waiting at the door, her wedge sandals dangling from her grip by their ankle straps, when Jordan re-emerged in cargo shorts and a long-sleeved T-shirt.

'You don't have to walk me back,' she said. 'It's not far. Stumbling distance, if I recall.'

'That may be true, but I made a promise to the jewel sisters, and they don't seem like the sort of people a guy wants to double-cross.' He stopped and picked his sweatshirt off the floor, and then handed it to her for the second time in 12 hours. 'It's chilly in the morning here.'

'Like I said, sweet,' said Pearl, pulling it over her head before following him back to reality.

They retraced Pearl's path in reverse, although she had to rely on Jordan's memory since she had little recollection of how she'd gotten from point A to point B. She only remembered aimlessly walking along the beach. But apparently, she'd had an aim, and it was the guy grabbing her hand and pulling her to a sudden stop.

'Here,' he said, keeping her hand tucked in his.

She looked around at the sand and the sea before shaking her head. 'Here what?'

'Here's where I first spotted you,' he said with a goofy grin that surely matched the one on her own face.

Just as he'd promised, Jordan walked her all the way back, still holding her hand on the winding path that led from the beach to Top's clifftop mansion overlooking the sea. He didn't blink an eye at the large historic home, which Top had received as a parting gift from her stepson in exchange for agreeing to fade into the background.

Before they could say their goodbyes, the voices of the jewel sisters carried through a nearby open window. Suddenly, exchanging phone numbers or even last names wasn't as much of a priority as getting inside and up to her room before anyone saw her.

With a quick kiss pressed to Jordan's lips, Pearl stole away like a thief in the night.

She and Di had their own bedrooms in the clifftop mansion Top had lived in with her late husband. 'I want you to feel at home here,' Top had told them the first time they'd visited the newlyweds. It's too bad the sweet gesture had come with period antiques and themes – pineapples for Di and songbirds for Pearl.

She tiptoed up the stairs, her heart pounding, making as little noise as possible until she reached her bedroom. Then, like a teenager, she slammed the door loud enough to announce that she'd returned but, under no circumstances, wanted company.

'Very mature, Pearl,' she said to the bright yellow canary on the wallpaper above the light switch.

Her suitcase and carry-ons were on top of the bed, not downstairs where she'd left them. She dug her cell phone out of her purse to find it was dead, so she plugged it into the charger Top always had waiting for her. It sprang to life with a flurry of texts. There was one from Millie, wondering how the flight was, but most were from Di and Top. They'd messaged on the family group chat and their solo text chains while she was with Jordan.

Jordan.

Did she really just leave him on the porch with hardly a goodbye? Between that, the jewel sisters' early morning pop-in, and her ramblings about the big family secret, she'd pretty much guaranteed that she'd never see him again.

Pearl moved her bags instead of unpacking them. She hated living out of a suitcase – even for a single night in a hotel – but this may be a much quicker trip than planned. After a massive flop onto the bed that had her nose to beak with some sort of finch, Pearl rolled onto her back and did some quick time zone math. Not that it mattered what time it was on the other side of the world, she needed to talk to her best friend. Now.

Millie picked up on the second ring and, as always, was instantly wide awake. 'This had better be an emergency.'

'Top's my mom and I just spent the night with some random guy in a beach hut,' Pearl blurted out.

'That qualifies,' Millie said. 'Meet me in the virtual conference room in ten minutes.'

It took almost that long for Pearl to brush her teeth and wash her face in the en suite, dig out her computer, and tuck herself in under the covers. She logged on to find her roommate already there, drinking coffee in their sage green living room. If only Millie could teleport her a cup, too. Although if that were the case, Pearl would teleport herself home.

Leaning toward the screen as if that allowed her to see Pearl better, Millie asked, 'First, are you okay?'

Pearl shook her head. 'I don't know. Seriously, I have zero clue how to feel about any of this.'

'All right, let's hear it from the beginning, and I don't want the CliffsNotes version. I'll work from home today if I have to.'

Pearl shared how she'd rushed in to find Top lounging on a crushed velvet chaise in her parlor. It was the opposite of what she'd expected to find after the urgent 'textagram' the morning before:

30 JULY

REGRET TO INFORM YOU THAT I AM HAVING
SURGERY THIS WEEK STOP YOUR PRESENCE
IS REQUESTED STOP HAVE BOOKED YOU AN
OVERNIGHT FLIGHT

Okay, so maybe Top hadn't used the word 'emergency,' but that was splitting hairs – it was implied as far as Pearl was concerned. So much so that Pearl had nearly exploded when she found out the actual reason she'd dropped everything and jumped on an aeroplane.

'Are you telling me that I risked life and limb to travel halfway across the world, at the drop of a hat, because you're having a boob job?'

'I believe the preferred terminology is "breast augmentation," dearest,' Top had said, smoothing the long skirt of a pale lavender floral day dress.

Pearl had arched an eyebrow and let slip her first curse word in months. 'Hmm. Ask me if I give a fuck.'

Which had clearly shown the impact of being awake for more hours than she'd cared to count. Pearl had never directed an ounce of irritation at the woman in front of her.

No, that was reserved for Top's twin. Aside from their shared beauty, Di was the yin to Top's yang. Opposites who somehow complemented each other, just like the Chinese symbol.

'Life and limb? Good Lord, child, you always have been prone to drah-ma.'

The too-familiar voice that had drawled from the next room overemphasized the first syllable of the word, barely acknowledging the 'ma.' Fitting, considering how Di had approached the role over the years.

*

'Wait, *Di* is there?' Millie interrupted.

If anyone understood her complicated relationship with the woman who raised her, it was Millie. She'd long been an odd wing-woman of sorts when Di visited and managed to find Pearl's last nerve. Once, Millie had diffused a tense situation by asking Di for a new look and then, several hours and pounds of makeup later, had even agreed to 'test it out' at happy hour. Pearl could've hugged her – but didn't for fear of Millie's face cracking.

'In the flesh, or at least that's who I assume is under all that foundation,' Pearl said. 'I walked in during happy hour on the Welsh Riviera.'

'Let me guess – red wine and brandy?' Millie asked.

The woman knew the Carrington family too well.

'Even though I know better, I had my fair share,' Pearl said.

'Oh, dear, although that may explain the second part of the story,' Millie said. 'Let's skip the booze and get back to the breast augmentation. I mean, isn't there a corset for that?'

Pearl sat up. 'That's what I said!'

'What's wrong with your breasts anyway?' Pearl had asked Top after she'd filled a goblet to the rim with the jewel sisters' go-to concoction.

Top had shifted over, patted the spot on her chaise, and waited until Pearl sat down before continuing. Di had pulled a nearby chair closer and grabbed her sister's hand once she, too, was seated.

'I'm afraid the girls never quite recovered from breast-feeding,' Top had said. 'They've been flat as a pancake ever since.'

Pearl had frowned. If there were a family secret she wasn't aware of, Top having a secret love child wouldn't have been on her bingo card. Her aunt had always embraced a childless-by-choice lifestyle, not to mention the many fruits of her non-labors. 'Breastfeeding? Were you trying to get in character as a wet nurse? Because that's not how it works. You kind of need to have a baby to breastfeed.'

Top had snuck Di another look. 'I did. 34 years ago. On the 14th of March.'

'But that's my birthday.' Di had reached out and attempted to wrest the wine glass from Pearl's grip, but that only made her hold onto it more tightly. 'How could you have—'

Top had given her a shy smile. 'It's you, dearest. You're actually mine.'

A slack-jawed Millie leaned into the screen again. 'That's how she told you? That is messed up, even for the jewel sisters.'

While her roommate drank multiple cups of coffee, Pearl shared how she'd stumbled out of the house, onto the beach, and into Jordan. She didn't have to spare any details about their night together in the beach hut since Jordan had cleared up what had — or hadn't — gone down.

'And?'

'That's it. Like I said, he walked me home, I ducked inside, and now I'm talking to you.'

On the other side of the world, Millie rolled her eyes. Between her eye rolling and Pearl's eyebrow arching, the two of them had been butterfly-effecting weather patterns since college.

'Was he a good kisser? Was he nice? What does he look like?'

'Yes, yes, and, hands down, the most beautiful man I've ever seen in real life.' Pearl gulped. 'Too bad I'll never see him again.'

Chapter 5

The teacup was almost to Jordan's lips when he heard the screech.

'Nooo! Stop! Not tea. Not tea!'

Above his chair, a wild-eyed Pearl appeared ready to knock the antique porcelain from his grip. He gently set the teacup onto its equally delicate saucer, wresting his thumb from the tiny handle before smiling up at the face of the woman he hadn't been able to stop thinking about since she'd pulled a kiss and run on Top's doorstep the morning before.

When Jordan left the cottage an hour earlier, he'd told himself he was simply going out for a mid-afternoon stroll and definitely not headed anywhere in particular. He didn't need to check in on Pearl – she'd assured him that she could handle the jewel sisters, and he believed her. But as he'd wandered the streets of the small seaside village, he wanted to.

How could he have known that knocking on Top's door would lead to him being the Mad Hatter's guest of honor?

Before Pearl's name had left his lips, Jordan had been ushered through the house to a small alcove overlooking the sea. There, at a table set for afternoon tea, Top had poured him a cup of what could best be described as brandy with a shot of Earl Grey before launching a fact-finding mission thinly disguised as polite small talk.

He'd never been so excited to see a party crasher as he was to see Pearl, who was shooting daggers at his tablemates. But thankfully, not him.

'How are a cup of tea and a few finger sandwiches *naughty*?' he winked. 'Seriously, I'm dying to know.'

'Not *naughty*. Not. Tea,' she said, elongating each word. 'As in, there's something other than leaves steeping in that pot.'

'Oh, I'm fully aware. It's quite nice, actually.' That was a lie, but at least the second cup was proving smoother than the first. 'No offense, but you look like you could use a shot of tea yourself.'

Judging by how dramatically Pearl plopped down in the remaining chair, she didn't disagree.

Top fetched another place setting. 'We'd been waiting for you, dearest, when we received the most delightful visitor,' she said, handing Pearl a teacup filled to the brim.

He should've guessed the hot seat didn't originally have his name on it, given they had no idea he would show up on their doorstep.

'Is that any way to greet a guest? Especially one this handsome?' Di asked. 'I raised you better than that.'

Pearl took a loud, long slurp from her teacup. 'Did you though?'

'She most certainly did,' said Top, who adjusted the blue satin ribbon on her long floral dress before sitting back down on his right. 'In fact, I think she did a fine job.'

Top's outfits reminded Jordan of a streaming series he'd binged while recovering from his crash. They also made him curious about that family photo Pearl mentioned, but given how Top's comment had caused her to smash her teacup onto its saucer, he was guessing now wasn't the time to ask.

'You two are real gems,' Pearl said.

'And so are you, in case you needed a reminder,' Di said.

'As I've been telling you since the seventh grade, the jury is out on whether a pearl is truly a gem,' Pearl said. 'It grows inside a living thing, not the earth. I wish you'd done a bit more research before bestowing me with a name best suited for a schoolmarm's great-grandmother.'

'Well, it's a gem in my book,' Top said. 'And so are you.'

'Did you even consider Emerald? It's *actually* a gem, and I could've gone by Em,' Pearl said.

Even though Jordan liked the name Pearl, he wondered why she hadn't considered Ruby.

'Emerald? That's a lot of name to live up to.' Di motioned from herself to her sister and back again. 'Just look at the pair of us.'

'I'd rather not, thank you very much,' Pearl said.

For the first time, Jordan had a front-row seat to family drama that didn't star him. He couldn't say he was enjoying the show, but it did shed light on how many uncomfortable people he'd left in his wake over the years. If he were a guy who dealt in apologies, he'd have more than a few to pass out – hundreds for the Rubie Racing team alone. Although he should probably start with his sister and soon-to-be brother-in-law if ever he found an opportune moment. He had a feeling their wedding wouldn't be the right time and, even if it was, Jordan was already struggling with putting on a brave face given that it was taking place near the one-year anniversary of him nearly taking out the groom.

The tiered tray of finger sandwiches and sweets in the center of the table was a welcome diversion from both the voices inside his head and the silence around him. He inhaled a few smoked salmon with an egg salad chaser, then washed them down with more spiked tea. His gulps broke through the quiet and brought Pearl's gaze his way, her eyes like storm clouds.

'How are you doing?' he asked her.

'That's very kind of you to ask, my lord,' Top said, rewarding him with two more sandwiches and a lemon tart. 'I'd love to know as well.'

Pearl ignored Top as she answered Jordan. 'I'm fine. Really. I had some work to catch up on, so that's kept me busy.'

'Our Pearl writes an advice column,' Di said with a hint of pride. 'It's in the newspaper *and* online.'

He stretched his foot under the table and tapped Pearl's. 'Like Ann Landers?'

When ten-year-old Jordan had learned that the woman

who wrote Dear Abby was Ann Landers' twin sister, he'd written her a letter, asking if having a know-it-all copycat twin sister ever bothered her. Ann had never replied, likely because, at that point, she'd passed away, and her daughter had taken over writing the advice column. But he'd felt vindicated when he'd learned years later about Ann and Abby's longstanding feud.

'That would be the dream.' Pearl took another sip of tea. 'I realise it's hard to picture me having the moral high ground right now.'

'I'm sure I have no idea what you're talking about.' He turned to Top. 'As you're aware, a gentleman never kisses and tells.'

The corners of Pearl's mouth lifted in a smile so sad that Jordan fought an urge not to flip the table and carry her away. As Di and Top made small talk and Pearl ignored them, his brain tried to think of a way to cheer her up that didn't involve scattered sandwiches and shattered china. It latched onto what was quite possibly the most insane option.

Mia's wedding.

She could be his date.

Not only would it give Pearl a few days to get her head on straight, but it would also save him from having to face the who's who of Apex Racing alone. And as a bonus, he'd have time to figure out what was so intriguing about Pearl that he was still sitting at this table drinking highly flammable tea.

If she agreed to go, which he suddenly, desperately wanted her to.

With a clear of his throat, Jordan caught Pearl's attention and Top's and Di's, too.

'So, I was wondering if you might want to have dinner with me,' Jordan said. Before she could answer, he added, 'In Scotland. It would probably be more like three dinners and a couple of breakfasts.'

When the table went quiet, he continued, 'Lunches, too, and drinks.' Still nothing. 'And, I assume, wedding cake.'

Pearl drained her teacup and, for the first time, shared a willing glance with the women seated on either side of him before answering. 'You're asking me to your sister's wedding.'

He grimaced. 'And the pre-wedding stuff, too.'

'Isn't it a little late to invite someone?'

She may have a point there. Jordan shrugged; he'd worry about clearing a last-minute plus-one with Mia later. 'What's one more person?'

'You'll miss my surgery,' Top said quietly.

His gaze drifted around the table. 'Wait, what surgery?'

'It's nothing serious,' Pearl said. 'She's having a boo— breast augmentation on Friday morning.'

Without thinking, Jordan turned and gave the woman sitting next to him a once-over, earning him a solid kick to his right shin under the table. From whom it came was a mystery, given how all three women were glaring at him.

'I'll be with you,' said Di, reaching across Jordan's lap to squeeze her sister's hand.

Top sniffed. 'But we still haven't had a chance to talk about everything.'

Pearl's elbows dropped to the table, and her head quickly followed. 'Just because you're ready to dissect my origin story doesn't mean I am. You've known about this my whole life. I found out roughly 47 hours ago. I need some time and space.'

That had to work in his favor — there was little doubt she could get either here. Jordan crossed his fingers under the table.

'I'd say a whirlwind trip to Scotland with someone as easy on the eyes as this one sounds like just the ticket,' Di said.

As much as he agreed with the intent of Di's somewhat uncomfortable overture, he wasn't sure how to respond. While he and Top watched, Pearl and Di began a conversation using only head bobs, hand gestures, and eye movements.

After what felt like an eternity, Pearl turned her attention back to him. 'When would we need to leave?'

His heart nearly exploded with happiness. 'Totally up to you. Tomorrow's Wednesday and the wedding is Saturday, but I need to be there for the rehearsal dinner the night before, at the latest. If we leave in the morning, we could take the scenic route. But if that's too soon, we could leave Thursday or even push through on Friday. I can pack some sandwiches or something if you don't want to stop along the way.'

Sandwiches? Shut up, man.

'They have the castle all week, though, and there are some things planned for people who arrive early.'

Top perked up beside him. 'Castle?'

He should've led with that.

'Tomorrow it is,' Pearl said. 'Although I'm not sure what I'll wear. I assume that a wedding in a castle is fancy. Like, black tie fancy.'

Another wrinkle in his impulsive plan he hadn't considered. 'Scottish black tie.'

'You in a kilt?' Top asked, returning his once-over from earlier. 'You can raid my closet, dearest. Given how often my weight has fluctuated over the years, it's like a department store in there.'

A family photo was one thing, but real life was quite another. Jordan winced, picturing Pearl in a historical nightmare similar to the one Top was wearing, only with more ribbons. Maybe he should offer up his credit card. There had to be a dress shop in this resort town.

But beside him, Di clapped her hands and bobbed up and down in her chair. 'Don't worry, they're good,' she whispered.

His relief was short-lived.

'And you can borrow some of my makeup,' Di said.

From across the table, Pearl smiled and mouthed, 'Thank you.' And that organ he'd long lost hope of doing anything besides pump blood skipped a beat.

Chapter 6

'Now, this would do quite nicely.' Top unzipped what had to have been the twentieth garment bag to reveal an off-the-shoulder gown in a deep fuchsia. 'I wore this to an affair with the prince. The earl and I danced the night away.'

'Don't you have a little black dress in there somewhere?' Pearl asked. Her own closet was full of them. It was all she wore to formal events.

'No black,' shouted Millie from Pearl's laptop screen. 'Also, nothing gray or chocolate brown. You're stepping out of your dystopian wardrobe – for a few days at least.'

'Silver?' Pearl asked hopefully.

Millie rolled her eyes. 'Maybe.'

As Pearl hung the magenta nightmare on the rolling rack with the other possibilities, she realised that circling in her best friend for moral support may have been a mistake. Especially given that Millie was also the *Chicago Daily Times'* fashion columnist and had more than once threatened to set Pearl's closet aflame if only for a momentary glimpse of red.

'I agree that this girl needs to learn how to live a little, but an LBD is always on point,' said Di, sitting cross-legged on the floor with a champagne cocktail in hand. 'Especially when it's paired with the right makeup and CFM heels.'

Pearl had never been more grateful that she didn't share Di's shoe size.

Top's head stayed stuck out of the walk-in closet, and Pearl fought the urge to push it back in with a palm to the forehead. 'I agree with Millie – black just isn't done here like in the States. Also, dear sister, I think our Pearl is already out of her comfort zone.'

Our Pearl.

She'd never given the pet name a second thought. 'You're our pearl, and we're your oyster,' Top had told Pearl more times than she could count when she was a girl. As if she belonged to both sisters. The sentiment had always made Pearl feel special, as if it were the three of them against the world – which had been the case after a car accident took her grandparents and left them to fend for themselves just after she'd turned seven.

Would her grandparents have embraced their ridiculous plan if they'd known their role would be so short-lived? Until their death, Di had been more of a big sister she called 'mommy' when she wasn't at school, on a date, or at her after-school waitressing job. Her grandma had taken care of her, made her lunch, and kissed her good night after she'd said her prayers. Her grandpa had read to her from the Bible

45

and taught her how to ride a bike. They'd been the oars keeping the family moving forward.

Pearl could still picture the jewel sisters at the kitchen table after the funeral, deciding what to do while she'd played cocktail waitress. In the end, Top had returned to Boston to finish her senior year of college while Di had inherited their parents' house in the northern Detroit suburbs and raised her twin's daughter.

Di interrupted her memories. 'Yes, but these aren't stuffy Brits we're dealing with. He's an American, and a rich one, too. Your stodgy old rules don't apply to new money.'

The assessment brought Pearl to full attention. 'Rich? Why would you think he's rich?'

'Have I taught you nothing over the years?' Di said with a shake of the head. 'For starters, normal people don't get married in castles.'

Pearl shook her head. 'Not true. Destination weddings are super common.' She'd received plenty of letters about them, mostly from people wanting approval to tell off the soon-to-be brides and grooms who decided to completely inconvenience their guests in the name of love.

'Fine, he's too good-looking to be poor. He looks like he belongs on the cover of a magazine, and don't even get me started on that mouth of his.'

Before Pearl could argue, she flashed back to how soft Jordan's lips felt against hers.

'Are you okay, dearest? You look a little flushed,' Top asked, holding up another gown. 'Don't forget the beach hut. They're a rare commodity and hardly ever go on the market. The earl once tried to buy me one for my birthday as a surprise and was promptly shut down. Some motorsport driver outbid him. Paid nearly £200,000.'

Pearl thought back to the bare bones space she'd spent the night with Jordan in. Someone would need more money than sense to pay that much for four brightly painted wooden walls and a deck, regardless of where it was located.

'It's not his though,' Pearl said. 'It belongs to a friend.'

Millie gave a thumbs down to the latest dress, which somehow gave the illusion of a peacock. 'Doesn't matter,' said Di, shaking her head at the dress, too. 'Birds of a feather and all that.'

'Unless beach huts are like boats,' Millie interrupted from the laptop.

The confused looks on both jewel sisters prompted Pearl to explain. 'You don't need to own a boat. You just need a friend with a boat.'

'Exactly,' Millie said. 'Remember that sports reporter who managed to spend every weekend hanging out on a boat? She partied on six or seven boats in one summer.'

Making friends with someone with a boat was a life goal of almost everyone who lived in Chicago. There was nothing worse than sweating on shore while watching people bob up and down on Lake Michigan, having more fun in a single afternoon than Pearl'd had in her entire life.

'It sounds like your co-worker was looking to get herself compromised,' Top said.

Di refilled her own champagne flute, then made a champagne cocktail for Millie, who'd decided to drink it vicariously through Pearl. Even though Pearl rolled her eyes at that logic, and she was still a little buzzed from teatime, she took the glass and then a sip.

'Okay, enough talk about boats and beach huts. Even if he's not rich, and he is, you need to look fabulous all the same.' Di pointed to the full rack of dresses. 'Now, let's nail down this dress situation before the shops close, just in case we need to make a mad dash into town.'

An hour later, Pearl had three dresses, matching jewelry and fascinators, and a pounding headache with roots like a weeping willow – too close to the surface, spreading in every direction, and all sad. The last thing she felt like doing was mining her inbox for high-priority emails from her editor, but it gave her a much-needed opt-out from any more family time.

Although Pearl always worked a month ahead of schedule and had a stockpile of columns at the ready, she could count on Madeline for significant input these days. Her editor had always been the queen of 'helpful' suggestions, but since talk of syndication started, her edits had become heavy-handed. Instead of asking Pearl to consider looking at reader questions in a different way, it was Madeline's way. At first, Pearl put it down to wanting things just right for a possible syndication deal. But lately, Madeline's voice was coming through more and more – and just like her editor was in person, it was preachy and judgmental as all get-out.

Still, complaining seemed whiney at best and ungrateful at worst. As difficult as Pearl often found her editor, she was fortunate to have had the renowned Madeline Ryan on her side. Without a doubt, Pearl owed her success to the woman who'd made building Pearl's career her personal mission. There was simply no looking past the fact that Madeline was a force in the industry. She hadn't stumbled into becoming one of the top lifestyle editors in the country, she'd earned it – and now she owned it. Madeline had her finger on the pulse of America – or at least her version of the United States.

And it would all be worth it when Pearl could open up any daily newspaper in the country and find her own face staring back at her. When the deal was done, Pearl would work at regaining the ground she'd lost. Until then, she'd keep her mouth shut, her teeth clenched, and a smile plastered on her face.

Pearl had only pushed the envelope for this spur-of-the-moment trip because Top had needed her. If Madeline found out that Top's procedure was cosmetic, her overly Botoxed head would explode.

Just as Pearl hit send on the final email, there was a quick knock on her door. It swung open before she could answer.

'Peace offering?' asked Top, carrying a large tray. 'You missed dinner, and it was from that takeaway place you've always loved.'

Pearl pushed her laptop aside to make room for the tray on the bed, then watched as Top nervously neatened its contents. It was one of her favorites, chicken curry, which was always blessedly bland in the UK, and 'half and half,' a side of half rice and half fries. The Welsh and Brits could keep their black pudding and beans at breakfast, but two sides of starch at dinner was pure genius.

Instead of leaving, Top wandered over to the window and stared at the sea, her arms wrapping around her midsection. 'It's never been awkward between us. I'll be honest, I'm not sure what to do.'

To avoid answering, Pearl shoveled more fries into her mouth. Because the truth was, she was mad at Top for what seemed like the first time in her life. Plus, she'd always been one to let anger simmer quietly on the back burner than express it. Which is probably why it boiled over this time.

'Before I married the earl, I told him about you,' Top paused, 'being my daughter and not Di's. It was the best and worst moment of our relationship. I'd finally found someone I trusted enough to share this monumental secret with, which I'd never thought possible. But his disappointment… it was almost too much to bear. He begged me to tell you then, but I didn't know how.'

A college student at the time of Top's whirlwind romance, Pearl had been considering transferring to a college closer to home rather than deal with another semester of unexpected costs her scholarships didn't cover. But the earl had stepped in. He'd pulled her aside after the wedding and told her she was now his responsibility, which she'd argued against.

'You are,' he'd said in his very buttoned-up, no-nonsense way. 'And Topaz and I will see to whatever you need.'

There had been no sense in debating the topic any further. Whereas Top had been generous over the years when her novels were doing well, the earl had deposited a tidy sum in her bank account each month. Her dream of coupling a bachelor's degree in English with a master's in psychology became a reality – and eventually, having an advice column in a major daily newspaper. After grad school, she'd tried to return what was left over. But he'd refused, telling her to treat herself. She had, in a way, to a retirement account and, when she moved to Chicago, a hefty deposit on a vintage condo close to Lake Michigan, downtown, and the L train.

Pearl stilled with a fry in midair. There'd also been the earl's will, in which she'd been remembered generously. 'I guess this explains my unexpected inheritance.'

Top came back to the bed and sat down on the corner. 'He'd always wanted a daughter, but his first wife couldn't bear children after their son. And I wouldn't. Not after you.'

The two sat in silence as Pearl ate more of her curry. After she finished and pushed the tray away, Pearl mustered a weak smile. 'I don't know how to be mad at you. But I am. Mad at you.'

'I know, dearest, and I don't blame you,' said Top, wiping a tear away. 'I would be mad at me, too.'

'It's like my life is suddenly a game of 52-pickup, and I don't know what order to put the cards back in. Or if they're even from the same deck.'

At that, Top laughed. 'I'm sorry. I know this isn't a laughing matter, but you should've seen your face when Di taught you that game. You were so small and excited.'

The playing cards had sprayed across the living room floor and under furniture, and Pearl had learned what the word 'literal' meant as she'd picked up each card. 'I was just happy that she wanted to play a game with me. What's really sad is that I asked her to play it with me again, even knowing that the joke would be on me.'

With that, Top grabbed the linen napkin from the tray and dabbed at the corner of her eyes. 'I'm sorry, Pearl. This was never about you. It was about me, all me.'

Although she wasn't sure if she wanted to hear the answer, Pearl couldn't help but ask, 'Did you ever regret it?'

With her finger, Top traced a songbird on the duvet cover before answering. 'I tried to convince myself that I didn't. But I did.' Her voice quavered. 'Every day.'

'If you had a chance to do it over again, would you?' Pearl asked.

'Honestly?' Top shrugged. 'I don't know. I'd like to say no, but the truth is more complicated. In this case, hindsight still isn't 20/20.'

'Actually, the truth tends to be the simplest explanation,' Pearl interrupted.

'I wasn't ready to be a mother, and I don't know that I would've been a very good one,' she said. 'And I had my heart set on going to Emerson, and everything I'd done in my life up to that point was to make sure that happened.'

Not everything.

Pearl flashed back to her and Di's visit to Boston for Top's graduation. At age eight, she'd decided right then and there that she wanted to be just like the aunt she idolised. Go away to college. Live in a big city. Be everything Di wasn't and do what she hadn't.

And Pearl had never wondered why – or asked Di if she was happy with her lot in life.

'That still doesn't explain why Di was pulled into all of this,' Pearl said.

'I think Mom and Dad thought that the stigma of teenage motherhood would be enough to cure her of her wild ways. It's ironic, all things considered. But even back then, we were only identical in looks. She was outgoing and fun, and people were drawn to her like a moth to a flame. Especially boys. I was always at least two steps behind with my nose in a book.'

The sisters' relationship had always fascinated Pearl – along with one of her psychology professors after she wrote a paper on Top's gradual transformation into a lady of a bygone era. The two were as different on the inside as they were alike on the outside, or so Pearl had always thought. But now she wondered if Top had really been selfless and giving or if she was actually a more selfish and self-centered woman than Di.

'I always wished I was more like Di,' Top said. 'That's how it happened, you know. I went to a special creative arts camp that summer, alone. Once out of her shadow, I found I could shine, too. And I did. Too brightly, mayhaps.'

That's when a question occurred to Pearl. One she should've asked two days ago.

'Who was my father?'

Once, during an argument, Di had let it slip that her father was 'some' carnival worker. For whatever reason, the *some* had made the fact that her father traveled the countryside with a bunch of rickety rides seem so much worse. Di's questionable taste in men over the years had only added to the plausibility that, at 14, she'd allowed some rando to tup her in the fun house.

'He was a boy at camp, the Romeo to my Juliet – quite literally. I had a little crush, so I channeled Di when I overheard him say he was auditioning for the lead in the summer show. I couldn't believe it when I got the part! One afternoon, when just the two of us were rehearsing alone, he suggested we practice the kissing scenes.'

'Let me guess, you channeled Di again?'

With a wistful smile, Top gave a quick nod. 'One thing led to another, and well, I thought it was true love. We exchanged letters, but then ...'

'You found out you were pregnant with me?'

Top didn't need to answer the question. Her silence said enough. From what Pearl knew about her grandparents, they would've immediately nipped that teenage romance in the bud. Even without a pregnancy, but especially after their harebrained plan to swap baby mamas.

'What's his name? My dad?' she asked, stumbling on the D-word.

'Harrison.' Top smiled. 'Harrison Carter.'

Pearl fought an urge to immediately grab her phone and search the internet for any trace of the man.

'And he has no idea he has a daughter? That I exist?'

Top wiped away a tear, then another, before giving up and letting them stream down her face. 'No, he doesn't. I was forbidden from ever speaking to him again. Eventually, he stopped writing.'

'But you could've contacted him after Grandma and Grandpa died.' Pearl's short life had already changed in an instant; what would've been the harm in throwing a reverse *Parent Trap* into the mix, too?

With a small shake of her head, Top said, 'Everything was set in stone and, by that point, seemed impossible to change. It's hard to explain, dearest.'

She got that, truly, because it was even harder to understand.

Within seconds of the bedroom door clicking shut, Pearl was on her laptop, searching for Harrison Carter.

She had a father.

She'd always known she did, of course. Di had never woven fairytales or minced words about where babies came from. The first time Pearl had asked, she'd learned the ingredients essential for 'baby batter' along with step-by-step instructions and bake time.

But now he had a name. Her father. A somewhat uncommon name, but one still shared by many people in the world. Mostly dead people, judging by the plethora of formal black-and-white photos of mustached men in suits that filled the page when she changed the search results to images.

What if he were dead?

Wouldn't that be a kick in the balls, to borrow Di's favourite expression.

Social media proved more fruitful, in that all of the Harrisons smiling at her from her computer screen appeared to be alive. Although the resurgence of old-fashioned names meant that she had to wade through plenty of frat boys and high school football players to click on men in Top and Di's age range.

Disappointing, but at least she was having better luck than when she'd searched Jordan. But then, she hadn't had a lot to go on — she didn't even know his last name. Holy hell, did she really agree to spend five days with a man she knew so little about?

Yes. Yes, she did, and with the full support of her family and best friend.

And apparently her heart, considering how it had sped up when she discovered Jordan at Top's table earlier.

Finally, she found a Harrison who was from Michigan. She clicked through to his profile, enlarged the photo, and searched for any resemblance.

Maybe?

Pearl's heart raced in a different way as the pointer hovered over the button to send Harrison a message and clicked. Channeling what she might advise a reader, she typed out, 'Hi! Were you once Romeo to Topaz Carrington's Juliet?' and hit send before she could second-guess herself.

Chapter 7

The figure meandering down the beach was a far cry from the one who'd stumbled and mumbled across the sand the other day, but Jordan knew it was Pearl the moment he saw her.

'Ahoy there!' he called down from the deck of the beach hut as she drew closer.

When she reached the stairs leading to where he sat, her right hand snapped to her forehead in a mock salute. To his relief, the left one held his sweatshirt.

'Permission to board?'

Jordan settled back into his chair and propped his feet up on the length of rope serving as a railing. 'Are you here to back out? I can't invite you up if you're not coming with me to Scotland. Pride and all.'

When she shook her head, he smiled. 'Good. You may enter.'

Not that he would've blamed her for deciding that traipsing across Wales and England to Scotland with a virtual stranger was a bad idea. Hell, he'd checked himself on his cockamamie plan more times than he could count since their afternoon tea party, but he kept coming back to the same thought.

This was maybe the best idea he'd ever had.

He'd been dreading Mia and Luca's wedding, for the same reason he'd avoided all things Apex Racing since landing in Wales. Their nuptials were on the heels of the first anniversary of his and Luca's big crash at the last grand prix before Apex's mandatory summer break.

Jordan couldn't blame them for choosing this particular weekend to get married. There weren't many opportunities for time off during the nine-month racing season — with the exception of summer break, when drivers and teams couldn't even touch their cars for two full weeks. But he couldn't stop thinking that at this exact time last year, he'd been lying in a hospital bed in Budapest following his 'resignation' from Rubie Racing.

He wasn't worried about it coming up in conversation or anyone throwing the incident in his face. But it would be in the back of everyone's minds. How could it not be?

Pearl handed him his sweatshirt and settled into the deck chair beside him.

'How did the dress-hunting expedition go?' Even with Di's reassurance, he couldn't help but worry about what had been hanging among the skeletons in Top's closet.

Her eyebrows lifted. 'Well, let's just say that I hope you can tie a corset.'

Even though he wasn't sure if she was joking, he laughed. 'I'm sure I can untie one.'

Pearl turned a dozen shades of red and cleared her throat, then gulped in a hefty dose of sea air. 'About that.'

He reached over and grabbed her hand. 'I'm not expecting anything from you, Pearl. There are no strings attached to this invitation.' Not that he'd mind repeating their kiss from the other morning. 'Why don't we just consider this a date? Our first date.'

'Most first dates don't last days or involve sharing a room, which I assume we are?' she asked.

He nodded. Unsurprisingly, the bride-to-be had been frazzled by his last-minute plus-one. They had the entire castle, but space was at a premium, with only a handful of rooms reserved for family and close friends. Given everything he'd put Mia and Luca through, Jordan was lucky to be counted as part of that group – and unwilling to rock the boat any more than he already had.

'I did ask, but there are no more rooms to be had,' he said. 'Are you worried that you won't be able to restrain yourself?'

'Please,' Pearl said. 'I'm perfectly capable of keeping my hands off you. You're not that good-looking, you know.'

He lifted their clasped hands. 'In case you hadn't noticed.'

'It's called being polite.'

'Is it now? In that case...' He loosened his grip, only to have hers tighten. They stayed that way as the sky turned shades of orange and red, until she finally let go to stand up. But instead of leaving, Pearl put on the sweatshirt she was there to return.

The well-worn pale blue sweatshirt emblazoned with a single word, 'Silverstone,' had been a Christmas gift from his dad to commemorate the track where he'd stood on his first podium. There were few things or people he cared as much about as that particular item of clothing.

He liked seeing it on her. 'I'm never getting that back, am I?'

'Maybe, maybe not,' she said. 'But definitely not right now.'

'Are you cold?' Jordan asked.

He couldn't stop his brain from conjuring up more than a few ways he could take away the chill. Not that he'd go back on his promise mere minutes after making it. If a move were to be made, it would have to come from her.

But something about Pearl's quick head bob made him think she needed more than the comfort of his sweatshirt. And so he stood up and did something he hadn't wanted to do to a woman in a long time. He wrapped his arms around her, pulled her tight, and breathed her in.

Chapter 8

'I just heard the door and thought you might need some help hauling everything downstairs,' Di said from the doorway to Pearl's bedroom.

The two of them hadn't spent a moment alone since she arrived, not that their interactions the past few years could've been considered plentiful. She'd last visited Di back home in Michigan for Mother's Day almost three months ago, when they'd spent the entire weekend at a spa, only crossing paths between treatments.

It had been the ideal gift for a woman obsessed with her appearance and the perfect way to spend time together without actually spending time together. So, worth every penny. They'd decided on the spot to make it an annual tradition.

Or not.

'Are you sure you don't need me to stay?' Pearl asked, knowing there was no way Di would ever interfere with anything to do with a man – especially one who looked like Jordan.

Di shook her head. 'My sister and I have been taking care of each other our whole lives. Not that we've always done a bang-up job. I'm sorry, you know, about—'

There were probably a million ways Di could've finished that sentence, but Pearl didn't have the energy for any of them, at least not right now. She had enough to process as it was.

'Okay if we save this conversation for later?' Considering they rarely scratched the surface on any topic, choosing instead to bond over movies and reality TV, Pearl assumed it would be.

But still, she was relieved when Di nodded. 'Go and have your little dalliance. Lord knows you deserve it. Who knows? This guy could be the one. Crazier things have happened.'

'Dalliance? I think someone's been reading one of Top's romance novels.'

'If that were the case, he'd most certainly be the one,' Di said. 'No way would you have escaped the parson's mousetrap after being compromised in a beach hut.'

'Nothing happened.'

Well, almost nothing.

'Doesn't matter,' Di grinned. 'Even people thinking you might've been compromised was enough.'

'Seriously, no more old-timey romance novels for you.' Pearl handed Di the garment bag off the bed before grabbing the suitcase and heading toward the stairway.

Before they reached the main floor, voices drifted from the front room. Di stopped midway down the last flight of stairs and lifted a finger to her lips just as Pearl was about to call out that she was ready.

'I'm not sure if our Pearl mentioned, but we've had a stressful time over here,' they heard Top say. 'Whatever your intentions, I feel the need to ask that you please tread carefully where she's concerned. Although Pearl is an adult and clearly capable of taking care of herself, I'd hate to see her hurt. I'm afraid we've already wounded her enough for one lifetime.'

Her heart began to race, but Pearl couldn't decide if it was from Top's attempt at motherly concern or the anticipation about how Jordan might respond. Since Di refused to budge, she had no choice but to eavesdrop.

'I understand,' Jordan said. 'And while I'm not comfortable sharing what Pearl has told me in confidence, I will say that I have no intention of making anything worse for her.'

Di looked back at Pearl and mouthed, 'Good answer.'

Even though she thought it was, too, especially considering that Pearl couldn't remember exactly all she'd shared with him, she mouthed back, 'Move.'

But before they could continue down the last few steps, they heard Top's voice again.

'That's nice to hear because, and I'll only say this once, I wouldn't recommend messing with the jewel sisters. The crazy goes way deeper than the long dress.'

At that, Di picked up the pace all on her own, yelling, 'You won't know what hit you, and we won't even bother making it look like an accident,' as she reached the room.

Instead of finding Top and Jordan circling each other, about to throw down, they discovered Top smiling from her chaise like a Cheshire cat and Jordan at the fireplace, his elbow resting on the mantle. He winked at Pearl before turning to address Di. 'Trust me when I say I'll keep that in mind. In fact, I doubt I'll be able to forget it.'

He crossed the room to take the garment bag from Di, who followed Jordan to the front door. But before Pearl could take a step, a pair of arms wrapped around her from behind.

'I don't blame you for running away,' Top whispered, kissing the back of her head.

'I'm not running away.' Pearl turned around and looked the person she'd always loved most in the world in the eye. 'It's a lot to process. I just need to be somewhere else for a few days.'

And maybe be someone else, too.

'A little advice, if I may. Don't let it go on for too long. You can begin to forget who you actually are.' With a crooked smile, Top took both of Pearl's hands in hers and gave them a squeeze. 'I named you, you know. The very first time I held you, you looked at me with those gray eyes, so knowing, so wise, that I felt like the jig was already up. I told Di you were our little Pearl of wisdom, and the name stuck.'

Pearl let Top pull her in for a hug. 'I still don't care for it,' she whispered. 'But thank you.'

When they finally walked outside, Di and Jordan were standing next to a sports car straight out of a James Bond film. It was somehow both squat and sleek, had angled slats in lieu of a rear window, and probably cost more than her condo — maybe her entire condo building. Even the rarely fazed Di was dumbstruck.

No wonder he'd politely declined the offer of her economy-level rental car for the trip — and not just because she'd insisted they stop by a branch of the rental car company and add him as a second driver. After Jordan grabbed her suitcase and placed it in the trunk, Pearl automatically went to the right side of the car, realizing a second too late that she was about to climb behind the steering wheel.

From across the roof, Jordan winked. 'Are you volunteering to take the first driving shift?'

'God no,' she said, making her way around the car to the door he'd opened for her. 'Trust me when I say you don't have enough insurance to have me as anything other than a passenger. I'm so out of practice from living in the city that I'm a hazard even when the steering wheel and shifter are where they're supposed to be, and I'm driving on the right side of the road.'

'Point taken, and trust me when I say that I'm more than happy to play chauffeur,' he said, shutting her door.

As soon as he was out of earshot, Di leaned in through the open window. 'What did I tell you.'

When it came to men and money, the woman had a sixth sense. With a palm to Di's forehead, Pearl pushed her out of the car as Jordan settled into the driver's seat. She answered his questioning glance with a shrug before turning her attention back to Top and Di.

'I'll check in later,' Pearl said. 'I promise.'

Side by side, the sisters nodded in unison.

'You have fun, dearest,' Top said, dabbing the corner of her eyes with a monogrammed handkerchief that had appeared from the folds of her long skirt. 'I'll be fine.'

Beside her, Jordan pressed a button next to the gearshift, and the engine revved to life. He guided the car neatly onto the road like it was his job.

He glanced her way. 'Are you ready for this, Pearl?'

'Yes,' she said, even though she was suddenly even more unsure of what 'this' was.

Chapter 9

The car was too much.

Jordan had known it the second he'd walked into the dealership of one of Britain's most iconic luxury brands and laid eyes on what was basically a road-legal race car on the sales floor. When the starstruck owner – who also happened to own the dealership – had so readily offered up her keys, he hadn't been able to bring himself to say no. Especially since every part of his body had been screaming yes.

It had been far too long since he'd driven anything with this much power. If there's something every race car driver knows, it's the importance of getting right back up on that horse after a crash. Jordan hadn't been back in a race car since he'd literally been pulled from the wreck he'd made of his. By his calculations, 600-and-some horsepower should more than make up for those 12 long months – not that he was ready to go anywhere near that fast. That would take some time, which was something Jordan had plenty of.

But if he'd known how much it would throw Pearl off her

game, he would've borrowed the SUV Wyn kept in Abersoch and called it a day. For the last 20 minutes, she'd done nothing besides stare out the passenger-side window, her arms folded in front of her like she'd been warned to look with her eyes, not her hands.

Unless he could get her to relax, they were in for a very long drive. Too bad the lack of a backseat made his tried-and-true relaxation method out of the question.

'My sister and her fiancé are into naming their cars,' he said. 'Any thoughts about what we should call this one?'

Her gaze drifted from the window again. 'It's not yours?'

He wished. 'Nope, it's a loaner. I was thinking the green machine, but that might be a bit on the nose.'

She shrugged. 'It's all right. What's your sister's car's name?'

'The supercharged squash.'

The Apex Racing car — designed to fit him and his driving style to a T — had emerged from the flames of his dumpster fire of a career like a phoenix rising from the ashes.

Her eyebrow arched. 'I'm guessing it's fast? And orange?'

Pearl had no idea. 'That would be correct.'

The supercharged squash could clock more than 200 miles per hour in a straight line. With Mia behind the wheel this season, it was one of the fastest cars on the track.

Last season, it had gone through some things before Mia's best friend had christened what was technically the RR1 into the gourd family. Named in honor of his father, it had been the last Apex Racing car Rob Rubie had worked on — and the one he was most confident would bring the team a world championship. And it had, to Luca.

'And her fiancé's car? What did he name his?'

'The turbo pumpkin. For the same reason.'

'Wow, they must really like orange.' She laughed. 'And fast cars.'

Here's your opening, my man. Take it. Tell her. She's going to find out soon enough.

But he couldn't bring himself to launch into a literal crash course about all things Rubie Racing. 'You don't know the half of it,' he laughed.

As her gaze drifted out the side window again, Jordan began to think the car wasn't the cause of her discomfort. Her fingers finding her temples and rubbing them in a circular motion only confirmed his suspicion.

'You okay over there?' He pointed at the water bottles in the cupholder. 'One of those is for you. You're likely still jet-lagged, and you need to stay hydrated.'

'Thank you.' She opened one and took a sip. 'I feel bad leaving, but I couldn't stay. It's so weird there right now. I mean, Top and Di always bring a level of weirdness to everything, just by being themselves, but this is something else.'

Besides what Pearl had told him in the beach hut and what he'd seen with his own eyes at afternoon tea, he knew little about the sisters. But he'd been surprised when Top broke character and basically threatened him when he came to pick up Pearl. Impressed, too.

'I still can't believe that there are still earls and that Top married one,' he said. 'I'd assumed that world had gone the way of the horse and carriage.'

'Oh, yes, the aristocracy is still around – dukes, viscounts, you name it,' she said. 'Top's earl was very nice, and they were deeply in love. His title passed to his son when he died, of course, but Top was well taken care of. It changed her, though, losing the love of her life. It was as if she lost some of what made her sparkle, too.'

After watching his dad grieve for his mom for 20 years, Jordan was well familiar with how love lost can wreck a person. He'd always struggled to imagine finding a love so big and all-consuming, even though he grew up seeing that kind of love between his parents every day.

'What about Di? Did she ever get married?'

Maybe he shouldn't have assumed she wasn't married, given she was as beautiful as her sister. But he hadn't noticed a wedding ring.

'Di hopped from relationship to relationship,' Pearl said. 'Nothing ever lasted more than a couple of months. She called them her summer flings, regardless of the season. Although mostly, they happened over the summer.'

Jordan gulped. Di's relationship track record was more similar to his than he cared to admit.

'It seems like they're close, though,' he said. 'That's nice, especially since they're so different.'

He wished he could say the same for him and Mia, although, since the crash, they'd grown closer than they'd ever been.

And on the surface, they had more in common as fraternal twins than Top and Di seemed to as identical twins. Even from his brief interactions with the jewel sisters, they came across as polar opposites – Di pushing forward while Top hung back.

'They're thick as thieves. I dedicated a whole term of psychology research to personas and came up with no logical reason for their behavior. My professor insisted it was due to trauma, but I could never find any.'

Jordan's eyes widened as he nudged the side of her arm with his elbow. 'I don't know, do you think that maybe a twin-baby swap type of thing would qualify?'

She laughed. 'I may owe a certain psych professor a very long apology email.'

Pearl's eyes drifted out her window again, making Jordan wonder if she'd rather he stop talking. But he had one more question.

'Have you always called Di by her first name?'

Pearl took a deep breath. 'Di always joked about not having a motherly bone in her body. One day, she sat me down and said, "We're all adults here, why don't you just call me Di."'

'How old were you?'

'Nine.' She turned toward the window once more. 'A very mature nine, but then I kind of had to be.'

Nine? Jordan couldn't have imagined calling his dad by his first name at 29, and they'd worked together every day.

'What's catching your eye out there?' Jordan finally asked. The worldview from his side of the car was rolling green field after rolling green field, sheep and more sheep, and had been since the moment they'd left the village limits of Abersoch behind them.

'Sorry, I'm not trying to be rude,' she said. 'It's the sheep. I'm looking for any on their backs. If they somehow manage to roll onto their back, they can't right themselves again. They just lie there, stuck, with their little feet kicking up in the air.'

Pearl paddled her hands in front of her to demonstrate, even though her eyes stayed glued to the window. It may have been the cutest thing he'd ever seen.

'If no one finds them and flips them over, they suffocate.' She finally turned toward him again. 'Or worse.'

'What could be worse than suffocating?' he asked.

'A crow might peck out their eyes.'

Holy hell. Why'd she have to say eyes?

The image of a crow feasting on a sheep's eye had Jordan squirming in his seat. If there was anything that set his teeth on edge, it was an injury to the eye. When he was a kid, his dad had told him about a friend who'd tripped and landed eye first on a tent stake. He'd never wanted to go camping again. Add in crows and their sharp, pointy beaks, and he was about ready to lose the bacon sandwich he'd had for breakfast.

'Not on our watch,' he said, keeping one eye on the fields on his side of the car while the other stayed fixed on the road. After more than a decade of driving race cars, multitasking behind the wheel was second nature. Who knew that skill would be put to use rescuing sheep from death and blindness by crow.

For the next couple of hours, that's quite literally how they rolled – scanning the countryside for upside-down sheep as they chatted. Jordan learned that Pearl had grown up on the opposite side of metro Detroit, so their paths probably never crossed; that her grandfather had worked on the assembly line for one of the automakers, but she had zero interest in cars and didn't even own one; and that she'd basically raised herself, and Di, after her grandparents died.

Comparing his life to hers made him feel like something of a schmuck. He'd had everything money could buy and a professional driving career handed to him on a silver platter. And for reasons he still couldn't fully figure out, he'd been a miserable s.o.b.

A castle ruin in the distance interrupted his thoughts. High on a hilltop, it was hard to imagine what the crumbling pile of rocks had looked like in its heyday.

'I hope the castle your sister is getting married in is in better shape than that one,' Pearl said.

Knowing Mia, even if she'd fallen in love with a medieval fortress in shambles, she would've found a way to put it back together again. Probably better and more fortified than it had been in the first place. 'I'm sure it is.'

She arched an eyebrow. 'But you don't know for sure?'

'I looked at the website, but I didn't pay much attention,' Jordan said. 'I mean, if you've seen one castle, you've seen them all, right?'

'I'm not sure that's how that works.' Pearl gave her eyebrow a break and shook her head. 'Like you've seen a lot of castles.'

More than his fair share, actually, and some more than once. If there was a castle near a track on the Apex circuit, the Rubie Racing marketing team booked it for a sponsor dinner. He'd come to view them as nothing more than medieval banquet halls.

When Jordan finally left the motorway to take the scenic route through England's Lake District, he wished they had days to explore the national park instead of hours to drive through it. He'd chosen a route before they'd set off, and the two of them took turns pointing out whatever they were gawking at through the window. Just when they thought they couldn't see a more spectacular view, they were proven wrong. Each time they rounded the next bend on the mountain pass, a landscape more lush than the one before revealed itself.

'I didn't know this many shades of green existed,' Jordan said.

On a whim, they decided to stretch their legs on a short walk when Pearl spotted a sign for a car park and a trailhead. Although they weren't dressed for a hike, they ambled along the path in sandals and flip-flops, past old stone walls and fields of, thankfully, upright sheep.

When they reached a stone bridge that looked as if it had stood for hundreds of years, Jordan paused midway. As he peered at the water rushing over moss-covered rocks below, Pearl laughed out loud beside him.

'I feel like I've slipped into the pages of one of Top's

historical romance novels,' she said. 'I half expect a knight to come riding up on his steed and steal me away.'

'No way am I letting that happen,' Jordan said, turning toward her.

'No?' she asked, facing him.

'Absolutely not.' His hands lifted to cradle her face, his thumbs brushing her cheeks as he studied her face. 'I don't think I've ever met anyone with gray eyes. Although sometimes, they remind me of the lightest shade of the bluest sea, where the sun's rays reach the white sand, and I want to drown in them.'

As much as his lips wanted to feel hers again, Jordan reminded himself to let Pearl take the lead. Even if the strategy had resulted in a chaste good night kiss the night before. Just when he thought nothing would happen, Pearl leaned in. That was enough of a signal for him. He kissed her once and stopped, to make sure it was what she wanted, and then paused again after the second, slightly longer kiss, just to be sure.

When he clearly had a green light for a third kiss, it was 'lights out and away we go.'

And then he was drowning, and he didn't care if he ever came up for air.

Chapter 10

When they were back on the motorway and debating where to stop for the night, Pearl gasped and pointed at a sign. In a flash, Jordan manoeuvered them across two lanes, neatly dodging cars to make the exit.

'What's so special about this place?' he asked as they entered the village limits of Gretna Green.

As she was about to admit that she couldn't remember, Jordan pointed out the driver-side window. 'I wonder what's so famous about that blacksmith shop?'

That's when it hit her. Starting in the late 1700s, it had been the quickie wedding capital of the UK, the Scottish equivalent of Las Vegas. Only instead of cheesy wedding chapels with fake Elvises, there were blacksmith shops with smithies marrying couples hopelessly in love and, more than likely, lust.

Top had told her about the village's famous past when she was writing a novel where some lady – the kind with a capital 'L' – ran away to Gretna Green to marry a duke who'd ravished her in an orangery.

'This place is famous because it's the first village in Scotland across the border from England, and couples used to elope here. At one time, England had tight restrictions for marriage while Scotland's were far more loosey-goosey.'

'How exactly does the blacksmith shop fit into this?' He seemed genuinely curious.

'Blacksmiths performed the weddings over anvils,' Pearl said. 'And that's all I know.'

Well, that and if their mostly innocent night in the beach hut had happened a couple of centuries before, they may have taken this same journey in a horse and carriage.

Jordan parked in front of an inn that looked as if it had been around since the time of anvil weddings. Pink and white flowers overflowed from boxes outside every window. A weathered sign promising accommodations and ales – which Pearl decided she might need in the opposite order – stuck out from the stone building in an elaborate wrought iron frame.

He turned off the car. 'I, for one, will not be able to rest until I know the full story of old-timey weddings in Scotland, so I vote that we stop here for the night and explore.'

The inside of the inn was as rustic and charming as the outside, with low doorways and ceilings and dark wood trim and beams. A bar and dining area took up much of the main floor, and it was bustling with locals catching up over pints.

They took the only available room, which the innkeeper promised with a quick wink was the nicest and the largest.

He handed Jordan an actual metal key attached to a large wooden keychain and directed them to take a narrow staircase at the side of the lobby up to the second floor.

At just over five feet, Pearl wasn't always the best judge of height. But when they arrived at the door to number 11, even she could tell it wasn't a standard size.

'I guess people were shorter back in the day,' Jordan laughed, although he didn't have to stoop to enter the room either.

The ceiling also seemed too low, to the point that the top of the immense four-poster bed nearly touched it. They found a sitting room tucked around a corner, with embroidered wall hangings of hills and flowers and French doors leading to a wrought iron balcony that appeared original to the building.

It was quirky and strange, and Top would've loved it.

'You need to see this, Pearl,' Jordan called out from the bathroom.

A jetted bathtub large enough for two took up much of the small space and appeared in danger of falling through the dipped floor void of water or people.

'We're not getting in that thing,' Pearl laughed.

'Don't have to tell me twice,' he said.

They wandered back toward the door where they'd ditched their luggage. Jordan opened his small suitcase, revealing a condensed closet with his clothes folded neatly inside. He hung it and his garment bag in the wardrobe before disappearing into the bathroom with a toiletry bag. The entire process took less than two minutes.

The man was a master of efficiency.

Pearl was more than a little turned on.

She was still unpacking when Jordan emerged. Somehow, a day behind the wheel on narrow roads had energised him, whereas Pearl felt like she could use a yoga class and a power nap.

He took one look at her much slower progress, grabbed his backpack, and suggested he wait for her downstairs. Once he'd left the room, she sent a quick text to check in with Top and Di before tackling the rest of her suitcase.

Her phone dinged twice just after she'd freed the bottom of the evening gowns from the hanging garment bag.

Top: You ran off to Gretna Green? No need for such extremes in this day and age, dearest.

Di: Told ya she'd been compromised.

When Pearl's brain auto-responded 'not yet,' she stashed a few of the condoms she and Millie had vowed, as independent women, to always carry with them in the nightstand drawer. Just in case.

Fifteen minutes later, she found Jordan at the bar nursing a pint and scrolling on his phone. He slid the glass toward her, and they traded sips back and forth as they decided what to do first. The bartender, already on a first-name basis with Jordan, suggested the courtship maze, where couples started at separate entrances with the goal of finding each other at a bridge in the middle.

When they stepped outside, the day had turned gloomy and chilly. Jordan dug through his backpack and then held his arms straight out in front of him. She eyed the jacket in his left hand but grabbed the sweatshirt in his right. The same one she'd borrowed and returned, and then borrowed and returned to him again only a few hours ago.

He grinned as she pulled it over her head. 'I knew it.'

Even though she'd washed it at Top's, it already smelled like Jordan again. Clean. Musky. 'I'm cold, and this is the only thing available to warm me up.'

With a choking noise, Jordan grabbed her hand and pulled her in the direction of the courtship maze. 'I have an idea,' he said. 'We should time how long it takes us, then switch entrances and see if we can beat our time.'

Fortunately, Mother Nature had other ideas. Raindrops began falling within half a block, just as they stumbled upon the original blacksmith shop-turned-museum. They ducked inside before the heavy clouds completely let loose.

A man clad in a kilt greeted them as if they were the first people he'd seen in several hours, if not days. Through his thick brogue, they were able to glean that his name was Logan and his great-great-great-great-great-great-'granda' had been a blacksmith who performed marriages back in the day, in this very shop no less.

At least, that's what Pearl thought he'd said. Judging by how quickly Jordan grabbed her hand and squeezed, the struggle was real for him, too. When he didn't let go, their kilted guide gave her a knowing smile and showed them around, pointing out with pride a display of centuries-old marriage certificates. They nodded and followed along, still not completely understanding him – or realizing he'd led them into the original marriage room until they saw the anvil front and center.

When the great-great-great-great-great-great-grandson of the original smithy led them over to the anvil and re-arranged their still-clasped hands so they were facing each other, with Jordan's right hand to her left, she worried about what they'd been nodding along to. But when he took a length of tartan fabric from the small leather pouch attached to a belt around his waist and began to bind their hands together as he murmured words in Scottish, she had a good idea.

Above Logan's soft brogue, only Jordan's steady breathing filled her ears. Before she realised what she was doing, she'd matched her breaths to his.

This isn't real.

Her heart didn't care.

With each wrap of the tartan, it felt real enough. By the time their guide tied a knot with the two ends, her heart was ready to explode out of her chest.

You barely know this person.

Except her heart felt she did, in all the ways that mattered.

When Logan said, 'You can kiss yer bride,' Pearl finally lifted her gaze from their bound hands and locked eyes with Jordan. As his head dipped and his lips touched hers, she wondered how this was happening to her, an advice columnist who had once told a reader to keep her libido in check because lust wasn't love. Because she'd be damned if she could tell the difference right now, as she was literally and figuratively bound to Jordan.

Then his mouth fully took hers and his free hand went to the back of her head, combing through her hair and pulling her closer. Pearl's lips parted on instinct, welcoming him in.

Her brain may not have understood how so many couples once upon a time pledged themselves to each other after only a few days, but in that moment, her body got it.

When they finally broke apart, Jordan rested his forehead on hers. The man they'd forgotten was even in the room cleared his throat to get their attention. With his right hand tapping his chest over his heart, Logan declared, ''Tis no legal anywhere but in here.'

That was enough for Pearl, who was still struggling to catch her breath. As if the kiss hadn't been enough to bring her to knees, Jordan handed over a wad of notes for the length of tartan that still bound them together and led her out into the rain, where he pinned her to the side of the building with his body and blue eyes swimming with desire and emotion.

His mouth slid up her neck until it hovered over her ear. 'Pearl, trust me when I say that I want you more right now than I've ever wanted anything or anyone.'

No one had ever spoken those kinds of words to her,

wanted her that much. She turned her head to look at him, only to have his lips catch hers again.

'Jordan,' she gasped, lifting their bound hands to where they could both see them, 'please tell me you can run with this on.'

Chapter 11

It was hard to say who won the race back to the inn, but for what had to have been the first time in his life, Jordan didn't care who came in first. He was a winner regardless.

They slowed to a stroll as they walked into the lobby and toward the stairs, connected by the tartan and a burning need to remove it and everything else they had on. But of course, the room key was in the front pocket of his jeans, just out of his reach.

'A little help here, Pearl?'

Her hand explored his backside as her mouth found his, even though he knew damn well she'd seen where he'd put the key. When it came up empty, she grazed the front of his jeans on her way to search the correct spot.

A very thorough search.

He lifted his head and whispered, 'Wrong wood.'

She finally pulled out her hand and pressed the key in his. 'Open the door, Jordan.'

They stumbled into the room half wrapped in each other's

arms, only coming to a stop when the backs of Pearl's legs met the edge of the bed. With his available index finger, he tilted her chin until her eyes finally met his. 'Bound or not bound?'

'Bound. Definitely bound.'

The woman may kill him.

His left hand dragged slowly down her back, settling on a cheek and tugging her against the hard length of him. With another brush of his lips, he asked, 'Do you know what I'm thinking, Pearl?'

With a slight nod, she fell back onto the mattress, taking him with her.

'Tsk tsk,' he teased. 'Not yet. First, I need to do everything I've been dreaming about for the past three days.'

Jordan slid down her body until he'd settled between Pearl's legs.

He couldn't remember ever feeling such a driving need to be inside someone. He had to tap into a level of control typically saved for the racetrack as he single-handedly unbuttoned her shorts and then slid them, and himself, down her body. He showered her feet with kisses when a silky thong finally passed them by, and then tossed it aside before sinking onto his knees.

All the while, their hands stayed clasped and wrapped in the most beautiful tartan ever woven.

Before Jordan could lean forward and pull her closer, Pearl scooted toward the edge of the bed and lifted her hips, bringing the sweet center of her so near that he only had to stick out his tongue to touch it. When he didn't within five seconds, she nearly pushed herself right into his mouth.

He couldn't help but laugh, especially when she nudged his right shoulder with her big toe.

'It seems someone needs a lesson in patience,' he said.

But one thing was for certain, Jordan Rubie was no man to teach it.

At least, not now, as he kissed up the soft skin of her inner thigh. He listened for her quickened breath and marked certain spots with an X on the map he was charting in his mind. By the time he reached his final destination, she was nearly there.

'Pearl, relax.'

'I don't think that's possible at this point,' she said. 'What you're doing is probably classified as torture in some parts of the world. Maybe this part. I don't know the laws here.'

Jordan laughed. 'Remind me to ask you later what other countries I should include on the must-visit list I'm definitely making for us.'

Pearl's groan morphed into a moan when – done torturing them both – he finally took her fully in his mouth. Another X to mark on his map, not that he could forget this particular spot or the one slightly above it that made her back arch. But hearing his name spill from her lips caused his own need to hit him like a brick wall. His intensity must've been contagious because she almost immediately shouted and shattered.

In what felt like an instant, they were a tangle of arms and legs, helping each other take off what clothes they could with their hands still tied together with the tartan. His jacket and shirt were three-quarters of the way off, having been stalled just below his shoulder above the length of plaid.

'My sweatshirt—'

He growled. 'My sweatshirt, and leave it on.' There was something about seeing this woman in his most prized piece of clothing that he was beginning to like. Even more so when she straddled him.

Another growl escaped his throat when he realised the condoms were still in his bag. 'We need to get up and grab—'

Pearl chose that moment to lean toward Jordan and suck his nipple. *Holy hell.* He nearly came right then and there. Before he could drag them off the bed and across the room, she reached into the nightstand and grabbed exactly what they needed.

'Is this what you want, Jordan?' she asked, a mischievous smile spreading across her face.

'Yes, please,' he said, his voice suddenly hoarse.

Pearl sealed his mouth closed with hers before taking care of business and then slowly easing them together.

Jordan used to kid that sliding into his race car for the first time each season was better than sex. Everyone would laugh, but for Jordan, it was the truth. But now he knew the joke had been on him all along.

This, with this woman, was as close as he'd ever come to an out-of-body experience, and that was saying a lot. In his career, he'd totaled seven race cars while going more than 150 miles per hour.

Pearl leaned over him, but before he could find her mouth, she gripped every inch and ounce of him. And just like that, he was gone.

'I don't know how you can eat that.'

They'd woken up starving and, after satiating their most immediate hunger, headed downstairs to the dining room. The traditional Scottish breakfast seemed like the best idea based on the quantity of food alone.

And when Pearl did a very couple-y thing – sliding a pile of what appeared to be crumbled hamburger onto his plate from hers – Jordan didn't think the morning could get any better.

Until his chewing prompted fake gagging from her side of the table.

'What do you mean?' he asked, taking another bite. After years of traveling the Apex circuit with food flown from home and a set menu to ensure foreign fare didn't disrupt his diet, he'd been enjoying trying whatever was placed in front of him this trip. Taco-type meat on a breakfast plate was weird, but he'd rolled with it. At least until he saw how wide Pearl's eyes were.

'Do you really not know that you're eating haggis?'

As he shook his head and willed himself to swallow, she arched an eyebrow – which was never a good sign, he was realizing. After washing the mouthful down with a half cup of coffee, he posed the question he wasn't sure he wanted the answer to.

'What is it? Seriously, you need to tell me.'

'To be honest, I'm not entirely sure because it's a number of things,' she said. 'But definitely sheep's lungs. According to Top, that's why it's banned in the States. Which is nutso considering what we eat. I mean, hot dogs?'

As she rambled on for a few minutes about what other sheep parts might've been used in the inn's recipe, he ate some traditional bread and drank the rest of his water and Pearl's, and then both of their coffees to try and get the taste out of his mouth.

An hour later, the mystery mutton was sitting like a rock in his stomach. Still, knowing he was full of various sheep organs wasn't enough to cast a dark cloud on the morning, especially given how it had started.

Jordan glanced over at Pearl, whose head was leaning against the window with her eyes half closed. He was about to pat himself on the back for so thoroughly wearing her out when she shouted, 'There's one!'

He veered to the side of the narrow road, and in a flash, she was out of the car, tumbling over a fence and running across a field. He raced after her, arriving at the downed black sheep only seconds after she did. The animal was definitely trapped on its back but still breathing, at least. In memory of its brethren's lungs making their way through his digestive system, Jordan made a silent vow that this one's would continue to pump air.

Jordan rubbed his hands together as Pearl circled the sheep, assessing the situation. 'Okay, what do we do?'

'I don't know!' she said. 'This is the first time I've actually found one.'

He took a step closer. To his relief, the animal still had both its eyes, although the narrow slits parading as pupils would surely take top billing in his next nightmare.

'Stay there,' he said once Pearl was opposite him. 'You push, and I'll pull.'

'Baa,' the sheep said.

'Well, that's enough for express verbal consent for me.' Jordan gripped its fleece while Pearl knelt down and pressed her hands into its side. 'On the count of three. One, two—'

'Three,' she screamed.

But the damp wool slipped through Jordan's fingers as soon as he began to pull, and his feet slid on the wet grass. He popped up within seconds of his ass hitting the ground to find all of Pearl's concern directed toward the sheep.

'What do we do?' she asked, patting its head.

Both Pearl's and the sheep's heads turned his way as he paced around the field. If only he hadn't left his phone in the car. There was surely at least one video on the internet about how to flip a sheep. Although he shuddered to think of the Pandora's box of perversion he wouldn't be able to unsee after searching 'sheep on its back.'

'The fleece is too slippery for me to get a good grip,' he said. 'I'm going to pull its legs this time. You still push.'

He took hold of the sheep's ankles. 'Ready?' Jordan said to both Pearl and the sheep.

'Baa,' the sheep said.

Pearl patted its side. 'We're ready.'

This time, they both screamed on three, and to their amaze-ment, the sheep was on its side and then up on all four legs within seconds. After a brief wobble, it ran off to join the rest of its flock, which, unbeknownst to Pearl and Jordan, had been watching the entire scene from a distance.

'We did it!' Pearl squealed and flung herself into his arms.

He caught her, and as he lifted her off the ground, her legs wrapped around his waist. Laughter bubbled up inside of him as his mouth found hers.

Clapping and cheering alerted them to an audience behind them, too. Jordan set Pearl down and took a bow as she curtsied for the small group of bystanders.

The two of them were the definition of the worse for wear. The sheep had streaked Jordan's crew neck with its hooves, and Pearl's floral top was grimy from leveraging her entire body on the beast's fleece during their heroic effort. He offered her a grubby hand, which she accepted with a smile.

'At least now your outside matches your inside,' she said as they walked back to the car. 'You know, sheep-wise.'

'Wonderful,' he said. 'I hope they send a thank you note.'

Jordan didn't notice the guy recording the entire scene with his mobile phone until they climbed over the fence. He gave him a quick nod as he rounded the rear of the sports car, having deposited Pearl safely in the passenger seat and shut her door.

'Nice going, mate,' the stranger said, still filming. 'Looks like you haven't lost your touch for flipping things over.'

Jordan's hand hovered over his door handle as he waited for his old friend, anger, to boil over. But for the first time in recent memory, the only thing simmering under the surface was a bubble of laughter.

'What can I say, it's a skill for life,' he shrugged. 'Have a great day.'

They stopped in the first village they came to, when Pearl spotted public restrooms with her eagle eye. Jordan scrubbed his hands and face the best he could, but getting the dirt and smell out of his clothes would take more than a surface cleaning. When he exited to find the sidewalk empty, he ducked into a nearby souvenir shop.

'Here,' he said, handing Pearl a bag five minutes later before heading back into the men's room. 'It's not perfect, but I'd rather not dig into my clean clothes until I've had a shower. I didn't exactly overpack for this trip as it is.'

When they met up on the sidewalk again a few minutes later, after he'd attempted for a second time to remove the sheep smell from his body, Pearl was wearing a bright red sweatshirt with what the woman in the shop had informed him was a Highland cow with Royal Stewart tartan horns plastered on the front.

She pointed at his sweatshirt, which was identical except for the tartan balmoral hat atop his cow's head. 'Nice green pom.'

He pulled her in for a kiss. 'Before you ask, the options were limited. It was either these or the Loch Ness Monster.

And as intrigued as I am by Nessie, I've suddenly developed quite an attachment to tartan.'

'Agreed,' Pearl said, following his kiss with one of her own. 'But I think we should probably get a moo-ve on.'

Since sheep-saving had lost them an hour, they decided to eat on the road and hump the rest of the way to the castle. While Jordan topped off the fuel tank, Pearl ducked inside the station's market. The bulging bag she returned to the car with was slightly worrisome.

'There'd better not be more haggis in there,' he said.

'I wouldn't do that to your stomach twice in one day,' Pearl said. 'Plus, convenience store fare is miles better here. You'll see.'

Not only had she managed to find her favorite sandwich, which was a sort of magical combination of roast chicken and stuffing, but she'd also bought an assortment of others with chicken, bacon, egg salad, and smoked salmon. After she'd gone over all of the options, he pointed at the Thanksgiving-esque one.

Pearl shook her head. 'This was the only one they had.'

His original plan had been to tease her a little, but now he was genuinely intrigued. 'It's your fault for selling it so well. I have to try it.'

'Fine,' Pearl said, opening the triangular container. But instead of handing it to him, she stuck her tongue out and licked both halves.

If she thought anything she did with her tongue would deter him, she was about to be sorely disappointed. 'I did grow up with a sibling, you know. Mia once farted on a brownie, and I still ate it.'

'Your mother must've been very proud of the two of you,' she said, making a show of sighing deeply as she handed over half. 'Don't even think about asking for any of the smoked salmon and butter.'

Pearl didn't give him a choice of chips. It wasn't until he cracked open the bag she handed him that he noticed her less than conspicuous attempt to hide her small bag from his view.

'I can see what you're doing over there.' He reached over to try and grab the bag out of her hand, but she moved it between the seat and the door and then shoved a handful of chips in her mouth.

'Stop,' she mumbled, her mouth full.

'What was that? You want me to stop the car so I can force you to share whatever it is you're hoarding?'

She shook her head and inhaled another handful.

'You're going to hurt yourself over there.'

'Am not,' she said, her mouth still stuffed with chips.

'This is not a good look for you,' he laughed, then pointed his hand out the window. 'Sheep down!'

In the one second she lowered her defenses, he snatched the nearly empty bag from her grip. After a quick glance, he threw it back on her lap. 'Marmite? That's what you were protecting? Trust me when I say that it's not necessary. I think I threw up a little just thinking about eating one, and that's saying a lot considering all I've had in my mouth today.'

When he noticed Pearl's blush, he backtracked – slightly.

'You're being a little melodramatic, don't you think?' She held a chip up for display. 'For the record, these are delicious.'

He imitated her fake gag from breakfast. 'For the record, you could not be more wrong. Keep them away from me. Actually, I'd like you to stay away from me, too. Don't even breathe in my direction.'

Pearl rolled her eyes and made a display of licking the chip before putting it in her mouth, then polished off the rest of the bag in silence. But a few minutes later, she grabbed his arm and screeched, 'Pull over, now!'

The car was barely off the road before her mouth was on his. If her goal was to be funny, she failed in the most spectacular way. Even with the lingering taste of Marmite, the kiss went from zero to infinity in passion within seconds.

'Fine, you win,' he gasped. 'But I have to warn you, if you keep that up, you're going to get a bigger prize than you bargained for.'

She planted another kiss on his lips, letting it linger a few tantalizing seconds too long, before settling back into her seat and refastening her seat belt. 'In this car? I don't think so.'

'Oh, you have no idea what I'm capable of in a car, Pearl.'

He pulled back onto the road and let pass what was likely the last perfect opening for letting her know she was about to walk into a castle filled with royalty of the auto racing variety. There would be a virtual minefield of drivers, present company included, considering how close he'd just come to exploding.

But when Jordan looked over and saw how pleased Pearl seemed with herself as she pulled out a second bag of Marmite chips and winked, he couldn't bear losing a moment where he was just a normal guy unexpectedly taking a funny and gorgeous woman to his sister's wedding.

A woman who just happened to make a living telling people the difference between right and wrong.

A woman who thought he was sweet, who laughed at his jokes, and who drove him crazy in the best way.

A woman who had no idea he was the racing world's most infamous bad boy, who'd left a trail of broken hearts, cars, and, at times, people behind him.

'How much longer?' Pearl asked, finishing the second and hopefully last bag of toxic chips.

He checked the navigational screen, knowing that whatever it said wouldn't be nearly long enough.

Chapter 12

'Oh, thank God!' wasn't the greeting Pearl had expected from the woman – Jordan's twin, she presumed – who rushed out to meet them in the castle's parking area.

'Pardon?' Pearl asked.

'It's just that we thought you might be Julia Sullivan,' she said, making a show of grabbing the shoulder of the man now standing next to her for mock support. 'There's even a betting sheet going around about it.'.

The guy nodded in agreement, as if thinking Pearl might be one of the world's most famous models somehow made sense. 'I believe everyone except Barb and I lost.' He smiled and extended a hand. 'Luca Toscano, groom. And this lovely woman is Mia, my soon-to-be bride.'

She shook both of their hands before turning to Jordan, expecting her confusion to be mirrored on his face. It wasn't.

'Did you really think I would do that?' he said quietly. 'Seriously?'

If there was an emotion Pearl was in tune with, especially

this week, it was tension. And as much as she had a sudden urge to pull Jordan down to the nearest loch and hold his head underwater until he shared why he kept company with models, she was, at heart, a pacifist.

And it was her turn to help diffuse whatever was happening with his family, just as he'd managed to with hers. She grabbed Jordan's hand and gave it a squeeze.

'Did my outfit give it away?' Pearl asked. 'Or the fact that I'm a full foot shorter than most models?'

Mia laughed. 'Well, since you brought up the sweatshirts... what exactly is happening here?'

Pearl began sharing the story of the sheep in distress but within seconds, Jordan added his own commentary until they were rushing to finish each other's sentences. At one point, she made Jordan turn around and show off the grass stains on his butt, but he baaed like a sheep all on his own.

By the end, they were all almost doubled over.

'So, I think it's pretty clear that I'm not a supermodel in sheep's clothing,' Pearl finally managed to say.

'Are you comparing models to wolves?' Jordan asked. 'Because you should probably know that our mom was a supermodel.'

That's when it hit her. Not only was Jordan ridiculously good-looking, but they all were. The phrase 'cute as a button' had clearly been invented to describe Mia, whose wavy blonde hair was pulled back into one of those messy buns that Pearl could never master or pull off, even at the gym. Luca looked like he'd just rolled out of bed in the best way.

Standing in front of an actual castle in Scotland, the three of them were an ad for a reality TV show about the rich and famous. As usual, Di was right on the money in every way.

Pearl's mind was still spinning when she heard a shriek. The whole group turned to find a middle-aged woman making their way toward them. After she hugged Jordan and pecked him on the cheek, she looked at Pearl and smiled.

Jordan grinned. 'Barb, this is Pearl.'

She hugged Pearl, too. 'Well, that's a name you don't hear very often anymore,' Barb said.

'Don't even get me started,' Pearl laughed. 'Although it does come in handy for work.'

'Are you a jeweler?' Mia asked.

'Or the Pearl of Wisdom?' Barb added in.

'Actually, yes.' Noticing the confused looks on the faces around her, she added, 'To the Pearl of Wisdom, not the jeweler.'

The clarification didn't help the confusion for anyone besides Barb.

'You're kidding!' she said, clapping her hands. 'You're the actual Pearl of Wisdom?'

'Wait, you've read Pearl's advice column?' Jordan asked.

Pearl was as stunned as Jordan. She rarely met readers in the wild.

'I love advice columns. I read as many as I can online.' The woman who was practically dancing with excitement turned her attention back to Pearl. 'I wrote you once, maybe a year or so ago. You probably don't remember, with all the letters you get, but I was so pleased to get a note back even if it wasn't in your column.'

Pearl wasn't clear who this woman was, given that Jordan's mother had passed away and, even if she hadn't, Barb was also on the short side for a supermodel.

'Pearl, meet our surrogate mom,' Mia said. 'Everyone's surrogate mom, actually. Watch out. She's always on the lookout for new marks.'

Pearl smiled. 'Sorry, but I'm full up in the mom department at the moment. But I have to say, I don't write people back very often. I hope it was helpful.'

Even if she remembered the contents of Barb's letter, Pearl wouldn't have revealed what she asked or pressed her to do so. But under everyone else's intense stares, Barb turned 50 shades of red.

'Is there something you'd like to share with the class, Barb?' Jordan asked.

'Not really, but you'll find out some way,' she said, then turned to Pearl. 'Worst kids in the world. I, um, was considering embarking on a new relationship with my deceased boss's best friend, but I wasn't sure if I needed to get the permission of his children. Not the best friend's kids — he doesn't have any — the boss's.'

Pearl's mouth fell open. Barb should specialise in writing CliffNotes, if the letter she was referring to was the one Pearl thought it was. The three carefully handwritten pages were among the most bizarre she'd received in all the time she'd been doling out advice, which was saying a lot. The writer had been overly concerned with the feelings of adult children who weren't hers but felt like hers, of a dead husband, and of a dead boss. It was far too confusing to print but so sweet that Pearl couldn't help but send off a few words jotted on a card.

'Actually, I do remember,' Pearl nodded. 'I hope it all turned out well?'

Jordan shot his sister a look. 'Well, if your advice was to start holding hands with said best friend until those children figured it out for themselves, then yes, things are perfect.' He put an arm around Barb. 'Awkward, sure, but also perfect. Speaking of, where is Cliff?'

At the mention of the name Pearl could only assume was the best friend-turned-boyfriend, Barb's whole face seemed to break into a wide smile. 'Oh, he's resting.'

Everyone's gazes suddenly found everything and anything else extremely interesting – a blade of grass, their shoe, or, in Pearl's case, the castle's two towers soaring above them into the afternoon sky. 'You know what,' said Barb, 'I think I'll join him. Mia, I'll track you down in a couple of hours.'

As they watched Barb skip away, Jordan leaned toward Pearl. 'I can't believe you're the one responsible for that.'

Mia coughed out a laugh. 'Me either, but I'm impressed – even if your wisdom has led to me being seriously uncomfortable 98 per cent of the time I'm around them.'

Jordan nudged his sister. 'If you're looking for two more per cent to make an even 100, Pearl and I really need a shower.'

Now it was Pearl's turn to blush.

After promising to meet up for the pre-dinner mixer Mia's maid of honor had planned, they walked through a stone arch into the great hall of the medieval castle. Pearl could almost picture the long-ago lord and lady of the manor sitting at either end of the massive table, a collection of silver platters between them and a fire roaring in the massive fireplace.

As much as she wanted to explore, her desire to find out what exactly Jordan had been keeping a secret was greater. She had a gut feeling that Julia Sullivan was the tip of the iceberg.

'My lady.' Jordan offered her his arm and then practically dragged her up a snug spiral staircase to the top floor of the castle's north tower, where Mia had told them they would find the Sir Walter Scott Room.

When they reached the door, Jordan swept her off her feet and into his arms. 'I meant to do this last night after our anvil wedding,' he said.

The goofy grin that spread across his face was hard to resist, along with the memory of being bound to Jordan with the length of tartan. She wrapped her arms around his neck and let him carry her across the threshold.

Inside, a crackling fire provided the only light besides what came in through the tall, narrow windows and from sconces above the beds.

As in, twin beds. Each with ornately carved wooden head- and footboards with posts rising ten feet off the stone floor.

Jordan stopped in his tracks. 'Well, this sucks.' After a

quick peck, he set Pearl on her feet and went to the nearest bed. 'I'll shove them together.'

He gave the bed a push, but it didn't budge. It also didn't move an inch when Pearl added her weight to the effort.

Pearl finally gave up and, after taking one look at the clean, frilly bedding and then a second at their clothes, sat down cross-legged on the floor in front of the fireplace and patted the hearth rug. Jordan kicked off his flip-flops and joined her.

'Jordan,' she said.

'Yes, Pearl.'

'Would you care to explain?'

His long sigh confirmed that she didn't need to elaborate on what.

'Okay, it's not a big deal,' he finally said. 'I'm a race car driver or, rather, I was a race car driver for Rubie Racing, my family's Apex Racing team, which my dad left to Mia. The family business part was all true. Also, Mia is a race car driver, the first female driver in years, and Luca retired from racing last year after winning the world championship. I'm not totally sure who's on the guest list, but you're bound to meet more drivers this weekend.'

'Jordan, I think we've already learned that I wouldn't know a race car driver if I fell over one,' she said.

'I'm aware.'

They shared a smile over that memory, which seemed like months instead of days ago. Somehow, Pearl felt more comfortable with Jordan than she had with her last boyfriend, and they'd dated for two years. Maybe that's why his omissions stung a little more than they should have.

Well, that and the fact that everyone in her life seemed to lie to her about who they really were.

At least his masterful driving skills made more sense. But Jordan being a race car driver still didn't explain why he cavorted with models or why his family thought he might show up with a particular one.

'So, I'm not often mistaken for Julia Sullivan. We both know that's not even remotely possible.'

'You're right,' he said, looking straight at her. 'You're far more attractive.'

Chapter 13

Of all the things Jordan regretted about his last season in Apex Racing, his relationship with Julia was close to the top.

There was a lot he should've told Pearl, but this wasn't even on the list. He still couldn't believe Mia thought Julia might be his possible date. Their fences needed more mending than he thought.

'Full disclosure, Julia and I were a thing for a second,' he said. 'It wasn't serious, but it was pretty messed up. Also, race car drivers dating models is far from unusual. I mean, my dad was a race car driver, and my mom was a supermodel, along with Miss Universe.'

But unlike Julia, his mother, Trish, had been beautiful both inside and out.

'Luca actually dated her first, before he and Mia got back together,' he said.

When Julia had reached out to say she'd broken up with Luca to be with him, Jordan had believed her. Like a fool.

Then his dad had died and he'd learned that while Mia had been given the keys to the Rubie Racing kingdom, he'd needed to either shape up or ship out to get his inheritance. It had wrecked him, or so he'd thought. His actual reckoning – when he'd learned the true meaning of the phrase 'fuck around and out' – had occurred months later.

'Do you keep in touch with her?' Pearl asked.

'Julia? Absolutely not,' he said. 'I can say with 100 per cent certainty that she's not pining for me, and I'm definitely not pining for her.'

That was an understatement. Julia was one of the few people in the world that he hoped never to lay eyes on again. He had little to worry about there – last he'd heard, she'd moved on to dating hockey players.

'Do you drive race cars anymore?'

He shook his head. 'I left the team after I caused a crash that put both Luca and me in the hospital. It was pretty bad.'

Pearl's hand found his and forced the fist he didn't realise he'd made to unclench.

'I'm sorry, Jordan, but I don't get all the cloak and dagger. Why didn't you just tell me?'

'You said I was sweet,' he said.

That was the crux of it, not that he expected her to understand. At least, not without knowing the whole story and the racing world's take on him. With a reluctant release of her hand, he pulled his phone from his pocket, connected it to the Wi-Fi, and handed it over.

'Trust me, there aren't many people who think I'm sweet.

If you google Jordan Rubie, with an 'ie,' you'll see what I mean.'

Jordan laid down on his back, closed his eyes, and waited for her to gasp when she learned who she'd been sharing a bed with. Instead, his phone hit the floor with a thunk. Pearl's body molded into his, her head landing on his chest, her hand sneaking under his sweatshirt in search of bare skin.

'I don't need the internet to tell me who you are, Jordan.'

With a sigh of relief, he kissed the top of her head.

'Not when you're right here to tell me yourself,' she said.

Maybe if Pearl hadn't tilted her head up and brushed her lips lightly against his, Jordan would've sought a familiar escape route, most likely Asshole Avenue. But instead, Jordan took a deep breath and told her. He didn't sugarcoat how he'd treated people, even those he loved. How he'd blamed Mia for all of his problems and failures in and out of the car – during the years when she hadn't been involved with Rubie Racing and especially once she'd taken over leadership of the team. How on that one fateful day on the track in Hungary, the only world he'd ever known had imploded in a single second.

Jordan was in a foul mood at the start line of the Hungarian Grand Prix – fouler than usual. His morning had started with his usual race day routine of drinking one cup of coffee with five sugar packets, just like he had as a teenager before he'd acquired a taste for the real thing, and jerking off in the shower, for much the same reason. But then he'd found Julia with his phone, copying down the contact info of a certain young driver Jordan had caught her flirting with a couple of times.

It hadn't taken Jordan long to figure out that Julia was only with him to stick it to Luca, and only a little longer than that to realise that Luca couldn't care less – and why. He'd only kept on with her to avoid looking like a fool, but there wasn't a chance in hell he could continue this sham relationship now. He'd broken up with her right there and then.

But then, after she'd left, he couldn't find the St Christopher medallion his mom had given him before his first kart race. Odds were good that it was in one of the thousand suitcases he'd seen Julia pack and haul into the elevator.

Watching Mia and Luca's pre-race hugging routine had been like pouring salt in an open and festering wound. No one at Rubie Racing had been surprised when they'd announced they were together – especially him. Not when he'd had a front-row seat to their teenage romance.

Jordan still couldn't believe they'd thought they could keep their relationship a secret. He'd considered Luca decent enough until the guy had started screwing around with his sister – his twin sister – but he'd kept his mouth shut.

Until that fateful night at the 24-hour Daytona race.

Jordan had been pissed when Mia disappeared after her shift in the car, and Luca had taken off after her like a love-sick puppy. Although they'd been driving in junior Apex races, the sports car race had been his and Mia's debut in the big leagues. Their dad including his twins as part of Rubie Racing's four-person team for one of the biggest endurance races in the sport had been a huge deal for her to be literally fucking around during. Then their top driver had started feeling unwell and their dad had been frantic, trying to find Luca to take over Scott's drive. Jordan had no choice but to tell him where to look – the parking lot. How could he have known that Dad would catch them with their pants down.

Maybe if Jordan had gone after the two of them himself, the rest of the story would've played out differently. Luca wouldn't have been sent packing – although Jordan hadn't minded that one bit. Dad wouldn't have essentially shunned Mia, who, in some sort of weird retaliation, shunned the sport altogether. It wouldn't have taken the old man dying to bring her back into the fold.

Jordan may never know why a switch flipped inside him that day at the Hungaroring, from pure adrenaline to the worst kind of aggression, the type fueled by jealousy and at least two other deadly sins. But it grew with each lap. After a large crash and an all-course yellow put Luca in his cross-hairs, it reached a dangerous level. He rarely saw his teammate on the track unless Luca was lapping him.

Finally, he had his chance to show the guy who'd been pissing him off for years what he was made of. But he couldn't pass his car's twin, no matter how hard he tried – and oh, did he try. He blocked out the radio transmission telling him to back off, his father telling him to know his car's limits, and even his mother begging him to calm down. His sole focus was besting Luca's turbo pumpkin.

He knew his failed attempts to pass were annoying Luca. At last, Jordan found a possible opening. Maybe. If he could only squeeze by.

But he couldn't. He didn't.

He slammed into Luca and braced himself for the crash and the physical pain it promised. Welcomed it, even. He wanted the outside of his body to, for once, match the inside. His wish came true.

Only as the rescue teams worked to free him and Luca from their cars did he realise the full extent of what he'd done.

'Luca had a concussion and a lot of bumps and bruises. I ended up in the hospital for a week, and had three surgeries before all was said and done.' He hesitated before saying the next part out loud. 'Honestly, we're both lucky to be alive.'

Not that luck had much to do with it. Safety changes to Apex cars had saved their lives. Fans may hate how the curved bar looks over the cockpit, but it had kept Luca from literally losing his head after Jordan metaphorically lost his.

'They always talk about rock bottom, but mine was more a mixture of sand, stone, and gravel,' Jordan said dryly. 'Good old asphalt. I thought the worst days of my life were behind me. Turns out, I was just getting warmed up.'

He'd talk about those low months later, which led him to heal his body and then his mind. Or, at least, try to.

Pearl was quiet for a beat before she spoke. 'I'm glad you

told me but I'm not going to lie, you don't come off great in that story. That must've been one hell of an apology tour.'

When Jordan didn't respond, she sat up and poked at the Highland cow on his sweatshirt. 'Tell me you apologised.'

He wished he could, if only to get her to stop. 'The timing's never been right.'

'Like it wasn't right to tell me all this stuff?' Pearl kept poking. 'Because we both know you had plenty of opportunity during the hours we spent in the car. Apologies are important, Jordan, and not just for the people who need to hear them.'

She was right, of course, but he'd had a hard time working up the appetite for a hearty helping of crow. But maybe starting with an appetiser would help him work up to it.

'I'm sorry I didn't tell you earlier.' He eased her back next to him to kiss her and was grateful when her lips moved against his. 'I should have.'

When she laid her head back down, Jordan felt like he'd traded some of the weight on his shoulders for one he much preferred on his chest. His hand found a place to rest on her lower back, and he realised that, at nearly 35, he'd found the peace he hadn't realised he was looking for.

Chapter 14

Star, the woman serving as Mia's maid of honor, introduced herself to Pearl as soon as she and Jordan showed up in the baseball jerseys that had been delivered to their room. Jordan's was personalised on the reverse with 'hot shot' in all capital letters, which apparently had been his childhood nickname. Hers said 'plus one' in Sharpie and was at least two sizes too big.

The jerseys made more sense once they saw the makeshift baseball diamond, which someone had created in a wide-open green space using bright orange bases. But Pearl traded a confused look with Jordan when Star asked each of them to name their favorite song to swing to.

'Excuse me?' Jordan asked, then turned to Pearl and, with a wink, added, 'I swear I didn't know it was that kind of party.'

Pearl struggled to hold back a laugh.

'A bat, Jordan. Swing a bat,' said Star, pointing at the assortment of wooden and metal baseball bats lying next to an official-looking home base, a large box of baseballs, and a T-ball stand much like the one that had dominated Pearl's nightmares one childhood summer.

'I can't believe they schlepped all of this gear over here,' Pearl whispered as she tried to think of a song.

'Pfft, this is nothing,' Jordan said. 'Apex teams drag two race cars and thousands of pounds of equipment around the world for months on end.'

He had to be exaggerating.

Once they'd both written down songs on pieces of paper, Star instructed them to join the others and await further instruction.

'It's best to do what she says,' Jordan whispered, leading Pearl over to where Mia, Luca, and about ten other early wedding guests were gathered in the castle's shadow.

'I heard that hot shot,' Star called after them.

The group greeted Jordan with handshakes, pats on the back, and questions about his ankle and recovery. He introduced her to Wyn, another race car driver, and his wife, Alys, after he thanked them for letting him use their cottage and beach hut.

'We're glad you liked it,' Wyn said.

'Best days of my life,' Jordan said, smiling at her. 'So far.'

Just as Pearl thought her heart might burst, an ear-piercing whistle cut through the chatter.

'One, two, three, look at me!' Star yelled, her arm up in the air.

Considering how quickly all eyes snapped to the maid of

honor, Jordan wasn't the only one who'd figured out the easiest way to deal with Mia's best friend.

The absence of baseball gloves made sense as soon as Star explained the rules of the simple game she claimed to have invented. But given the questions she was fielding, no one besides Pearl and the guy standing next to Star were grasping them. Which were, essentially, going up to home plate when your name was called, swinging at a baseball on the T-ball stand once your song started playing, and then taking a home run lap when you hit the ball.

'What if you hit the ball on your first swing?' Jordan asked from beside her.

'You run around the bases,' Star said. 'Also, it's a T-ball stand. It's pretty much a given that you're going to hit the ball on your first swing.'

Obviously, Star hadn't been repeatedly struck out by a T-ball stand in the first grade.

'Some of us here have never swung a bat!' someone yelled out.

'Speak for yourself,' said an Australian from the back.

'Can I use a cricket bat?'

Pearl would've easily recognised the Welsh accent if she hadn't just met the man behind it.

'Anyone else wonder why Wyn travels with a cricket bat?' Star asked. 'Also, the answer is no. It's my game and my rules, and we're playing with good ole American bats. Any other questions?'

Although Star's tone dared anyone else to pipe up, the

groom-to-be cleared his throat. 'How fast should we run?' Luca asked. 'Who's timing us?'

'As fast as you want to, and no one, literally no one, gives a shit about how fast you run.' Star was no longer hiding her annoyance. 'It's not a race.'

'I'll time you.' Jordan gave his soon-to-be brother-in-law a thumbs up, which Luca returned.

'No,' Star said. 'No one is timing anyone.'

'She said no timing people,' the guy next to Star echoed.

'Come on, Brian. How will we know who wins?' Luca again.

'There's no winner,' Star shouted. 'This is just for fun. Have none of you ever played a game just for the fun of it?'

Given the blank stares around her, Pearl guessed the answer was a collective no.

'I'm sorry,' Mia said. 'I appreciate what you and Brian are doing here, but it doesn't sound like a game. You keep score in games. I mean, even Yahtzee has a score.'

'Uno, too,' Jordan said. 'And, games have winners and losers.'

'It is so a game!' Star yelled.

'Oh, yeah? Then what's it called?' Jordan asked.

'At. Bat.' Star gave him a smug smile along with the middle finger.

Pearl's arm went up in the air, and Jordan tried to pull it down. 'You don't have to raise your hand.'

But Star gave an approving nod in her direction. 'Finally, someone with manners. Go on, Pearl.'

'Two questions,' Pearl said. 'Are we allowed to cheer for each other like normal, rational people who aren't borderline-psycho competitive? Also, is alcohol involved? Please say yes.'

Star dropped her clipboard on the spot, ran over, and hugged Pearl. Looking straight at Jordan, she said, 'Well done with this one. If we were swinging not with bats, I'd pick her.'

Mia cleared her throat. 'That is odd but high praise indeed. I can't say I'm not a little hurt, but everyone, let's play along.'

A cooler appeared out of nowhere, which was a welcome addition to the party considering Pearl's heart was already pounding in her chest. A little liquid courage might help bury those childhood memories from the one season Di made her play T-ball so she could flirt with the coach. A chorus of six-year-olds chanting 'hey batter batter' still rang in her ears on occasion.

Pearl made a beeline to the drinks as everyone else fought over the bats and practiced their swings.

'Good Lord,' Star said, appearing next to Pearl as she sorted through the options in the cooler. 'I don't know what the hell I was thinking. These people wouldn't know fun if it hit them in the head. And I'd venture to guess they've all had their fair share of concussions at some point or another.'

Pearl's eyes found Jordan, who was intently studying every inch of one of the wooden bats while keeping it more than an arm's reach away from his sister.

'I'm betting not a single person over there was ever picked

last for anything,' Pearl said, choosing a canned gin and tonic and cracking it open. She waited until Star had picked her drink so they could clink their cans together before taking a sip.

Star took a substantial gulp from her cocktail. 'As the great Ricky Bobby said, "If you ain't first, you're last."'

The line from *Talladega Nights* brought a grin to Pearl's face. The year the movie came out, Di's only request for her birthday had been for the two of them to see it together – and they'd ended up staying in the theater through the next two showings. She'd felt so guilty afterward that she'd mailed a note with enough cash to cover her and Di's additional ticket prices to the movie theater manager.

'Oh, wait! Are *those* the kind of cars they all drive?' Pearl asked.

That was all it took for Star to spray light pink liquid all over the lid of the cooler. 'You know what? You're officially my new favorite person.'

Ten minutes later, Star called the group to order. Bats dropped to the ground, and those who'd been frantically trying to figure out the mechanics of a perfect swing made a mad dash to the cooler. When everyone was finally gathered around her, Star announced that they'd be choosing teams after all, and declared herself the captain of one and Jordan the other.

'But we're the bride and groom,' Mia said, throwing her hands up in the air in a dramatic show of exasperation.

'Yes, *mija*, and you're receiving all of the attention you

deserve and then some, and you can give this one to your always-a-bridesmaid best friend and your twin, can't you?'

Mia folded her arms across her chest, Luca grunted, and Star ignored them both.

'I pick first,' she said. 'Pearl. Over here. You're on my team.'

But before Pearl could walk to stand beside her, Jordan grabbed the crook of her arm. 'Wait, what? No. Pearl's on my team.'

'Afraid not, hot shot.'

'Afraid so, Star.' His grip tightened.

'I will cut you, Jordan. Let. Her. Go.'

Apparently, no one doubted that might be a real possibility because the entire group took a step back at the same time Jordan released his grip. Pearl, almost giddy about being fought over, and not because she was the last person left and someone was being forced to take her, dashed over to Star and was rewarded with a high-five.

Jordan then picked Luca, mumbling something about a pink dress when Mia protested, and Star told her best friend to 'get your ass over here.' After the rest of the teams filled in and an overly enthusiastic 'let's play ball!' from Star, the game began.

Mia and Luca each hit first, earning an abundance of oohing and aahing when it was revealed that they'd unknowingly chosen the same Motown favorite for their song. Thankfully, no one minded listening to Stevie Wonder croon 'Signed, Sealed, Delivered (I'm Yours)' twice in a row. During the second playing, everyone gamefully joined in as the bride and groom sang along.

Jordan was up next. He made a show of making sure the stand was placed where his front foot would land after hitting the ball, finding the exact spot by demonstrating a textbook swing and follow through. When he was ready, he gave a nod to Star, who hit play on her phone.

The song that blared from the nearby Bluetooth speaker was one that had, coincidentally, been on constant replay in the Carrington house the summer of Di and the T-ball coach. 'Dirt' by The Stooges, which she hadn't heard in the nearly 30 years since.

As a child, she'd thought the song was about someone who was dirty, as in filthy. As an adult, she realised it was true, but in a far different context.

Jordan stood in perfect position as Iggy Pop snarled but, at the last second, took his eye off the ball and put it on Pearl. *Swish*.

No one clapped. Or laughed. Iggy continued on as Jordan tapped the bat on the base. Barb, who'd arrived late and declared herself the 'baller,' much to everyone's chagrin, replaced the baseball on the stand with a new one and gave Jordan a reassuring pat on the shoulder before he crouched down again.

Pearl didn't look, but she heard the second *swish*. They all waited, most of the group shuffling uncomfortably in place and looking everywhere but at Jordan, who was casually tapping the bat on the base in time to the music. When he finally settled into his batting stance for the third and final time, Pearl's heart thumped for him. She half wondered if he was putting on a show so she wouldn't look like an idiot when she whiffed her turn at bat.

She didn't plan to watch again, but her head jerked his way on its own when he began to sing along. Jordan's eyes locked in with hers and stayed there.

Thwack.

Neither of them saw how far the ball went, but judging by the cheers, it was a more than a respectable distance. Jordan dropped the bat, walked over, and grabbed her hand, and together they rounded the bases. Only after clearing third base, they didn't run home. They veered off the makeshift ball diamond and headed toward the castle.

'Come back or we're giving you a DNF,' someone shouted.

They kept running, even when Star called out, 'Hey! Pearl's up next!'

'Later,' Jordan yelled, then glanced at Pearl. 'Much later.'

Their breathing grew heavier as they made their way inside, across the well-worn stone floors, and up the tower staircase. By the time Jordan pushed open the heavy wooden door to their room, they were both gasping – for each other.

Her mouth found Jordan's, and they tumbled onto the first twin bed they came to.

'Should we try again to push the beds together?' Pearl asked when he sat up, straddling her, and pulled his baseball jersey and then a T-shirt the same shade of blue as his eyes over his head and tossed them on the floor.

'No time, and I honestly can't stress that enough,' he said.

He didn't need to tell her twice. As soon as he shot up to find a condom and take off his pants, she made quick work of her own clothes. Within seconds, he settled himself between her legs, but it was her urgency, her legs wrapping around him, that pulled him deep inside of her. And held him there.

'You're not dirt, Jordan Rubie,' she whispered.

He had no choice but to still, his blue eyes burning like molten copper. 'Pearl,' he gasped.

'Say it.'

His breathing deepened as he fought to stay in control. 'You're killing me.'

Her hands went to his face. 'Say it.'

She tightened around him, and he broke. 'Not. Dirt,' he said, his voice shaking along with his entire body.

Her legs set him loose. Over and over again, he slammed into her, repeating her name, not stopping until she was screaming out his. Thank God this castle had thick stone walls.

When he finally collapsed on top of her, his fingers nestled in her hair as his thumb brushed against her cheek, keeping their faces close. 'How is this happening?' he asked, his lips lightly brushing hers. 'Seriously, is this real?'

She couldn't pretend to know the answer or stop herself from running her hands up his spine and then back down again until he shivered. 'I have no idea. Nothing like this has ever happened to me before.'

'Some Pearl of Wisdom you are,' he said, his laughter

shaking both of their bodies. He rolled off her and made his way to the en suite.

The small bed felt empty without Jordan in it, and the room was cooling down quickly with the setting sun. Pearl climbed under the covers. When Jordan reappeared moments later, she pointed to the fireplace. 'Do you know how to make a fire?'

'Oh, I think I've already proved that I can, Pearl,' he said, lifting the duvet and sliding in next to her. 'But in all seriousness, I'll keep you warm.'

Within seconds, her backside was molded into his front, his top leg wrapped around hers. Her body shivered anyway.

'You're still cold?' he asked, tucking her closer.

'No,' she yawned. 'I don't think that's it.'

They lay there together, pretending there wasn't a flurry of pre-wedding activity happening outside their cocoon.

Just as she drifted off, he said sleepily in her ear, 'I'm glad this has never happened to you before. Because it's never happened to me before either.'

When they woke up, the room was pitch black, the castle was eerily quiet, and they were both starving. It wasn't until Jordan found the switch on the wall sconce above the bed that they noticed someone had slid a note under the door.

'Barb's saved us.' He flipped the note around so she could see a hand-drawn map. 'She hid a tray in the kitchen.'

As anxious as she was to explore the castle, the middle of the night wasn't the ideal time for a tour. Their footsteps echoed in the ancient corridors, with the wall sconces providing enough light to see where they were walking but not what was lurking in the shadows. (Pearl's guess: the ghosts of lairds past.) When multiple clocks chimed, seconds off from each other, Pearl attached herself to Jordan's side.

They finally found the modern-day kitchen, where Jordan installed her on a stool in front of a stainless steel worktable and located the food Barb had hidden for them. As he prepared their spread, he caught her staring.

'I'm an okay cook but a master at reheating,' he said. 'Barb's a feeder. I don't think I would've survived this long without her.'

While they ate, she learned that Barb had taken over running the Rubie household after Jordan and Mia's mother died of breast cancer. His voice cracked as he talked about the woman who'd left them when they were far too young.

'I take after her in looks and personality, and Mia is more like our dad,' he said. 'When I started racing, I couldn't believe how quickly the season went by, knowing how painful and slow those same number of months could be.'

They were almost through the assortment of dishes from the traditional Scottish dinner they'd missed when Luca wandered in, looking a little worse for wear himself. He scowled at the sight of them sitting side by side, but especially at Jordan, who was scraping the last of some sort of chowder from the bottom of a bowl.

'Well, you've done it now. Mia's already mad that you ran

off and skipped dinner. Wait until she finds out you ate the leftovers Barb set aside.'

Jordan's mouth fell open. 'They were for us. I can prove it. There was a note, Luca.'

'And a map,' Pearl added.

'Relax,' he said, pulling out a stool across from them and plopping down. 'As long as I return with shortbread, you're good.'

'This shortbread?' On instinct, Pearl grabbed the last cookie on the plate and shoved the whole thing in her mouth. Both men stared as she slowly chewed and swallowed. It was a classic Di move akin to the one she'd demonstrated in the car earlier – licking something you wanted to claim.

'I'm sorry; I don't know why I just did that,' Pearl said once she'd washed it down with a gulp from her bottle of bubbly water. 'If it makes either of you feel better, I'm sad the shortbread is gone, too.'

Luca looked at Pearl, then Jordan, in amazement. 'Is it weird that I'm low-key impressed?'

Jordan shook his head and leaned closer to Pearl. 'Not as weird as me being turned on, especially since I'd called that cookie.'

Within seconds, Luca was up and out the door, nearly knocking over the stool he'd been sitting on in his rush to leave. 'Well, then, I'll leave you two to it,' he called out over his shoulder. 'Good night.'

Jordan also got up, but only to begin clearing their plates. Pearl couldn't help but study him as he stacked the empty dishes neatly by the sink, clearly considering whether or not to wash them, and then found a cloth to wipe the crumbs off the table. Their time together hadn't included a shred of normalcy, and for whatever reason, watching him tidy an industrial kitchen like it was his own made her realise how little she knew about his life in the real world.

'So, where do race car drivers live, Jordan?'

'In general, or this one in particular?' He laughed and leaned against the sink. 'It depends on the racing series. It's mostly Europeans in Apex – that's the racing my family does – and they typically have places in Monaco or near their factories, and houses in whatever country they're from. But I only have the one house in Michigan. Rubie Racing is the only American team in Apex, and my dad thought it was important to be based in Detroit.'

'In the city proper?' she asked.

Large tracts of now vacant land in what was once one of the largest cities in the United States had been converted to working farms, but she couldn't imagine there being enough land for a bunch of race cars.

'No, but my dad grew up there, on the east side. The team complex is about 45 minutes west, in the suburbs. But the lake I live on is even further west, in the Irish hills, if you know where that is.'

She nodded. Di had conveniently dated a guy with a cabin on a small lake out that way, along with a pontoon boat, one very hot summer when Pearl was ten. As a kid, she'd loved the touristy area, which felt like northern Michigan with its kitschy tourist attractions. She wondered if he lived by the Old West theme park or if it was even still in business.

'Do you have a boat?' she asked.

'Almost,' he said. 'I ordered a pontoon, but it hasn't come in yet, so I've been mostly casting from the dock this summer.'

'What about the other summers?'

'As a race car driver, I was never home enough to enjoy a boat. The crash happened last summer, and then I was recovering.' He lifted his left leg and showed off by rotating the foot at the ankle. 'They weren't sure if this would heal correctly, even after three surgeries. It was questionable if I'd walk again, let alone race again.'

If Jordan hadn't told her he'd been injured, she never would've guessed. 'And will you? Race again?'

'That remains to be seen.' He walked over to where she sat and pulled her to her feet. 'Now, I think someone owes me dessert.'

Chapter 15

After years of manoeuvering a car going a couple hundred miles an hour, Jordan knew a thing or two about blind spots. But the past week had proven that he was losing his touch.

Exhibit A: Pearl.

Exhibits B and C: Barb and Mia.

He could cut himself some slack for not seeing Pearl coming, but he definitely should've anticipated Barb and Mia cornering him the first time the three of them were alone.

The great room's long table allowed everyone staying in the castle to dine together, and no one left breakfast the next morning hungry. A sideboard had been loaded with eggs prepared in every imaginable way and more sweet and savory dishes than he and Pearl had been able to work through.

Pearl had headed back to the room to check in with Di about how Top's surgery was going that morning, leaving him to linger over his coffee and catch up more with a couple of the guys he used to race against. People peeled off one by one, and before he knew it, the room had cleared of everyone except for him, Barb, and Mia.

The two had been huddled together at the other end of the table for the last hour. There was probably a signal he'd missed — another sign his instincts were failing — given how they swarmed in on him. Before he'd even registered that they'd gotten up, Barb was in the chair on one side of him and Mia had flopped down on his other side.

'Spill,' Mia said, refilling her cup from the silver coffee pot he'd hoarded for him and Pearl.

Conjuring his seven-year-old self, Jordan lifted his cup and tilted it until the amber liquid was millimeters from spilling over the edge and onto the crisp white tablecloth.

His sister wasn't amused. 'Not that, hot shot. Pearl. What's the deal?' she asked, her voice raising an octave on each word. The curiosity was clearly killing her. Too bad the truth — that he'd brought a woman he barely knew to her small and intimate dream wedding — might involve her killing him.

Theirs was a fragile relationship. Even if they'd grown closer and texted somewhat frequently over the past year, it was a work in progress. And not only because he'd almost taken out half the wedding party in one reckless move — his own jealousy and insecurities had taken a massive toll on their relationship since they were kids.

It's amazing what a near-death experience and therapy can help make a person realise. The fact that he was now sitting next to Mia in Scotland, the day before her wedding, and happy about it was nothing short of amazing.

Jordan went with the most straightforward answer he could think of. 'I like her.'

'Well, that's obvious.' Mia's eyes rolled up toward the ornate tile ceiling. 'I don't think I've seen you smile so much since, well, ever.'

No arguing with her there. He'd caught himself smiling and whistling – *whistling* – in the shower that morning. Although that may have been due to the pre-shower activities.

Barb patted his knee. 'Well, I, for one, am thrilled to see you so happy. You've kept your smile hidden for long enough.' She hesitated. 'It's just that you don't seem to know each other very well.'

Mia snorted. 'Oh, I think they know each other well enough.'

Even a minor comment like that would've been enough to raise the old Jordan's hackles, and he knew neither Mia nor Barb would've been surprised if he said something shitty and stormed out. Disappointed, sure. But it had been months since he pulled such a classic Jordan move, and he found that he no longer had it in him.

So, he sighed and launched into the story of Pearl falling over him on the beach and the next couple of days, leaving out her family drama about learning Top was her mom, not her aunt. That was her story to tell.

'So, you're right,' he said. 'We don't know each other well, but it doesn't feel that way. It feels like I've always known her. I can't explain it. It's weird.'

'I don't think "weird" is the word you're looking for.' Mia

grabbed the linen napkin on his lap and dabbed at the corners of her eyes. 'It's amazing, Jordan.'

Barb pulled a tissue from her sleeve and did the same. Jordan put his arm around her, which only made her cry harder.

'I'm sorry,' she said. 'They're happy tears, I swear; I'm just so happy to see you both happy. I only wish your dad were here.'

'Me, too,' Mia said. 'But let's be honest, we probably wouldn't be here if he hadn't died. Me and Luca? There's no way I would've let him back into my life if Dad's death hadn't forced us together.'

'And there's no way I'd be out of a drive if Dad were still alive,' Jordan said.

Mia shrunk back in her chair. In their text messages before and after races and during his visits and phone calls with Barb, no one had brought up the race car-sized elephant always parked nearby. His sister had fired him, kicked him off Rubie Racing, and severed his connection to their family's legacy.

Of course, there was something else left unsaid. He'd deserved it, and it had been the best thing Mia could've done for him. Not that he'd ever admitted as much, and not that the women on either side of him would ever expect him to. But maybe Pearl had a point when she'd admonished him for not apologising.

He sighed and forced himself to look Mia straight in the eye. 'But then we both know that I never would've pulled a stunt like that when Dad was around. I crossed a dangerous line that I'd been edging toward for months, if not years, and I'm so thankful that I didn't manage to kill myself, Luca, or both of us. You were right to kick me off the team.'

Even though he hadn't said the words 'I'm sorry,' it was likely more than she ever expected to hear from him. He could stop there.

But Jordan's brain flashed back to a day it refused to stop revisiting. Only this time, it skipped over the crash with Luca and fast-forwarded to him lying in the hospital bed in Budapest. To his first visitor.

Mia.

He hadn't been in the mood to mince words that day. He'd told her that he hated her, himself, everyone, and everything. It had all been true, in that moment and countless others. And especially where his twin sister was concerned.

It wasn't that their parents had played favorites. But when he and Mia had competed side by side, Mia had almost always come out ahead. It didn't matter how good he was; she was better. How could they not have cheered a little louder for her? Looking back, he couldn't blame them. Mia had been a natural, a winner – at almost everything – and she still was. Only half over, Mia's first full racing season had already been filled with more trips to the podium than he'd seen during his entire career.

Somehow, that childhood jealousy had grown into an emotion he couldn't quite put his finger on or control, on or off the track. Sometimes, it felt like envy; other times, resentment; always, emptiness. It fed on the grief and anger from losing their mom. It hadn't been quelled after the crash that changed Mia's life and caused her and Luca's hasty exit from Rubie Racing, paving the way for his career. Because even without her on the track, he'd still felt her presence. Jordan had continued racing against her, as if he had something to prove.

Until Hungary. It had all ended there, when Mia had literally shut the door and he'd found himself alone in that hospital bed, unable to move. Escape. Run away. With no other choice, he'd had to lay there and experience every conceivable type of pain. Most people probably assumed the crash had been the pivotal moment in his life. In reality, that happened as the hours on his back stretched into days.

And above all expectations, he could feel another pivotal moment coming on.

He folded his hand around Mia's, remembering the ultrasound photo their mom had treasured of the two of them in utero, their tiny hands pressed toward each other as if they couldn't wait to rid themselves of their amniotic sacs and finally touch the person who'd been growing next to them.

'I'm sorry, you know,' he said. 'About the crash, what I said at the hospital, and a thousand other things.'

One thing in particular.

Say it. Just do it. Apologizing for almost killing Luca shouldn't have been easier than this. But then everyone had seen it happen; they knew he did it. If he didn't share this one thing, they wouldn't actually know – even if they suspected.

But he would.

'The reporter from 411.com who broke the story about you and Luca at the 24-hour race in Daytona. It was me.' Jordan's stomach churned, and he didn't have haggis to blame. 'At least inadvertently. I told Julia, like an idiot, in the early days before I realised what she was about.'

Julia had lapped up the story, practically purring for every juicy detail. And he'd given them to her, not knowing she'd been amassing ammunition to take Mia and Luca down. But that's exactly what Julia had done, at Mia's first press conference as owner and team principal of Rubie Racing no less.

Pre-season testing in Catalunya, Spain, had taken place only a month after their dad's unexpected death. Out of the blue, a seemingly fresh-faced reporter had point-blank asked Mia about the fateful night Rubie Racing's top driver had crashed and the role she'd played. Jordan was ashamed to admit it, but he'd been gleeful at seeing his dad's golden child finally getting her due.

To distract from the situation, their team manager had shoved Mia in the Rubie Racing car for the first drive of testing. She'd done more than that – in a single afternoon, she'd shown the world, along with her brother, which Rubie twin had inherited Rob Rubie's natural abilities behind the wheel. Unable to beat her time when he'd taken his shift the next day, Jordan had fled the country in a fit of pique with Julia in tow.

Those had been dark days indeed.

'It had to have been her,' he said. 'The only other person in the world who knew besides me and Dad was Cliff.'

'But how did you know?' Mia asked.

He leveled her a look of disbelief. 'You two weren't as sly as you thought you were.'

At that, Barb piped in. 'Your brother's right there.'

Again, Jordan looked his sister in the eye. 'I'm so sorry, Mia. I really am.'

Mia's mouth opened and closed a couple of times before she visibly gulped down emotion. 'I never understood why you hated me and who I was so much.'

In that moment, the truth hit him like another brick wall. 'It was never about you and who you were; it was about me and who I wasn't. Always.'

She squeezed his hand. 'I'm sorry, too.'

'For what?' he asked. Anything Mia had ever done was child's play, especially compared to the stunts he'd pulled during those months after she'd taken leadership of Rubie Racing. 'Seriously. In the grand scheme of things, you have nothing to apologise for.'

Mia shook her head. 'The crack about the little pink dress in Spain last year for starters.'

Ah, yes. There was also that at pre-season testing in Catalunya. After the drive, she'd reminded him of the girl who'd once kicked every boy's ass in a 100-mile radius in her pink kart and was crowned champion in a frilly pink dress their mother had picked out.

'Maybe it's time we both stop looking in the rearview

mirror.' He squeezed her hand. 'You're getting married, Mia. *Married*. It's a whole new chapter for you and Luca. Let's make it one for our family, too.'

He watched as Mia made eye contact with Barb, who'd mostly sat in silence as the children she'd help raise truly and finally made peace. She answered his sister's silent question with a nod and a watery smile.

'I wanted to ask you before,' Mia said, 'but I was wondering, would you give me away tomorrow?'

It was his turn to grab the napkin and wipe the tears spilling from his eyes. 'Seriously? How can you want that after' – his voice broke – 'everything?'

They stared at each other for a few moments before Mia, through her own tears, gave him the famous Rubie grin, the one she'd inherited from their father. 'I didn't forgive Dad, and now it's too late. He never apologised, but then neither did I. By staying away, I pretty much made sure neither of us had the chance. You're my brother, my twin brother. You and me, we're all that's left of the Rubie family. I don't want to make that same mistake again. I won't. Ever.'

'Me neither,' he said. To both of their surprise, he pulled her in for a hug. 'And I'd be honored.'

Chapter 16

Besides *Talladega Nights*, Pearl's knowledge about auto racing of any kind came from another of Di's summer flings – Greg, a guy whose family owned a small dirt racetrack in northern Michigan. Her 12-year-old self had considered the hours she spent in the bleachers, enduring waves of dust every time a car rounded a corner, to be a decent trade-off for an unlimited supply of snow cones from Greg's parents, who not only owned the speedway but also a string of small lakeside cabins.

Pearl had more than a strong suspicion that what she'd watched Greg do in his multicolored beater was far different than Jordan's version of auto racing, and she needed to know what she was dealing with before even more people arrived for the rehearsal dinner and the wedding. Not that she expected a pop quiz on all things racing, but if she could glean enough information about exactly what these people did, she could save herself from making another Ricky Bobby-type reference, like the one that had caused the maid of honor to spit out a perfectly good beverage.

If she'd learned anything from the jewel sisters, it was that alcohol was for drinking, not spraying.

And now that she knew Jordan's last name, searching was easy. Too easy. It would take days to get through the tens of thousands of search results.

She'd hoped to bang out this little research project while Jordan was still down in the breakfast room, but her phone call with Di had taken longer than she'd anticipated. Everything had gone well – Top was already in recovery and since the surgery was outpatient, they'd be home in a matter of hours. Jordan had walked in as Di was sharing every gory detail about what she needed to do to keep the incisions clean, and only headed into the en suite for another shower after Pearl had given him a thumbs up.

The first link Pearl clicked on showed Jordan standing next to a car unlike anything she'd ever seen. It was sleek and sexy as hell and looked as if it could go a million miles an hour. Her finger absently traced the outline of Jordan in his racing suit.

Focus, Pearl, focus.

Clicking through one article after another, she quickly fell down the rabbit hole. When Jordan emerged from the bathroom, she was so engrossed in an article about his family's legacy in the sport that she didn't even register his presence until he was standing next to her.

'Here we go,' he said with a sigh, the air escaping his lungs like a bounce house deflating at the end of a birthday party.

She blindly reached for his hand, or at least that's what she aimed for. When she got a handful of something else, her surprised gaze met his. He'd obviously had something else in mind.

He cleared his throat and ran his fingers through his wavy blonde locks. 'I'm not saying that wouldn't help, but...'

Pearl let go, sensing that the off tone of his voice wasn't only from her hand placement. 'I need to get you a bell.'

He slid into his boxers and perched on the edge of the bed. 'I hate to ask, but what are you doing?'

Considering that she'd asked him to share his history first-hand only 24 hours before, she understood if he felt let down after finding her cruising the internet. 'If you must know, I was cramming for possible small talk and rehearsal dinner conversation. I prefer not to look like a total idiot, and when it comes to all this racing stuff, I'm way out of my league.'

'Fair enough,' Jordan said. 'What'd you find?'

'You don't know?'

Jordan looked out the window. 'Not anything recent. I put myself on a strict media and social media diet several months ago.' He paused. 'On the recommendation of my therapist.'

Impressed by his honesty about his mental health, especially given his obvious discomfort, Pearl made a note to circle back to this conversation. She knew from too many letter writers how many men struggled and suffered alone because of the stigma of seeking professional help.

'That makes sense. If you're trying to figure out who you are, you don't need any outside noise weighing in. I mean, these people don't know you, Jordan. At least not like I do.'

He cocked an eyebrow.

Pearl returned an arched brow of her own. 'Stop. I know you. Better than these people, at least.'

The guy she'd read about was a different person than the one now lying back on the bed, his feet on the floor, his chest rising and falling in equal measure. Apparently, race car driver Jordan had had a permanent chip on his shoulder and a supermodel on his arm. The black sheep of the Rubie family, although even Mia didn't come across great – unsurprisingly, people didn't like female drivers in the traditionally male-dominated sport.

No wonder Jordan took her family drama in stride. His family could write a book on theirs.

'Keep going,' he said quietly. 'Seriously. I'd rather you did it while I was in the room.'

When Pearl changed the search results to show videos, she gasped. Jordan covered his head with a pillow and muttered something that sounded slightly blasphemous.

'Jordan, it's us! Saving the sheep.'

She crawled down to the end of the bed, tossed the pillow away, and held her phone above them. A still photo of them filled the small screen. Jordan's head jerked up as they read, 'Jordan Rubie, a hero to animals! Former bad boy driver shows he can flip more than a car.'

Pearl hit the play arrow, and they watched themselves attempting to right the sheep before finally succeeding. She'd been oblivious to anyone recording them, but then her eyes were either on Jordan or the sheep for the duration of the video. Mostly on Jordan. She read aloud the video description, which referred to her as a 'mystery woman.'

'I wonder how they knew it was you?' she asked.

'Oh, I'm sure the car caught the guy's curiosity and he pulled over to look at it. You don't see that model on the road every day. And Apex is big over here – a couple of teams are based in England – so drivers don't have the same anonymity they have in the States.'

Pearl was rarely recognised – probably because she'd relented and let Di do her makeup when she'd had the head-shot for her column taken. And also because the photo ran about an inch high and in grayscale.

'I hate to say this, Jordan, but when you spoke to the guy recording the video,' she paused to make sure she had his attention, 'you seemed a bit, I don't know, sheepish?'

He groaned but laughed and turned her toward him. 'Actually, Pearl, I'm a hero. The internet says so.'

'Oh, it's more than the internet,' she said. 'I bet there's a few sheep in these parts. What do you say we patrol the countryside for a few hours? Save some more lives.'

Jordan got up and began getting dressed. It was strangely intimate, watching someone put on clothes – maybe more so than helping them get undressed – and she couldn't make herself look away. She wanted to soak in as much of this man as she could, in case this fantasy world of castles and race car drivers was only just that.

Chapter 17

Before anyone could push back their chairs from the long dining table, Star announced that the men would gather in the library with Luca for an after-rehearsal dinner drink while the women toasted Mia in the parlor.

'It's some old-timey thing the bride read about in a romance novel,' Star said. 'Ladies, I managed to talk her out of serving tea, so you're welcome.'

This was an unwelcome development, considering Jordan had been plotting to skip out on any planned evening activities since before they'd left the Sir Walter Scott Room. Specifically, since the moment Pearl had emerged from the en suite and asked him to tie her up. As if her phrasing hadn't been enough to pique his interest, she'd spun around to reveal that the upper part of her dress was a corset.

A corset.

Keeping his hands to himself and off the strings crisscrossing her back had been a serious challenge – and one he'd failed multiple times throughout the seven courses. His fingers were itching to untie them. It certainly didn't help that, beside him, Pearl was alternately scraping the last of the traditional Cranachan from the bottom of her dessert glass and licking every last bit of the raspberries and cream off her spoon.

His head tipped toward hers. 'How bad would it look if we ducked out?'

Before Pearl could respond, there was a quiet voice in his ear. 'Don't even think about pulling another runner, hot shot.'

Jordan didn't need to turn around to know who was lurking behind him or that there was a snowball's chance in hell – perhaps less – of him and Pearl escaping without anyone noticing.

'Wouldn't think of it, Star,' he said. 'As a matter of fact, I was just about to escort Pearl to the parlor.'

To prove he wasn't lying, even though he definitely was, Jordan got to his feet and then helped Pearl to hers, too.

'Well, aren't you sweet,' Star said, linking Pearl's arm with hers. 'But since I'm headed that way, she and I may as well walk together.'

Right there and then, apparently. Pearl glanced over her shoulder, her amused look saying, 'What's happening here?' Jordan could only watch as she and those damned corset strings exited the dining room.

Before he could head to the library for what he hoped involved a stiff drink, a hand landed on his shoulder. He wasn't surprised to find that it belonged to Brian; Jordan had noticed that wherever Star happened to be, Rubie Racing's team principal usually wasn't too far behind.

Considering how thick Brian and Mia were and how close he'd been with their dad, Jordan and Brian had never really connected. Odd, considering the guy had been around Rubie Racing since he was a teenager. A brainiac at one of Detroit's top high schools, he'd written to the late Rob Rubie about his research on building a faster race car for a class project. Dad had been so impressed that he'd decided to make Brian his protégé, and the two struck up an unlikely friendship over the years. Brian had worked at Rubie Racing through college and grad school, and at the end of last season, Mia had promoted him to the top rung of the team ladder.

But Jordan had always gotten the feeling that Brian didn't care for him much. Not that Jordan could blame him – Brian had seen him at his worst more times than either of them could count – and not that it ever bothered him. Now, though, it kind of did.

The two made small talk as their footsteps echoed on the castle's stone walls. As it turns out, they were both somewhat anxious about the formal Scottish attire for the wedding, although for reasons other than wearing what was essentially a skirt. Brian thought a Black man in a kilt was probably some sort of sacrilege, and Jordan was weirded out by the high socks.

Jordan and Brian entered the library to find Wyn pouring and passing out glasses of Scotch, and they were soon joined by a group of Apex drivers staying in a nearby village. They greeted him with handshakes that evolved quickly into man hugs, and Jordan realised the weirdness he'd anticipated had been more about him than them. He'd known most of these guys since they were kids in karts, and they'd all checked in with him over the past year, calling and sending messages even though he rarely responded.

They were people he'd entrusted his life to for years on racetracks, and they to him. They were his friends, and they hadn't shut him out. He'd closed the door.

After Wyn brought around the decanter to top off everyone's glasses, he called those gathered to attention. Jordan wasn't surprised – Luca and Wyn had been best friends for as long as he could remember.

'Luca, after competing against Mia this season, I can confirm that you've met your match in every way,' Wyn said. 'I'm hesitant to use my go-to Welsh wedding toast, which translates to "two hearts, one wish," since we all know what their one wish is.'

The uncomfortable laughter that filled the room made Jordan thankful he wasn't on the track with his sister this season. Every driver present realised there was a strong possibility that Rubie Racing's wish – a second world championship, two years in a row – could come true.

'But what the hell. *Dwy galon, un dyhead.* To Mia and Luca!'

They all drank to Luca's impending marriage, with Jordan lowering his glass to notice the eyes in the room had shifted to him. It took him a few seconds to realise why, given their history.

They were about to become family. Tomorrow, he was handing over his sister to the guy – not that Mia was his to give away, of course, but the sentiment held. It was time to turn the page and start their relationship anew. But first, there was something he needed to do.

Jordan cleared his throat, and the room quieted. His gaze met Cliff's, who nodded.

'Luca.' *You can do this.* 'I'm sure I'm the last guy you ever wanted for a brother, considering what an ass I've been to you over the years.' *Don't cop out.* 'But I want you to know that I'm sorry. Truly.' *Just a bit more.* 'I don't expect you to forgive me, but I do hope we can find a way to move forward, for Mia's sake.'

Wyn broke the silence that had enveloped the library. 'Do you two need to *cwtch* it out? I know I'd like a nip, but it's bad luck until the toast is finished. Not that I'm superstitious.'

A ripple of laughter broke the tension in the room – race car drivers gave new meaning to the word.

To Jordan's surprise, Luca crossed the room and gave him the hug Wyn had suggested. 'If your sister has taught me about anything, it's forgiveness.'

After the two men stepped back and gave each other a nod, Jordan lifted his glass. 'To Luca and Mia.'

Chapter 18

If there was ever a man made to pull off a kilt, it was Jordan Rubie. Pearl could hardly keep her eyes off him, but maybe it was because she knew what was under that length of green and blue tartan.

Nothing but Jordan.

He'd seemed almost bashful getting dressed, even after Pearl pointed out how muscular his calves looked in the matching tall forest green socks. So, she'd decided it was her duty, as his date, to build up his confidence before he met up with the wedding party. Judging by how he was marching his sister across the great hall, Pearl had more than accomplished her goal.

But as they drew nearer, she couldn't help but notice how overcome Jordan was by this special moment with Mia. As much as he appeared to be trying to swallow down his feelings, they were bubbling up and spilling out in the obvious, tear-filled way as well as in subtler tells. Pearl wanted nothing more than to grab the clenched fist at his side, open his fingers, and hold his hand in hers.

Not that anyone but her was likely to notice. All eyes were on the other Rubie twin. Pearl truly had never seen a bride who sparkled like Mia Rubie. It wasn't what she was wearing, although the draped satin of her wedding dress, in the palest of pink, reminded Pearl of perfectly chiseled marble on a museum statue. Or her wavy blonde hair, the same shade as Jordan's, which was pulled back in a simple knot with a few loose tendrils surrounding her face. Or her bouquet of orange poppies with sprigs of white heather sprinkled in.

It was just her. From head to toe, Mia glowed.

When the siblings reached Luca, the significance of Jordan giving his sister away wasn't lost on the wedding guests. Barb, sitting on the other side of Jordan's empty chair, openly cried as the siblings hugged. And when Jordan clasped Luca's hand for a lingering handshake, a collective gasp reached the rafters – one nearly echoing Pearl's reaction to the video of the two men crashing. Apparently, for those gathered, what was playing out in front of them was just as shocking.

Jordan had told her about his apology toast when he returned to the room the night before, after finally tackling the corset strings he'd been so obsessed with throughout dinner. But instead of having sex right away, they'd talked until the wee hours of the morning – sharing their innermost thoughts about their hopes and fears, their families and friends, and their lives. When their souls were laid as bare as their skin, they'd finally reached for each other.

Pearl had never experienced intimacy with such intensity. She felt it again as she watched Jordan make his way to his seat, his glistening eyes only on her. He immediately took her hand and lifted it to his lips for a kiss.

When Top had married her earl, a local registrar officiated the ceremony, and similarly to that ceremony, the formal legalese couldn't take away from the pure joy that filled every nook and cranny in the cavernous space.

If Jordan hadn't shared about how Mia and Luca had re-kindled their teenage romance after she'd inherited the racing team, Pearl would never have guessed that the two people staring into each other's eyes like they were the only ones in the room were anything but meant to be – always. They certainly erased any doubts she'd ever had about second chances at love.

There wasn't a dry eye in the castle as their vows echoed off the ancient stone walls, and that included the bride and groom. As Jordan lifted their joined hands to his cheek to wipe away his tears, Pearl's heart clenched.

When Cliff got up to give the reading, Jordan whispered in her ear that in addition to being their father's best friend and Barb's boyfriend, he was Mia's godfather. He retrieved a folded piece of paper from this coat and read an E. E. Cummings poem that began with the words Jordan's mom had engraved inside their dad's ring, 'i carry your heart with me.'

Mia's gaze broke from Luca's for the first time since they pledged themselves to one another and shifted to her brother. Jordan gave a brief nod in return and then squeezed Pearl's hand, as if their connection was the only thing holding him together.

After the ceremony, while everyone gathered around the happy couple, Pearl took a moment to herself. She wandered around the room, stopping in front of an immense and intricate tapestry that covered a significant portion of one wall and featured a unicorn, the national animal of Scotland.

She sensed Jordan before she heard him walk up behind her, and the arm that wrapped around her held a sprig of the white heather.

'It's for luck and for wishes coming true,' Jordan said, even though the story of a Scottish woman who turned purple heather white through her tears over her lover's death seemed the opposite of a happy wedding tradition.

When she turned toward him, he bent down and lightly brushed her lips with his and whispered. 'You look beautiful, by the way.'

As he had left the room early to find Mia before the ceremony, he hadn't seen the full effect of her dress. The strapless ballgown she'd chosen from Top's closet was periwinkle and would've been out of her comfort zone if not for the layer of tulle with silver beaded embroidery and petal appliqués. The sheer fabric draped across one shoulder and the opposite arm in the most romantic way.

Feeling like a woman of the Regency period out for her first season in society, Pearl couldn't help but dip into an extravagant curtsy. 'Why thank you, kind sir.' When he laughed, she added, 'And I must say, you're not so shabby yourself. We might need to find a kilt for you to take home.'

Considering that they hadn't talked about anything past

going back to Wales after the wedding, she wanted to take the words back as soon as they'd left her mouth. To her relief, Jordan bowed and then kissed her square on the mouth.

'As you wish, my lady.'

It wasn't until much later, after they'd both drunk too much champagne and were dancing in the castle courtyard under strings of twinkling lights and a sky full of stars, that she realised how much she wanted to have a conversation about what came next. Because whatever was happening between them didn't feel like a dalliance. She was falling.

Chapter 19

The banging pulled them from a deep sleep. That's when they noticed the pieces of paper shoved under their door, which Jordan stumbled toward as he pulled on a pair of boxers. He steadied himself on the doorframe and shook away the cobwebs before turning the doorknob to find Barb, wringing her hands, on the other side.

In times of trouble, she made handwringing an art form. Something was wrong – very wrong – and his brain went straight from barely coherent to wide awake. 'What's happened? Where's Cliff? Is it Mia?'

Before his mind could race any further, Barb cut him off. 'I'm sorry to wake you two, but someone named Di keeps calling for Pearl. It sounds urgent.' More handwringing. 'She's very upset.'

Pearl was beside him in a flash, wrapped only in the bed sheet. 'Did you say Di's upset? She's never upset.'

Barb nodded. 'Distraught, actually. We were downstairs for breakfast, and the staff wasn't sure what to do, so they handed the phone to me. They said she started calling early this morning, so I promised to find you myself.'

The notes on the floor drew Jordan's gaze, and he bent down and scooped them up. The staff had left three, apparently taking the do-not-disturb sign to heart. They all said the same thing: *Please call Di at your earliest convenience.*

Reading over his shoulder, Pearl pointed at the phone number scrawled under the message. 'I think that's Top's number, but I don't know. I always just hit her name. Wait, where's my phone?'

After assuring Barb that he'd check in after Pearl reached Di, Jordan helped her search the room. They finally found her phone on the floor, under the kilt he'd worn the night before. The mad dash to get their clothes off and into bed seemed like a distant memory not — he checked the clock on the nightstand — six hours ago.

'Damn it, the battery's dead.' When she fumbled to insert the tiny connector into the charging slot, Jordan took over and handed her his phone.

As Pearl punched in the number on the note, he debated whether to give her privacy. But before he could turn away, she grabbed his hand and held it tight. Together, they waited for someone to answer.

Barb was wrong. The voice that answered wasn't distraught. It was hysterical.

Even if Pearl hadn't put Di on speakerphone, her shrill 'Pearlllll' would've still echoed through the room and in his brain. Between sobs, they learned that Top had been fine when Di had brought her home after surgery the day before. But a few hours later, she'd spiked a fever that kept climbing. No matter what Di did, it refused to break, so she'd finally called an ambulance.

'It's an infection, sepsis they called it, but nothing's working.' Di was barely holding it together. 'I wonder if we should ask them to bleed her, you know, like they do in her books.'

Pearl gasped as Jordan leaned into the phone speaker and yelled no.

Through sobs, Di said, 'I don't know what to do. Can you come back now? Please, Pearl. I need you.'

Beside him, Pearl cried, too. Jordan squeezed her hand and took the phone from her. 'Di, we'll be there as soon as we can.'

He hung up and called Barb, who started running when he asked her to find them something, anything to eat on the drive. And coffee. Lots of coffee.

Pearl, on the other hand, wasn't moving at all.

Jordan wrapped his arms around her. He wanted to tell her everything would be okay, but he knew from experience that wasn't always the case.

'I wanted something bad to happen, like for one of her breasts to be larger than the other.' Her head shook against his chest as she whispered, and he tightened his grip. 'I was mad at her; I didn't want her to die.'

He kissed the top of her head. 'Of course you didn't.'

'I made fun of her, Jordan.'

As much as he wanted to do nothing but stand there and hold her, they needed to get on the road back to reality. Regardless of what had gone down with Top and Di, Pearl would regret not being there if the unthinkable happened. Both he and Mia had missed their dad's final moments on this earth, and he wouldn't wish that regret on his worst enemy.

Whatever Pearl was to him was far from that.

'I've been where you are before, and we need to go.' He planted another kiss on the top of her head. 'Now. But since we can't really leave wearing boxers or a bed sheet, do you think you can be ready in 15 minutes?'

When he felt her nod, Jordan released Pearl with a squeeze and headed for the shower, leaving her standing in the middle of the space they'd more than settled into over the past few days. Clothes were piled on the floor, atop the second twin bed they'd never slept in, or wherever else they'd landed after being torn off each other every time they'd found themselves alone. Their frantic search for her phone hadn't improved the situation.

The mess was still there minutes later when he emerged from the bathroom towel-drying his hair. Pearl was where he'd left her, still clutching the bed sheet. This wasn't going to be easy, Jordan thought as he herded her into the shower and turned on the water, only leaving her to get himself dressed when she grabbed the soap and lathered it between her hands.

His master packing skills honed from years traveling

around the world went out the window — there wasn't time to be neat about it, or so he told himself as he began stuffing clothes into whatever suitcase or bag was nearest. Knowing that their wedding attire was crumpled and destined for the dry cleaners was all the justification he needed to wad the dress Pearl had borrowed from Top into a ball.

Jordan scanned the room for anything he'd forgotten to pack beyond clean clothes for Pearl. His eyes landed on the length of tartan still tied to the bedpost from the night before, and he quickly untied it and placed it in the front pocket of his suitcase. What he wouldn't give to go back to Gretna Green, to when it had fastened their hands together over the anvil, and repeat the last few days.

He wouldn't change a single thing except for how it was ending.

Once Pearl had dressed, he grabbed his favorite sweatshirt off the bed and held it up. 'You might get cold on the drive. Arms up.'

Once he'd pulled it over her head, Pearl finally broke her silence. 'I don't want to leave. I want to stay holed up here forever.'

'Me, too,' he said. But the real world was already seeping in, and they couldn't do anything to stop it.

If any sheep were in distress on the ride home, they were on their own. Jordan set the navigation system for the most direct route to the hospital and, for the next nine hours, only took his eyes off the road to check on Pearl, who rested her head against the window and stared blankly ahead.

If only he could drive this almost-race car like an actual race car. But these roads weren't meant for that kind of speed, and the day was as gloomy outside of the car as it was inside. Rain and wet asphalt had never been his favorite driving conditions.

Di called again about halfway through the drive. Top wasn't worse, but she also wasn't better.

'Stupid boob job,' Pearl said when the call ended.

Jordan had planned on talking to her about where they went from here on their way back to Wales. That didn't seem like an appropriate conversation now.

He reached over and squeezed her hand. 'Are you hungry?'

Her hand squeezed his back twice. 'Not really. Are you?'

'Not yet, but I will be in a little while,' he said. 'We can go through what Barb packed when we stop for fuel.'

Jordan pictured Barb barging into the castle kitchen, elbowing their chef out of the way, and taking over. Food was her love language. He couldn't begin to count how many meals Barb had popped over with since he'd moved out of his dad's house, especially in the past year.

She'd wanted him to recover at her house – the estate he and Mia grew up at, which their father left to Barb in his will. But he couldn't.

It had nothing to do with her having inherited their family home. That had been a sore spot at first, but what wasn't in those days, and he may have reacted poorly when Cliff read that section of the will out loud. But Jordan had come to realise that it was now Barb's home more than his or Mia's.

Plus, it was reassuring to know he could always visit because she would always be there. If only he and Mia could convince her to redecorate their bedrooms, which had been frozen in time since their teenage years. When he'd spent the night last Christmas Eve because he'd had one too many spiked eggnogs with Cliff, Jordan had woken up in the middle of the night thinking he'd either dreamed the years from 18 to 34 or had stumbled through a wormhole during a nighttime trip to the bathroom.

Neither would've been a bad thing.

If he was 18 again, Jordan could change the night that derailed Mia's life. If he could go back in time to the 24-hour Daytona race, he would've challenged Rubie Racing's top driver, who'd seemed off before climbing into the sports car for his relay shift. But Scott had insisted he was fine, and Jordan, technically an adult but still really a kid, had been too intimidated to push Scott on it.

So, Scott had gotten in the car and soon started feeling ill. Then Dad had found Luca and Mia naked in that random backseat, Scott had crashed, and everything had fallen to pieces.

If he could go back, at 33, he would've answered the phone instead of ignoring the six early-morning calls and increasingly frantic voicemails from Barb. When he'd heard the doorbell ringing and the banging on his front door and discovered her sobbing, he'd told her in a panic that his ringer had been off.

How could he have known that a heart attack would take the great and seemingly healthy Rob Rubie? By the time they'd reached the hospital, he'd died. Alone.

It had killed him, knowing his dad hadn't been surrounded by family during his final moments on earth. It still did.

When he and Pearl finally drew near the hospital in Bangor, he called Di, who'd continued giving them updates from Top's bedside. Pearl practically leaped from the car as soon as he shifted into park, and he was right on her heels.

But as they neared the entrance, Jordan's heart pounded. Through the revolving doors, Di's face came into focus, then blurred. His stomach rolled, and he bent over and placed his hands on his knees. Why were his palms so sweaty?

'Jordan?' Pearl asked, her voice sounding too far away.

After attempting a deep breath that wouldn't fully come, he managed to stand up. But instead of Pearl standing at the revolving door, he saw Barb, her face awash in tears like when they'd learned his dad had died. He shook his head, hoping to erase the memory like a bad drawing on an Etch A Sketch, but the pain wouldn't go away.

And so he did the only thing he could think to do, the only thing he'd ever done when his emotions overwhelmed him. He turned around and ran away.

Chapter 20

After the third surgery on his ankle and then more time in a cast and physical therapy, Jordan had found himself climbing behind the wheel of his SUV for 'Sunday drives' most days of the week. It was to make sure his ankle still worked like it should since Apex drivers needed full use of both feet for the gas and brake pedals during a race. At least, that's what he told himself.

But in reality, the driver's seat had been the only place where he felt at home.

As the hours multiplied, he'd started packing a bag for longer drives. On one, he'd headed to Chicago to stay at Mia's condo for a change of scenery. While wandering the Windy City, he'd stumbled upon the road sign for the beginning of Route 66. How had he forgotten that the historic United States highway began there, in the middle of downtown?

Standing amid the skyscrapers, a seed had been planted. And much like those tiny sprouts that manage to find light and life in the cracks of busy sidewalks, this one had quickly grown into a full-blown, cross-country road trip for the ages. Jordan hadn't even headed back to Michigan first – there hadn't been anything at home he needed that he couldn't buy in the third-largest city in the United States.

For nearly two weeks, Jordan had followed Route 66, barely registering the states rushing by outside and stopping only for food, gas, or a place to sleep. Every few hundred miles, he'd glance at the empty passenger seat and wonder what it would be like to have someone riding shotgun. But each time, he'd brushed away the feeling before he could dwell on it.

Racing was a solitary sport, and his life had simply followed suit. With the exception of – and maybe because of – a few women, like Julia, it had been the only life he'd known. He was good with being alone.

Or so he'd thought. Until he'd reached the end of the road.

After nearly 2,500 miles, Jordan had parked his car near the Pacific Ocean, jogged across a beach and down the Santa Monica Pier, and slapped the sign announcing Route 66's official end.

'I did it,' he'd said to no one in particular.

And that's when it hit him, harder than the cement wall he'd crashed into in Hungary. He wished there was someone in particular, someone special, in his life.

He'd gotten right back on the road and headed back to the Midwest – this had been about the journey not the destination, after all – but he'd hardly made it out of California before pulling into a roadside motel on Route 66. It was one that had gone to ruin in the years following the creation of the interstate highway system but saved by one person. That guy, a hipster named Phineas, had been in the process of restoring the 14 rooms, one by one, modernizing what needed updating while keeping as much of the old school charm as possible.

Little had Phineas known that the guy in room five was a washed-up race car driver in need of the same treatment.

Three days later, Jordan's phone had rung. He hadn't needed to look at the screen to know who was calling. Barb had strong-armed him into having his phone share its location with hers after the first time he'd gone off her radar.

'Are you sick?' Barb had asked. 'Is your ankle bothering you?'

Although caring for him and Mia had stopped being her responsibility more than a decade before, she refused to quit. No matter how many times he'd pushed her away over the years, the woman was a glutton for punishment.

'No, I'm fine,' he'd said. 'I'm just ... lost.'

At that admission, a dam had broken inside of him and out had spilled a river of tears. For hours, with Barb on the other end of the line, he'd blubbered, at times almost incoherently, about his parents, Mia, racing, and even love.

'One day,' Barb had said to the emotionally wrought Jordan, 'the right person will fall in your lap when you least expect it.'

Damn if she wasn't always right.

*

'And then what did you do, Jordan?' his therapist asked.

He'd started seeing Adam on the heels of his Route 66 meltdown. Then, like now, he was in crisis.

Jordan gulped. 'I left. Well, first I went to the emergency department to make sure I wasn't having a heart attack. But then, I got the hell out of Dodge.'

His dad having died of a heart attack had only worsened what he now realised was an anxiety attack. His first. To ensure it was also his last, he'd called Adam for an appointment before boarding his flight in London and had driven straight to the office when he'd landed in Detroit.

'I thought I'd changed.'

'What makes you think you haven't?' asked Adam, leaning back in an iconic Herman Miller Eames chair that matched the one in Jordan's own home office. It had been one of only a few things of his dad's he'd asked Barb for.

'I ran away. I left her with only the clothes on her back.'

Since he'd packed in such a hurry, mixing up their things in the process, both suitcases and garment bags had made the trip home with him. Loading everything into the back of his SUV in the airport parking garage had nearly broken him.

'You had an anxiety attack, Jordan.'

'I'm an asshole.' He choked up, picturing Pearl's shocked face, which had been burned into his retina. 'Always have been and, apparently, always will be.'

He had to give Adam credit for not quitting on the spot when hearing that old self-descriptor come out of Jordan's mouth. They'd both assumed – hoped – Jordan's asshole days were behind them.

Instead, Adam set his notepad and pen on the table next to his tea, leaned forward, and said three words Jordan had hoped never to hear again: 'Let's dig in.'

For as many times as Jordan had dug into his emotions in this room, he should have a shovel in the corner with his name on it. The work had been necessary and painful but, as it turns out, unfinished.

And so he talked. He was relieved he wasn't dying because he wasn't ready – not many people get to choose when they draw their final breath – and relief begot relief. After the crash, when Luca didn't move at first, Jordan had had fleeting thoughts of wishing he was the one lifeless in a mangled orange race car.

He was embarrassed about breaking down mentally in a public parking lot in front of Pearl as well as Di. Shame piggybacked a ride on the emotional rollercoaster at that point since embarrassment had led to him not being there for Pearl when she'd needed him.

Just like he hadn't been there for his dad, who'd had an actual heart attack.

'My dad died alone.' Jordan wiped away a tear streaming down his right cheek and the others that quickly followed. 'I could've been there, I should've been there, but I wasn't there. And now I've gone and done the same thing again. Like I said, I'm an asshole.'

Adam retrieved a box of tissues from the other side of the

room. They'd already blown past the standard 50-minute session, but Jordan knew Adam wouldn't cut him off while the tears flowed. Which was good because Jordan wasn't sure he could get them to stop.

'Jordan, no two situations are the same – these two especially,' Adam said.

'Maybe not, but there is one common denominator,' Jordan said, 'and it's me.'

Dear Pearl of Wisdom,

A very wise woman once told me that it's important to say you're sorry.

I'm sorry. So very, very sorry.

Always,

Heartbroken (JR)

PS I miss you.

Chapter 21

In the end, Pearl decided to bring Top back to Chicago. She couldn't stand the thought of leaving her by herself in Abersoch. Peeling Di from Top's body had already taken all of the physical and emotional strength Pearl had in her; there was no way she could bear prying an urn containing Top's ashes from her grip, too.

For what had to be the millionth time in two weeks, Pearl pushed aside the image of Jordan standing outside the revolving doors and turning around instead of following her in. Pearl wasn't sure what she would've done if Di hadn't pulled her deeper into the hospital, to Top's deathbed.

It was a good thing she was already heartbroken.

She looked down at the woman who'd hardly moved from the sofa since five minutes after they walked in the front door of Pearl's condo – a woman who bore no resemblance to the one who'd raised her. No makeup. Not a hair in place. A St Patrick's Day bar crawl T-shirt paired with bright pink sweatpants that said 'LUCKY' plastered across the rear end, which she'd unearthed from the back of Pearl's closet.

'Are you sure you'll be okay?' Pearl asked Di again.

Not that she could do anything about it if Di's answer was no. She'd taken every day of bereavement leave available and then some. It had been just over three weeks since she last saw the inside of her office. If she didn't show up at work this morning, she could kiss goodbye her days of being the Pearl of Wisdom.

'Yes, for the hundredth time,' Di said. 'We're going to rest today.'

As if Pearl didn't know who 'we' was, Di's hand snaked out from under the blanket and came to rest on the urn beside the sofa. For sisters who lived on different continents for most of their adult lives, they were now proving inseparable.

'I'll call at lunch,' Pearl said, at a loss for what else to say.

At least it was Friday, and she only had to endure one day back at work before having two days to figure out how to deal with Di's grief. Not to mention her own.

Considering that Madeline rarely left her office, preferring to summon people to hers, Pearl was surprised to get a 911 text from Millie that their editor was heading her way. Perhaps she wanted to express her condolences now that she could do so in person, although she'd had all morning to do that.

On impulse, Pearl shoved the day's batch of reader letters

into her tote to get them out of sight. While she'd b
Madeline had been screening what arrived via snail
email, which an editorial assistant printed out. Pearl
to nip that in the bud.

Not two seconds after she'd turned her attention bac.
her computer screen, Madeline appeared in the doorw
cleared her throat, and waited until Pearl's gaze met hers.

'Apparently, a conversation is warranted,' she said.

Leave it to the woman to speak both passively and
passive-aggressively. She was nothing if not efficient.

'Pardon?' Pearl asked, hitting save on the document she'd
been working on before giving Madeline her full attention.

'I'm confused,' Madeline said, even though she looked
nothing of the sort. Thanks to regular Botox treatments, her
face rarely displayed any emotion at all. 'I was under the
impression your aunt was gravely ill when you requested
time off to be with her.'

It was more than an impression; it was what Pearl had told
her and believed to be true at the time. But she hadn't updated
Madeline when the storyline had changed – or that Top was
her mother, not her aunt.

'As it turns out, she was undergoing surgery and simply
wanted her family by her side,' Pearl said.

'What type of surgery?' Madeline asked.

'Cosmetic surgery.' Her editor could hardly judge, given
that she'd flown to Europe with miles earned from her last
facelift. 'Very serious cosmetic surgery.'

'I see.' Madeline reached into her cardigan pocket, took

out her phone, and after a few clicks, set it on Pearl's desk. 'Then perhaps you'd care to explain this.'

Pearl froze when she saw what was queued up on the screen: the video of her and Jordan saving the sheep. Madeline didn't need to hit play – Pearl had been there – but she did, and didn't hit stop until Jordan had deposited Pearl in the sleek, green sports car and turned to face the person recording the video.

Her brain went into overdrive with some immediate thoughts.

One: *Green bean.* That's what they should've named the car. It was a perfect fit with the turbo pumpkin and supercharged squash. Not that it mattered now. The odds of her ever seeing the man dominating the phone screen again were slim to none.

Two: Why did Jordan have to be so damn good looking? And why did she still want to kiss that smug smile right off his stupid jerk face?

'Pearl, would you care to explain' – even Botox couldn't hide how much Madeline was enjoying this – 'why you asked for time off for one thing when you clearly had plans to do something far different?'

That's when Pearl noticed the security guards lingering in the hallway outside her office and the file folder on the side chair beside the doorway, and she had another thought.

Three: She was being fired – *fired* – from her dream job.

Madeline picked up the file folder and handed the papers inside to Pearl. In bold letters across the top page was 'Termination Agreement.'

'This deception is completely inexcusable for a professional in your position, and you, more than anyone, know that actions have consequences,' she said, holding out a pen. 'We're releasing you from employment at the *Chicago Daily Times*.'

Pearl shook her head. 'But I'm Pearl ... of the Wisdom.'

Madeline sniffed. 'Are you quite certain of that?'

Pearl numbly thumbed through the packet. But when she found the lines for her signature and the date on the final page, she paused. If she'd learned anything from Top, who'd been royally screwed over early in her publishing career, it was that legal documents should never be signed on the spot.

Waving away the pen, Pearl folded the papers in half and stuck them into her tote. 'I'm sure you understand that I'll need my attorney to review this.'

Within seconds, a member of the maintenance staff arrived with a dolly and boxes and, along with the security guards and Madeline, watched as Pearl packed up the few personal items she'd accumulated in her office – her favorite pens, which the newspaper had refused to spring for, the tin of tiny paperclips Top had put in her stocking last Christmas, and her planner. She kicked off her heels and added them to the box, along with a handful of succulents on the windowsill and a textbook on moral philosophy. When her work life fit neatly into a single box, the maintenance guy gave her a sympathetic nod, took his dolly, and left.

Once Pearl had shut down her computer and slid back into the Birkenstocks she'd walked to work in, she tossed her tote bag over her shoulder, picked up her box of belongings, and followed Madeline into the open office space. With the security guards in tow, they headed to the elevator, her coworkers stopping to stare as she walked past.

Madeline tapped the down button, and Pearl watched as the indicator lights counted down the floors. When the doors opened, she stepped inside with the security guards and waited for the door to close on the face of the woman she hoped never to lay eyes on again.

Once outside, Pearl decided to walk home, even though she was more overloaded than a pack mule. She followed the path she'd taken too many times to count over the past ten years. A decade of her life. Done. Kaput. The box was more awkward than heavy, and from time to time, she'd stop to sit on a bench and rest her overstretched arms.

When Millie caught up with Pearl and her box, they were parked on a bench in front of the Victorian fountain at Washington Square Park, staring at the historic Newberry Library across the street. At one point, she'd thought the building seemed ancient, but it couldn't compare to a Scottish castle.

Nothing did.

'How'd you find me?' Pearl asked.

'I followed the breadcrumbs,' she said, holding out a handful of the multicolored paperclips shaped like tiny animals before dumping them in Pearl's tote bag. 'There must be a hole in that box; you've been dropping them for blocks. Not that it was hard to figure out which way you'd head home.'

The park had been Pearl's favorite since they'd moved into the quirky vintage condo in the nearby Gold Coast neighborhood. And not just because it was small and quaint and never crowded like Lincoln Park, which stretched for miles along Lake Michigan north of downtown. It was the kind of park where older people sat quietly on benches with equally aged dogs.

It was also famous for being where soapbox orators would stand on small wooden shipping crates and speak their minds. For decades, people shared their opinions on politics to poetry and everything in between.

Pearl didn't have an old wooden crate. But she did have a box and something to say.

Under the watchful eye of her best friend, Pearl moved the box to the ground, climbed atop it, and screamed, 'This sucks!'

'You've certainly got that right, missy,' an older gentleman called out from the other side of the fountain. In a huff, he got up and shuffled away with his Jack Russell.

'Sorry!' Pearl bellowed after him and then sat down on her box and cried.

'Stop kicking me,' Di said. 'Better yet, go to your own bed.'

After Pearl had dumped the box and her tote bag inside the door and dragged herself down the long hallway to the living room, she'd made herself at home at the other end of the sofa.

That was 18 hours ago.

'You're the one taking up too much space,' Pearl said. 'You always do.'

'Always' was a stretch, considering it had been at least 25 years since she and Di had shared a sofa. For once, though, Di was right. She should go to her own bed, especially since sleeping in such close proximity with someone else reminded her of the twin bed in the castle – and Jordan. He was the last person she wanted to think about.

But each time Pearl considered shifting from the sofa, she couldn't muster the energy. She'd barely been keeping her head above water after Top and Jordan. Losing her job, too, felt like she'd been fitted with a pair of cement shoes.

She must've fallen asleep again because the door to the condo opening and closing woke her up. Within seconds, Millie appeared in the doorway of the living room with multiple shopping bags, including two from the fancy grocery store where they only shopped for special ingredients. Pearl yawned and shoved Di's legs away from her face.

'What time is it?' Pearl asked, realizing she hadn't heard her roommate leave.

'It's afternoon,' Millie said. 'I figured that if you two slug-a-sofas were going to lie around all weekend, we needed some provisions.'

After so many years of friendship and sharing a space,

Millie knew her better than anyone. Whatever she'd bought promised to be worth-getting-off-the-sofa good.

Di finally stirred. 'Did you buy wine?'

Millie nodded. 'In honor of Top, I have wine *and* brandy, along with the makings for a charcuterie board for the ages. But it's only for people who take showers and put on clean clothes.'

Although that comment was directed at Di, Pearl knew she could also use a freshening up. Before crashing on the sofa the day before, she'd changed into yoga clothes. Although she hadn't managed any poses beyond savasana, she was still in them – and had been lying next to Di. Even if the charcuterie ended up being nothing more than bologna and plastic cheese, she owed Millie for initiating the stinky-kid-in-gym-class conversation.

As usual, Di drove a hard bargain. 'Is there chocolate, too?' she asked.

'Dessert is a surprise,' Millie said, 'but trust me when I say it's worth it.'

Three hours later, Pearl and a squeaky-clean Di gawked at side-by-side charcuterie boards on the dining room table. One was the typical cured meats and cheeses, only on steroids, but the other was a wet dream come to life for anyone with a sweet tooth. Mille had traipsed the Windy City seeking out Pearl's favorites, including pistachio old-fashioned doughnuts, chocolate cupcakes with brown butter frosting, and the cheddar and caramel mix from the gourmet popcorn shop that always had a line of tourists out the door.

'Worth the price of admission?' Millie asked.

'More than,' said Pearl, wondering what she would do without her friend for the millionth time since the housing gods at Northwestern University assigned them to the same dorm room. 'You're the best.'

Di harrumphed and said, 'I just don't know why you had to throw away those clothes.'

Still, she reached for the 'Polish roses' Millie had made just for her. The spring onions rolled up in paper-thin ham slices covered in cream cheese were a staple at any party in the Carrington house.

'No offense, Di, but they had to go,' Millie said. 'As a style expert, I couldn't have them in my home any longer. Plus, they smelled.'

Millie had gone as far as taking them out to the dumpster while Di was in the shower and then dressing her in a pair of her black jogger pants and a cropped teal sweatshirt. Between the outfit and her makeup-free face, Di looked like a woman about to turn 40 instead of 50.

The three of them sat around the table for a couple of hours, going back and forth between the sweet and savory boards until they were about to burst. By the time they moved the party to the living room, the brandy bottle was in the recycling bin, and they'd uncorked the last cabernet.

'This is what happens when you don't follow the rules,' Pearl said to no one in particular.

'You have days of mind-blowing sex with a gorgeous race car driver?' Millie asked.

That got Di's attention. 'What happens now?' she asked.

Pearl shook her head. 'People die.'

At that, Di slid from what would now forever be known as her spot on the sofa to the floor and draped herself over Top's urn. Her entire body shook with emotion.

'What is wrong with you?' asked Millie, hurling a throw pillow at Pearl. Ironically, it was one with a hand making a peace sign embroidered on the front. 'We just got her cleaned up.'

Di's face lifted, and to Pearl's relief and astonishment, her tears weren't from a sorrow backslide but instead, the kind of belly laughter that renders a person mute. When she was finally able to speak, Di lifted herself up and addressed the urn. 'Can you believe this girl never knew she was yours? So prone to drah-ma.'

There wasn't enough wine in France for whatever was happening here.

'I hate to break it to any of you, but your girl is 50-50 when it comes to the jewel sisters,' Millie said. 'You could be a case study for nature versus nurture, with your closet full of gray and black clothes and lingerie drawer stuffed with silk and lace.'

Correction: There wasn't enough wine in the world.

'I'm not discussing this,' Pearl said as another throw pillow came sailing her way, 'and you and Di dragged me into that lingerie store.'

'We didn't force you to buy any of it, or to throw away all of your old stuff,' Millie said. 'It was still perfectly good. You said so yourself. Many times.'

175

Di nodded in agreement as she wiped away more tears and caught her breath, her hand resting on the chest of her sweatshirt.

An image of Jordan in his Highland cow sweatshirt flashed in Pearl's mind. She found herself transported back to their room in the castle, in front of the fireplace, her fingers seeking the warmth of his bare skin under the fabric. In an instant, the memory was gone, leaving behind heat that traveled to her cheeks.

'Are you okay?' Millie asked.

'It's the wine. My red face.' Pearl redirected the conversation. 'Bad things happen. I didn't do what I said and look at what happened. I lost my dream job.'

Pearl caught a look between Millie and Di that, in their drunkenness, they'd done a lousy job hiding.

'What was that about?' she asked.

Unsurprisingly, it was Di who said the quiet part out loud. 'Dream job? Your dream was to sound like you had a stick up your ass? Or worse, like your grandparents?'

Millie shook her head at Di. 'No, not always. And I don't think I'd call running off to Scotland with Jordan breaking the rules. It was braving the rules. And look, I don't blame you for being excited about the syndication deal, but the column doesn't sound like you anymore. It's 99 per cent Madeline. Only the face and the name belong to you.'

Pearl didn't want what they were saying to be true. She'd made a difference – Cliff and Barb were proof of that.

'I was good though – I am good.' Pearl leaped up and

retrieved her tote bag from where she'd left it by the door. She walked back into the living room waving the letters she'd meant only to hide from Madeline but had instead taken home along with her personal items. The old Pearl would've put them into a manila envelope with her own letter of apology and sent them back to work. But that Pearl had left the building 32 hours ago.

'Ask me any of these,' she said, tossing them between Millie and Di on the sofa. 'Go ahead. Quiz me.'

'Oh, what the hell,' Millie said, setting down her wine glass to pick through the pile. The question she pulled was from a man considering calling off his wedding because his mother didn't think his bride would produce attractive enough offspring.

'Easy-peasy,' Pearl said with a sip. 'He needs to grow a pair.'

Di began picking letters from the pile, too. After reading a few, she looked at Pearl and, with a wink, said, 'Hoo boy, our family has nothing on some of these folks.'

She arched an eyebrow and pointed at the urn, which Di had moved to the coffee table so Top could see better. 'I'm not so sure about that.'

Millie grabbed one of the last letters remaining. 'Oh, thank God, a short one,' she said, then read, '*Dear Pearl of Wisdom, A very wise woman once told me that it's important to say you're sorry. I'm sorry. So very, very sorry. Always, Heartbroken (JR). PS I miss you.* Well, that's dumb. He didn't even ask a question.' She hiccuped. 'He misses you? Stalker alert.'

Pearl froze, staring at the sheet of paper in her best friend's hands. 'What are the initials again?'

'JR, like junior.'

'No, dummy,' Di said, grabbing the paper from Millie's hands and shoving it at a still-stunned Pearl. 'Like Jordan Rubie.'

Chapter 22

Only one person would continue to knock when no one answered the door. But then again, only one person knew with certainty that Jordan was home because he'd given her permission to track his location at all times.

It was also the last person he'd leave standing outside in the rain, which she knew. Not that it was raining, or at least he didn't think it was. He hadn't left the house in a few days.

'I can't believe you have the nerve to come over and not even bring me any food,' Jordan said when he opened the front door and found Barb standing there empty-handed.

He'd been on the treadmill for the last hour, attempting to lift his serotonin levels and sweat out his sorrow naturally. Given how soaked his clothes were, he should be the picture of mental health. Although exercise was helping, he had miles to go.

'I thought we'd go out and grab a bite to eat, but maybe ordering in is a better option,' said Barb, giving him a quick once over. 'Glad to see you're alive, by the way. Thank you for not returning my many phone calls and texts and scaring a woman half to death.'

After what ended up being a full week of daily therapy sessions, Jordan had shut himself off from the rest of the world to contemplate his past, present, and future. That deep dive had entailed a lot of time staring at the water from the end of his dock, the blank pages of his journal, and the back of his eyelids.

'I'm sorry,' he said. 'I had some thinking to do, but I should've let you know.'

'I just worry about you,' she said, reaching out and lightly touching his forearm with her left hand.

When he glanced down, a diamond sparkled from her ring finger — a stone so perfect and shiny that it couldn't have been out of its velvet box for long.

'Do you perhaps have something to tell me?' he asked.

With a blush, Barb shared that she and Cliff had been talking about getting engaged for a while. Not wanting to steal any of Mia and Luca's thunder, they'd waited until after the wedding to make it official and were planning something small during the Apex off-season.

'I'm happy for you, Barb,' he said, enveloping her in a sweaty hug. 'But this sort of news deserves more than carryout.'

Barb pulled away and wrinkled her nose. 'Like a shower, maybe?'

'Sure, if you want a bridal shower, I can make that happen,' he said, humming 'Here Comes the Bride' when she shoved him out of the way and marched inside.

After a quick congratulatory call to Cliff, Jordan snagged a last-minute reservation for the three of them at Mario's, the Rubie family's favorite old-school Italian restaurant in downtown Detroit. It's where they'd always celebrated birthdays, anniversaries, and every milestone in between. For Barb, he'd put on a happy face and a suit. Because if anyone deserved to find love again, it was her.

So later that night, once they were shoved in the old school burgundy pleather booth in the back corner of the restaurant, Jordan toasted Barb and Cliff's good news with a bottle of champagne and a gluttonous amount of antipasto and tried not to think about how he'd blown his chance at love. Big time.

'I'm glad you're making an honest woman out of her, even if seeing the two of you make eyes at each other does open up a very uncomfortable Pandora's box of emotions for me,' Jordan said.

He and Cliff laughed when Barb blushed and subsequently fanned herself with the dinner specials card and blamed the champagne, then the room being too warm, and finally, good ole menopause.

'I guess that answers my question about whether you kids have to get married,' he teased, pretending to pump a shotgun.

'Jordan Robert Rubie!' Barb said, her face turning an even deeper shade of red.

It was the best night he'd had since Mia's wedding, which

was coincidentally the last night he'd spent with Pearl. They'd been Prince Charming and Cinderella, only instead of her losing a glass slipper, he turned into a heel.

As if she could read his mind, Barb asked, 'Have you heard from your friend?'

There was no question about to whom she was referring and no sense in playing dumb. When Barb had returned from Scotland, he'd given her the abbreviated version of deserting Pearl without so much as a goodbye.

At least he'd learned what had caused his anxiety attack during his marathon sessions with Adam. How every emotion he'd buried along with his parents had come rushing back at about 300 miles an hour. How, one second, he'd been frozen in place, staring at Pearl, his heart pounding, and in the next, he was back in the car with his foot on the gas pedal.

He shook his head, as much to answer Barb's question as to clear the memory that had already gotten too much replay. Even though he was trying his best not to think about Pearl and the days and nights they'd spent together, he was failing miserably. He'd watched the video of them uprighting the sheep so many times that the ads stalking him around the internet for days afterward were interesting, to say the least.

'You know what? Tonight's not about me.' Jordan picked up his glass for another round of 'cheers' and pretended not to notice the look Cliff and Barb exchanged.

After rounding out a family style Italian feast with cannoli, tiramisu, and gelato, they were all so full that the car ride back to the suburbs was quiet, even before Barb conked out in the backseat.

Cliff turned around to check on his fiancée, then angled his body toward Jordan in the passenger seat. 'You sure you're okay with this?'

Jordan's eyes stayed on the road. He wasn't as close to Cliff as Mia, who was his goddaughter. His own godfather had been his dad's best friend on the racetrack, which is where he'd died in a fiery crash when Jordan was still a toddler. His widow, Jordan's godmother, had drifted out of the picture as the years passed.

Cliff, on the other hand, had always been around. He and Rob Rubie had grown up together on the east side of Detroit, where they'd raced karts against each other and forged a lifelong friendship. It had endured even though their adult lives couldn't have been more different, with one becoming an Apex driver and then a team owner and the other a lawyer.

His dad's will had strained his relationship with Cliff. Since he'd requested it be read aloud, Cliff had gathered Mia, Barb, and Jordan together the day after the funeral. In his dad's den, Jordan had learned that his father had left Rubie Racing to Mia with no strings attached. Apparently, he'd needed them all for his son's inheritance, which was more of a contingency clause based on Jordan either shaping up or shipping out.

But after the crash in Hungary, Cliff had flown to Jordan's bedside and stayed there until his release from the hospital.

Following that, the two had come to an unspoken mutual understanding, which had been helpful when Cliff and Barb began dating soon after.

And now he was marrying the woman who'd been mothering the Rubie twins longer than their mom had.

'Of course I'm okay with it,' Jordan said. 'I don't know if Dad would be surprised by all of this, but I'm sure he'd be pleased.'

Cliff sighed. 'He wouldn't have been surprised. Those letters he left all of us? Mine was all about Barb. He practically told me to get my head out of my ass.' Cliff shook his head. 'He knew long before we did. Bastard always thought he was so smart.'

Jordan thought about his own letter, or rather, the letter he still hadn't been able to bring himself to open in the 18 months since his dad had died. Cliff had passed them out after reading the will, but Jordan had been too angry to read it. The envelope with his name written neatly on the front in his dad's trademark script had nearly ended up in the fireplace that night.

If only he could bring himself to get it over with and open the damn envelope. But the more time passed, the less he desired to see exactly what Rob Rubie thought of his only son.

Cliff relaxed in his seat, and they finished the drive in a comfortable silence. When he pulled into the driveway of the house he'd grown up in, he fought a sudden urge to run inside and camp out in his childhood bedroom.

Barb stirred in the backseat. 'It's late, Jordan. Why don't you stay and leave after breakfast.'

Maybe the woman actually could read minds. He put the SUV in park but didn't turn off the engine.

'No, I have things to do,' he lied. 'But I'll call you tomorrow.'

With a kiss on the cheek and a shoulder squeeze, Barb was out the door. Cliff took her hand, and they walked together out of the beam of his headlights.

When Jordan reached his driveway 20 minutes later, he hesitated before clicking the garage door opener. As opposed to the house he'd just left, this was simply a place where he ate and slept. It could've been a hotel suite or a corporate rental, for as much as it matched him, his personality, or who he was.

He'd decided to buy the house before his real estate agent had opened the door, simply because it ticked all of the boxes.

On a lake. Check.

Private. Check.

Close to work. Check.

Big enough to impress. Check check check.

His father's housewarming gift had been the use of his interior decorator, and Jordan had promptly upped her budget. His only specification: Make the space look like it belonged in the pages of a magazine. She'd succeeded and then some, but it was no magazine he wanted to read. The interior was sleek, purposely sparse, and floor-to-ceiling bright white. As a result, no one felt comfortable touching anything or sitting anywhere – including him.

Inside, the full moon reflected on the walls and carpeting through the floor-to-ceiling windows, illuminating the entire house. He made his way to the master suite, which Barb had helped him de-sterilise and outfit with new furniture and bedding after the crash.

Jordan flopped onto his bed and grabbed his phone. After a quick time zone calculation, he pressed his sister's name. Mia picked up on the first ring.

'So, if I'm a ring bearer, are you the flower girl?' he asked.

'We're what now?' she asked.

'In the wedding.'

Nothing.

'Barb and Cliff's.'

Her scream spoke volumes. Several decibels worth.

'Oh, shit,' he said. 'You can't say anything. Promise you won't say anything.'

Mia promised, but they both knew she was lying. 'Tell me everything you know. How did Cliff propose? Did he get down on one knee? When's the wedding? What's the ring like?'

It was a miracle she didn't hang up on him and call Barb on the spot when he could only share that her diamond ring looked nice and the wedding would happen after the Apex season ended.

'I'm extremely disappointed in you, Jordan,' Mia said.

'How am I supposed to race today with all of these lingering questions?'

It was Sunday morning in Baku, where Mia, Luca, and the rest of the Rubie Racing team were for the Azerbaijan Grand Prix. Mia had stood on the podium again at the last race in Italy but was frustrated that she couldn't get past a certain French driver. It was only a matter of time before she figured out how to put Henri Aveline's red car in her rearview mirror, which he told her.

'But you've got to knock off the penalties, Mia,' Jordan said. 'You're not doing yourself or the team any favors there.'

So far this season, she'd touched wheels with another driver attempting to pass him, shoving him off the track. In another race, she'd sped in the pit lane. Even though they were only five- and ten-second penalties, she'd gifted that time to the drivers behind her and dropped a spot in the race results. At the end of the season, when all of the points from finishing in the top ten were totaled, a few seconds and a few spots here and there would matter — to the tune of tens of thousands of dollars.

It was something Jordan knew too well.

'I still say that was a racing incident at the Dutch Grand Prix,' Mia said. 'Watch the video again, Jordan.'

'Uh-huh.' He smiled, knowing his sister was stewing on the other end of the line, and would probably send him some specific video to prove her point. He cleared his throat. 'So, Grant Clark's team manager called me the other day.'

'From Clark Motorsport? Interesting.'

Like with Barb and Cliff's news, it was clear she didn't have a clue as to why a racing team in Pinnacle, the American series most similar to Apex, would be calling him.

'And?'

'I'm videoconferencing with him on Monday.' Jordan had a knot in his stomach already. He wasn't sure he could handle what Grant might say to him given how precarious his current emotional state was.

'Why don't you sound excited? Wait, hold on.' Even with her hand covering the microphone, Jordan could hear her talking to someone. 'Heads up, I'm putting you on speaker.'

'Hey, mate. Word is that a few Pinnacle teams are adding a third car,' Luca said. 'Good morning, by the way.'

'Pinnacle isn't limited to two cars like Apex,' his sister added.

He couldn't help but laugh. 'I'm aware, Mia. And I'm sure he's only checking in to see how I'm doing after Dad and the crash. Also, Luca, it's nearly midnight here, so I'm going to say good night to the both of you.'

'Call us as soon as you hang up with him,' Mia said. 'I'm serious.'

'Good night, Mia.' Jordan yawned. 'And stop giving away points. I'm serious.'

Chapter 23

'I've made a decision,' Di said Monday morning at the crack of dawn. 'We're heading back to Michigan.'

'Am I dreaming?' Pearl asked, pulling the covers over her head. 'If I am, please don't wake me up.'

After Saturday night's wine and charcuterie-palooza, they'd spent Sunday recovering. Pearl had reread Jordan's four-sentence letter at least a hundred times, and then Millie had streamed the sheep video on the television and they picked that apart, too.

She always circled back to the same conclusion. It didn't matter, especially when she looked at the big picture. He'd left.

Of course, it was easy think the situation was so cut and dried given that she had no way of getting ahold of him. Jordan hadn't included his address, the envelope was long gone, and she didn't have his phone number. His social media accounts had been dormant since his crash, just like he'd told her. She'd only checked to prove her point.

'Knock it off, you,' Di said, yanking back the covers before opening the window shutters. 'I said we, meaning you and me.'

Pearl rolled over. She'd been incorrect. This wasn't a dream. It was a nightmare.

'What I still don't get is why Grandma and Grandpa decided you should've been punished instead of Top,' Pearl said when they were two hours into the six-hour drive to Di's house in the northern suburbs of Detroit.

While Pearl was in the shower trying to figure out why she'd agreed to go or if she actually had, Di had tracked down a rental car. Since it was at the last minute and the downtown Chicago car rental agencies weren't flush with vehicle options at any given time, her choices had been at the opposite ends of the spectrum. She'd chosen an extra-large SUV over a compact car akin to the one Pearl had rented in the UK, likely because Top's urn fit neatly in the center console.

Pearl could only hope they weren't pulled over. It wasn't illegal, but there would be questions.

'First of all, "punished" isn't the right word,' Di said. 'You're going to end up in therapy if you start thinking you were a form of punishment.'

Considering how well Di had rebounded in the past 36 hours, Pearl decided it wasn't the time to share that she'd already had years of therapy. Her upbringing hadn't exactly been conventional, and she'd struggled with feeling like a burden to Di growing up. At least now she knew why, even if having validation was unsatisfying.

'They decided it was my fault,' Di said, fiddling with the GPS screen. 'Top told them she only did it to be more like me.'

The insane train of thought fit with what Pearl remembered of her grandparents. 'So, their thinking was that if you hadn't been such a poor influence on your sister, she never would've gotten pregnant?'

'Bingo,' Di said.

'Yeah, that's bonkers,' Pearl said.

'It's hard to explain what it's like for there to be two of you. For someone else to have the same face you see when you look in the mirror. As far as Mom and Dad were concerned, Top and I were more than a single egg that split and formed two babies – we were one person in two bodies. We may as well have been those good and bad angels that sit on your shoulder and whisper in your ear.'

There was no question which twin Pearl's grandparents had pegged as which angel.

'You know, even though Top threw me under the bus when she told them she was only trying to be like me, I was proud of her for going against them. I doubt this will come as a surprise, but Top was even more timid and sensitive as a kid. I tried to protect her as best I could, but she was different. I was shocked when she came home from camp and told me she'd lost her virginity. I hadn't even had sex yet. We were only 14.'

'Well, isn't that ironic?' Pearl asked, glancing at the urn of ashes between them. She almost felt bad talking so openly about Top when she was in the car with them. 'Who did you tell people the father was?'

'That I had a Canadian boyfriend,' Di laughed.

As far as Pearl could tell, her actual father hadn't read her message yet. She'd checked a dozen times and also looked through the few photos on his social media page. They offered few clues about him or his life.

'Did you know anything about Harrison Carter?' Pearl said. 'The guy Top said my father was?'

Di nodded. 'Top pointed him out when we picked her up at camp, but she didn't introduce him. If Mom and Dad had figured out what she'd gotten up to, they wouldn't have allowed her to go the next summer. Which, of course, is exactly what happened. From what I can remember, he was cute.'

After they stopped for lunch and were back on the road, Pearl realised they weren't taking the normal route home. When she tried to check the GPS screen, Di slapped her hand away.

'Don't mess with that,' she said. 'I need to know where I'm going.'

Something was up – way up. Di knew where she was going, always. If she'd been someplace once, the route was permanently programmed into her brain. And she'd been back and forth to Chicago plenty of times over the years.

'I thought we'd take a scenic route,' Di said.

Just as Pearl was about to blow up, she forced herself to pause and look at the woman behind the wheel. Di was wearing makeup for the first time in weeks – a fraction of her normal amount – but something else was different about her. Something Pearl couldn't put her finger on. So she kept her mouth shut until they exited the highway, and GPS said they were five minutes from their destination.

'We're going to Rubie Racing, aren't we?'

Di's hands gripped the steering wheel. 'I saw his face before he walked away, Pearl. The man was terrified, and a look that intense couldn't have had anything to do with you.'

'He left and took my stuff with him,' Pearl said.

'He wrote you a letter.'

Pearl swallowed. 'To say he was sorry.'

'He misses you.'

As much as Pearl had been trying to convince herself otherwise, she missed him, too. It was illogical, missing someone she barely knew ... except she did know him.

She did.

'What if it wasn't real?' Pearl asked. 'I don't want to go through what you did every September after Mr June, July, and August dumped you.'

While other people associate autumn with football, apple cider, and doughnuts, for Pearl, fall was heartache season. For years, she'd watched Di mope around until the first snowflakes flew.

Di shook her head. 'You've got it wrong. They never dumped me. I ended it, every single time.'

'But you were always so into them, and then you were always so upset when it was over. Why?'

As soon as the question left her mouth, she knew the answer. Getting close to someone would've entailed telling him the truth, and that wasn't something the Carrington family excelled at. All things considered, it was a miracle Top had told the earl.

How ironic that she'd built a career as a moral authority when her own life was based on a lie. 'You know you didn't do anything wrong, don't you?' Pearl asked.

Di did a quick check of her hair and makeup as she pulled into the entryway to a massive complex with a pond and Rubie Racing sign out front. When they reached a security guard shed, Di flashed a smile.

'We're here to see the race car,' she said.

Pearl slunk down in her seat. That was never going to get them in the door.

But apparently no man in uniform was immune to Di's charms because he returned a wide smile. 'Well, you've certainly come to the right place. The championship car is on display in the main lobby. Park in that small lot right there, and head through the doors. You can't miss it.'

Di drove to where he pointed and parked in a visitor's spot. 'Unfortunately, I didn't do much right, either,' she said. 'But that's going to change.'

Pearl wasn't sure why Di thought she could talk their way into getting Jordan's information from the first person they encountered at Rubie Racing. But she walked right past the roped-off orange race car and the massive trophy displayed in front of it and tried anyway.

The snotty woman behind the front desk wasn't buying what Di was selling. 'Ma'am, I just can't give our former employees' personal information to random strangers. You must understand why.'

That's right, Di got ma'amed. Pearl nudged her aside before she exploded and attempted to course correct. 'Of course we do. I only need to talk to him. I swear, I know him.'

'Great, now we sound like stalkers,' Di whispered.

Judging by the look on the receptionist's face, not to mention her hand inching toward the phone, Pearl was grateful she'd convinced Di to leave Top in the car.

Not one to give in easily, Di leaned in, like she was letting the receptionist in on a secret. 'They spent a week together. In Scotland.'

At that, the woman scoffed and gave them a look that made Pearl realise she wasn't the first person to show up claiming to have something special with Jordan Rubie because they'd slept together. Or that he'd simply 'forgotten' to give her his phone number.

Suddenly defensive over what she and Jordan had shared, Pearl wanted to scream. It had been more than sex. They'd done a handfasting ceremony. They'd saved a sheep. Pearl doubted banging her head on the desk's high counter would help the situation, even if it did make her feel better.

It was Di's forehead that hit the counter. 'But they were

there for his sister's wedding. It was in a castle. She was Jordan's date.'

'Yes, Mia. Is she here by chance? Or Luca?' Pearl asked.

As the receptionist picked up the phone, presumably to call security, the entrance door slid open and in strolled someone Pearl recognised in an instant. A person who instilled fear and awe in almost everyone she met.

'Oh, thank goodness,' she said. 'Star!'

Mia's best friend and maid of honor crossed the space between them in a flash. 'Pearl! What on earth are you doing here?'

After a quick hug, Star gave the receptionist a look that even made Di shrink back. 'Is there an issue, Olivia?'

The woman shook her head. 'No, no, not at all. They asked about Jordan, and I explained that he was no longer with the team.'

'She never got his phone number,' Di said, 'and she really needs to talk to him. I'm Di, by the way. Her – Di.'

Her eyes rounding, Star grabbed Pearl's and Di's hands and pulled them toward one of the doors leading off the lobby. She touched her badge up to the scan pad and led them through a maze of hallways, finally stopping to knock on a door with a shiny new plaque reading 'Mia Rubie-Toscano' and a well-worn sticker under it that said, 'Property of Mia.'

Star walked in before anyone answered. Inside, they found Mia at her desk, staring at a computer screen. Pearl couldn't believe Jordan's sister was in the country, let alone the building.

'Did you get everything?' Mia asked without shifting her gaze from her work.

'I did and then some,' Star said. 'Lookie who I found at reception, *mija*.'

It took a half second for Mia to register Pearl's face and squeal. 'Omigod, Pearl!' She rushed over and hugged her. 'It's so nice to see you. Is everything okay?'

Still wide-eyed, Star nodded. 'Pearl has something she needs to tell Jordan.'

At that, Di cackled. 'Sweet Jesus. Pearl, they think you're knocked up. Trust me, ladies, that's not it.' But then she paused and counted on her fingers. 'It's not, right?'

'No! Sorry. Wait, I'm not sorry and, to be clear, also not pregnant.' At least she didn't think she was. She fought a sudden urge to count on her fingers, too, even though she was on the pill and Jordan had used condoms. 'Anyway, this is Di, my … aunt.'

Although it was correct, the word felt wrong. She looked at Di, whose head bobbed in the tiniest of nods.

Given their warm welcome, Pearl hoped Mia would be willing to lead her to Jordan's door with little fuss. No way would Di give up until that happened. 'I do need to get in touch with Jordan, but we never exchanged phone numbers—'

'On account that they were joined at the hip the whole time they were together,' Di added.

Star snorted. 'Right. Hip.'

Pearl felt her cheeks warm. 'I know he hasn't been active

on social media, so I wasn't sure what else to do. He wrote a letter to my advice column.'

Before she could explain further, Mia stopped her. 'You know what? There's no sense in having you tell this story twice. How would you two feel about crashing a little party I'm throwing tonight? Ladies only.'

Chapter 24

'Can someone help me? I'm afraid to touch literally anything.'

Luca marched through Jordan's house with hands covered in pizza grease and tomato sauce raised in front of him as if he were a surgeon in need of latex gloves instead of a guy in search of a napkin.

'Even the kitchen towels are white,' Luca said. 'Do you have anything I won't ruin?'

Jordan ducked into the walk-in pantry and tossed out a roll of paper towels. 'Besides my sister? Afraid not. But if I go into the other room and you wipe your dirty hands on all of the things, I won't be mad. If anything, it will give me a reason to get rid of everything and start over.'

'You need a reason?' Cliff asked. 'This place is like a mausoleum, kid.'

'Seriously, if you looked up "man cave" in a thesaurus, this place would be the antonym,' Brian added.

Jordan wasn't surprised when Mia and Luca scrapped their plans to stay abroad until the next race and flew home immediately after Mia won the Azerbaijan Grand Prix to celebrate Barb and Cliff's engagement. Mia had planned a girls' night so she, Barb, and Star could flip through bridal magazines and drink wine. Not wanting to be any part of that, Luca and Cliff had invited themselves over to Jordan's and dragged Brian along.

Everyone was regretting that decision – Jordan included. After watching Luca's predicament, no one else would grab a slice. Pizza may have been a poor choice, but then Jordan rarely had people over. The last time had been for his dad's birthday almost a year ago when he and Mia had spread their parents' ashes in the lake while Cliff and Barb watched on. Against all odds, that final goodbye to Trish and Rob Rubie had proved to be a new beginning for his and Mia's relationship.

'Are we allowed to sit in these?' Brian stared at four white chairs grouped in what the interior designer had called a 'conversation area.' With their stocky round bases and curved backs, they were more fitting for a spaceship than a living room. Jordan had never sat in one, let alone conversed with someone while doing so.

'You know, I still have the card for the woman who helped me furnish my place top to bottom,' Luca said. 'You should give her a call.'

'Since this isn't something I ever thought you and I would discuss, I've made a decision. Everything goes, including us.'

Jordan headed back into the pantry for a cooler, then rallied the guys to help him move their sad, sterile party outside to the bonfire pit he'd had built near the shoreline.

Brian volunteered to make a fire while Jordan shoved a couple of tables together to create a buffet. Luca played bartender, and Cliff settled into an Adirondack chair.

'Now this is more like it,' Cliff said, taking a beer off Luca. 'Reminds me of the place in the Upper Peninsula. We should all go up there and call it my bachelor's weekend.'

When Jordan's dad left Cliff the Upper Peninsula retreat – a lodge and 85 acres of virgin white pines on the shore of Lake Superior – Jordan hadn't just been displeased. He'd been pissed and hurt, even though he hadn't accepted one of his dad's invitations to join him there during Apex's summer break the last dozen years his dad was alive. But Cliff had extended Jordan and Mia an open invitation and gave them each a set of keys. Jordan planned to use them soon, both to see the fall colors and clear his head on the nearly nine-hour drive.

'I'd like that,' Jordan said.

'Me, too,' Luca said. 'Mia and I were supposed to get up there last summer break, but I was—'

Brian jumped up. 'Who's ready for pizza?'

'I am, and it's okay,' Jordan said, dipping his head toward his brother-in-law. 'We're all aware Luca was in the hospital at that time because I put him there. Trust me, there are two things in my life that I'd do anything to take back, and that's one of them.'

He begged his brain not to think about the other one, but it conjured Pearl's shocked face anyway. What he wouldn't do to replace that final image of her with a different one.

'In that case, tell us what's going on with Clark Motorsport,' said Brian, handing Jordan a slice. 'Doesn't seem like a bad place to land.'

He was surprised they didn't know, considering Mia had texted every 15 minutes before Jordan messaged her about what Grant had proposed, and they'd all been on a flight together. The offer was far less than what an Apex driver made but more than enough to live on. Not that he wasn't set for life between savings and the inheritance he'd finally received after resigning from Rubie Racing.

'Seems like it could be all right,' he said. 'Grant's adding two new cars and thought my driving style might be a better fit for Pinnacle than Apex.'

'How long is he offering?' Cliff asked.

'Two years,' Jordan said.

'That's a good deal — enough time to get your feet wet, see if you like it,' Luca said. 'You worried about how the ankle will hold up?'

'Maybe,' Jordan said, not wanting to admit out loud that his lengthy hiatus out of a race car was his biggest worry. Pinnacle cars may be smaller and less powerful than Apex cars, but they were still fast. Even though the car he'd had in Wales could've done some serious speed, neither the roads nor the company had been conducive to opening her up to see what she could do.

What he could do.

'Not to change the subject,' Luca leaned forward, 'but you should call Pearl, assuming she was the second thing you'd change if you could.'

When Cliff nodded in agreement, Jordan realised word had traveled briskly through the Rubie family grapevine. 'Not sure how I'd do that, considering I don't have her phone number.'

He'd redialed the number Di had left at the castle from when Pearl had used his phone, but it was no longer in service.

Even in the firelight, Jordan couldn't miss Luca's one-shoulder shrug. 'You could write her a letter. I mean, isn't that what she does for a living – answer letters?'

Like he hadn't thought of that. He'd also looked for her on social media, but her accounts were locked down more than Fort Knox, which he assumed was to keep her personal life private from readers.

'What's the big deal? You obviously were into the girl.' Brian cringed. 'Poor choice of words, but from what we all saw, true on every level. If you like her, make it happen.' When everyone's jaws dropped open, Brian threw his hands in the air. 'What?'

Luca laughed. 'Maybe that's advice you should consider taking yourself, mate.'

Brian shook his head. 'We're just friends, Luca. And co-workers, I might add, thanks to your insane wife.'

'Funny you knew he was talking about Star,' Jordan said.

'Shut up, all of you,' Brian said. 'My point for Jordan is, if you like the woman, don't let a minor detail like not knowing where she is get in your way.'

Chapter 25

That morning in Chicago, when Di had practically dragged her out of bed, Pearl hadn't had an inkling of what the day would bring. But if she had, attending a slumber party celebrating Barb's engagement to Cliff wouldn't have been on her bingo card.

As they followed Mia from the Rubie Racing complex to Barb's sprawling estate, Pearl couldn't help but wonder what she and Di were getting themselves into. Or why Mia hadn't just given them Jordan's phone number and sent them on their way.

Di parked the massive SUV in the driveway next to a sand-colored sedan that didn't appear to have moved in months. It was covered with a layer of dust that people had taken to writing messages in, like 'wash me,' 'barely a car,' 'car of the year,' and 'what year???'

To Barb's credit, she wasn't at all fazed by the party crashers who walked into her kitchen — even the one in the urn — and immediately enveloped Pearl in a warm hug. 'I can't tell you how happy I am to see you.'

Barb turned to the only person she didn't know next. 'You must be Di. I'm the one you spoke to on the phone that morning when you called the castle looking for Pearl.'

A few tears slid down Di's cheeks as she clutched the urn. 'My sister passed away, but I'm so grateful for your help in getting our Pearl back in time to say goodbye.'

Barb wrapped an arm around Di for a side hug. 'Oh, my, I'm so sorry to hear that.'

At that moment, Star showed up with wine and bags of Chinese takeout. Reading the room, she unpacked the wine first, then coaxed Di into relinquishing the urn by creating a booster seat out of cookbooks for Top and setting a full glass at her spot on the island.

That's when Pearl realised no one was even mentioning Jordan. They were so close-lipped that she was starting to suspect the worst.

'Almond boneless chicken?' Mia asked, holding up a container of breaded chicken breasts in one hand and another with thick brown gravy in the other. 'I know you can't get this in Chicago.'

'Yes, of course, I love me some ABC,' said Pearl, momentarily distracted by the Chinese dish with Detroit roots that she always craved but couldn't find outside southeast Michigan. 'Extra rice and gravy, please, but skip the weird lettuce.'

Watching Mia, with wavy hair in the exact shade as her twin, prepare her plate only increased her need to get the information she and Di were there for in the first place.

Hearing Barb, Mia, and Star talk about anything and everything but Jordan made her suddenly lose her appetite.

As soon as Mia set the plate in front of her, Pearl pushed it away. 'So, who's going to tell me what's going on with Jordan?'

All motion in the kitchen stopped, causing Pearl's stomach to drop.

'Seriously, is something wrong?' she asked.

Barb leaned across the island and patted her hand. 'Jordan is fine, I promise. But let's have dinner first. As you know, we don't want to eat this stuff cold.'

'Or hot,' Star mumbled, digging into her personal container of sesame chicken.

'That's blasphemous, child,' Di said, accepting her own serving of almond boneless chicken.

Pearl mostly listened as Mia and Star peppered Barb with questions about her engagement. She shared that Cliff had proposed on the shore of Lake Superior, in the exact spot where they'd first kissed, and that they intended to have a small wedding.

'I know a great castle in Scotland,' Mia said.

'Or you could do an anvil wedding just across the border from England,' said Pearl, smiling to herself. 'Having our hands fastened together was—'

She gulped, remembering the intimacy of having Jordan's skin pressed against hers and the length of tartan that had joined them well into the night. For a brief second, she was there with him again, until Mia gently cleared her throat and she realised all eyes were on her.

'Excuse me?' Mia asked. 'Your hands were what now?'

Pearl shook her head and pointed her fork at what was left of the chicken on her plate. 'Later. We don't want this to get cold, remember?'

It wasn't until they'd shifted to the family room, taking with them the wine, a stack of bridal magazines, and a plate of brownies, that Mia spoke up.

'So, Jordan,' she said. 'He's a little… lost.'

Barb took a seat on the sofa next to Pearl. 'He told me what happened when he dropped you off at the hospital. And while I'm sure there are things about that situation he'd rather share with you himself, I think it might be best if Mia and I give you a little backstory before you see him.'

Mia took a sip of her wine. 'Which, sorry, won't be tonight. He's got the guys at his place celebrating Cliff with pizza and beer. But Barb, he sent her a letter.'

Although Pearl knew Jordan's letter by heart at this point, she didn't feel right repeating his words verbatim to his family, especially since Jordan hadn't shared with them that he'd written to her. 'He said that he was sorry,' she said, catching Di's eye and arching an eyebrow, hoping she'd pick up on the signal to say no more. 'That was the gist of it.'

'And that he missed you,' Di added, who'd either missed or chose to ignore said signal. 'It's amazing our little rule follower even got his letter, considering it arrived the day she was fired. If that's not fate, I don't know what is.'

From beside her, Barb gasped and grabbed Pearl's hand.

Considering the column's unexpected role in why Mia and Star were celebrating her tonight, her reaction wasn't a huge surprise.

'It was the sheep video. My editor saw it and thought I'd lied about the reason behind my personal leave.'

Star looked up from the bridal magazine she'd been flipping through. 'Last I knew, "personal" meant it's nobody else's business,' she said. 'Also, what sheep video?'

Barb and Mia also looked confused. Apparently, between Mia and Luca's wedding and Apex's summer break, when all things racing-related were forbidden, they'd all missed it. Only Mia had seen her and Jordan's reenactment of their heroic efforts that day.

Pearl brought the video up on her phone and let Star stream it onto the television. They were all laughing so hard that they didn't notice they had company.

'Sorry for crashing your party, ladies,' Cliff yelled over them. 'Jordan's house is too pristine to have any fun in, and the mosquitos got too thick to sit by the fire.'

He came to a halt when he realised the room contained two additional faces and registered to whom they belonged. Right on his heels, Luca and Brian had the same reaction.

Pearl's heart was pounding out of her chest, wondering if Jordan was there, too, and when he didn't walk in, she thought it might burst. Years ago, she'd read about a heart condition called broken heart syndrome and couldn't believe a person could have heart attack-like chest pain from severe emotional distress. She got it now.

Pearl closed her eyes, took a deep, calming breath, and willed her heart to beat normally.

'Hey, Barb! I'm almost afraid to ask, but who's in the urn in the kitchen?'

Her eyes flew open as Jordan walked into the family room and took in the scene. The video frozen on the television screen just at the moment she catapulted herself at him. His sister, Barb, and Star with their mouths agape. Her.

The color drained from his face, but unlike when they last saw each other, he didn't turn around and run away. In what felt like an instant, he was in front of her, pulling her up and smashing her into his chest.

'Oh my God,' he whispered. 'You're here.'

Chapter 26

Jordan could hardly believe Pearl was in his arms.

Pearl.

'I can't believe you're here,' Jordan said, his voice shaking. When her arms came around his neck, his entire body sighed in relief.

'I didn't know how to find you,' she whispered, 'or if you wanted to be found until I got your letter.'

He didn't want to let her go, ever, but he also didn't want an audience for what he wanted and needed to say. The only place he could think to take her for privacy was his childhood bedroom, which seemed presumptuous even if she had magically appeared in Barb's house.

'We'll leave you two to catch up,' someone said.

It took a beat for Jordan to realise who the voice belonged to since the sight of Pearl had stopped him in his tracks. But once he connected the voice to Di, he figured out the likely inhabitant of the urn drinking wine in Barb's kitchen.

Top.

Fuck.

And here he hadn't thought it possible to feel worse than he already did for deserting Pearl at the hospital. But knowing what she'd then dealt with was a double punch in the gut. When he finally let her go, the room was empty.

As they stood there, staring at each other, Jordan couldn't stop touching her. His hands ran up her arms until they cradled her face, his thumbs brushing lightly across her cheekbones. Her eyes seemed tired and sad. Pearl being sad added another gut punch. Right then and there, he made himself a vow that he'd never be the cause of this woman's grief again.

When Jordan finally opened his mouth to say something, the words came rushing out. 'Pearl, I'm so sorry. If I could go back—'

Her hand covered his mouth, and she gave her head the tiniest of shakes, her eyes wide. Even though he couldn't wait to have his lips on her, the palm of her hand wouldn't have been his first choice.

Jordan arched an eyebrow.

'It's too quiet,' she said, her voice barely a whisper.

He grabbed her hand from his face to hold it as they stood in silence, trying to detect any sign of life outside the family room. Even though it was a huge house, there was no way a group of people that included Star and Di could be so quiet. Without a doubt, they were all nearby. Listening.

His bedroom it was.

Tugging her close, he breathed into her right ear, 'Follow

me,' and sensed the chill that traveled up her spine. Pearl nodded.

He took the most direct route to his bedroom on the second floor, not spotting anyone as they headed toward the front entrance to the double staircase he and Mia had spent hours racing up. At the top of the steps, they turned left. His bedroom was at the end of the hallway.

'This is the most private place I could think of,' Jordan said before opening the door to his past.

Although he hadn't moved out until his mid-twenties, his travel schedule was such that the space had hardly changed since his mom had redone both his and Mia's bedrooms when they were 12. Given that she'd been diagnosed with breast cancer soon after, the heart of the Rubie family never knew if the adult versions of her children she'd imagined matched the people they became.

Looking at the room through Pearl's fresh eyes, he couldn't help but think his mom would be disappointed. The wood-paneled walls, heavy wooden furniture, and bed frame upholstered in rich leather exuded strength and confidence in a way that Jordan had never managed. Only the color palette – a moody deep blue – was spot on for the man he'd become.

Or, he hoped, had been.

Pearl sat on the king-size bed and patted the spot next to her.

Instead, he knelt down on the floor in front of her and grabbed her hands. 'I want to hear about everything, but first, I'm sorry I left you at the hospital that day.'

'Me, too,' Pearl whispered. 'Why did you take off like that?'

When Jordan told Barb what had happened, he didn't mention the panic attack, and her look of pure disappointment had almost killed him. For some reason, Barb thinking he'd treated Pearl poorly was more palatable than the truth. It wasn't until after a few digging sessions with Adam that he'd set the record straight.

But Pearl didn't know the asshole version of himself, and he didn't want her to. Even if he could never go back to being sweet in her eyes, Jordan wanted her to know the real reason he'd fled.

'I physically couldn't do it. My legs wouldn't move, and I felt sick, and my heart was beating out of my chest.' His heart rate sped up just thinking about it. 'I flashed back to the last time I rushed to a hospital, and I had a panic attack.'

'When your dad died,' she said.

'I didn't make it to the hospital in time, and it was all on me. I ignored Barb's calls until it was too late.' Jordan wiped away a wayward tear. 'Everyone still thinks my phone was on silent, but it wasn't. Not at first, at least. I turned off the ringer after her third call, and my dad died alone because of it.'

Jordan knew that, on some level, his guilt from that day would likely haunt him for the rest of his life. He'd been making headway in that department until the incident with Pearl in Wales, and even then, knowing he'd had an anxiety attack didn't make him feel any less guilty – only weaker.

'If I'd known—'

'There's no way you could have,' she said. 'I didn't know until I reached Top's room how bad things were.'

As soon as the tears started streaming down Pearl's face, Jordan took the spot she'd offered a few minutes earlier.

'Can I hold you?' he asked.

'Yes,' she said. 'Please.'

As he pulled her to his chest, Jordan realised he'd do anything to take away Pearl's pain – even if it meant taking it on himself.

Chapter 27

Pearl hadn't avoided grieving Top on purpose – her own heartache had simply taken a backseat to managing Di's heartbreak. But now, in Jordan's arms, the sadness poured out of her.

For the woman she'd known as her aunt, who'd always been her favorite person in the world, as well as for the woman she'd never known as her mother, and now never would.

Would the word 'mom' have rolled off her tongue eventually if Top's surgery had gone as expected? Would her return from Scotland have been marked with one of her and Top's late-into-the-night talks? Would she have told the woman who'd always been there to listen that she was falling in love, real love, for the first time in her life? How long might she have stayed angry if grief hadn't taken over?

When the tears stopped falling, Jordan dried her wet cheeks with the bottom of his T-shirt. 'Tell me everything,' he said.

So, she did.

How she and Di kept vigil in the hospital for a full day, their hopes dwindling with each passing hour.

How Top's body hadn't responded to the antibiotics, and the infection had weakened her heart.

How she'd gone into septic shock, and her organs had shut down.

How, for as long as Pearl lived, she would never forget the final scene between the jewel sisters – Di crawling into bed with Top when the machine's steady beeping slowed and then stopped, clinging to her twin and begging for her to come back, for her heart to start beating again.

How it had felt like Pearl's own heart had stopped beating at that moment, too.

'How could this have happened?' he asked. 'She went in for a boob job, not open-heart surgery. It just doesn't make any sense.'

Pearl shook her head and repeated what Top's doctor had told her when she'd asked the same thing. 'All surgery carries a risk, even an outpatient procedure like a breast augmentation. Although it's rare in someone as healthy as Top was, there's always a chance ...'

That the most horrible thing you can imagine might happen.

As she talked, they found themselves gravitating toward each other. By the time she finished, they were under the covers, face to face, taking up the same amount of space as the twin bed had allowed in the castle. Which somehow felt like yesterday, not weeks ago.

'So, how'd you end up here?' Jordan asked.

216

'Well, you're not exactly easy to find.'

'That may be by design,' he said. 'But if I'd known you were the one who'd be looking for me, I might have made it easier.'

'We went to Rubie Racing.' She wasn't sure she had the emotional wherewithal to go into her being fired and Di dragging her back to Michigan.

'Let me guess – Mia?'

'And Star,' Pearl said. 'Mia invited us here. I think she and Barb were protecting you.'

Jordan rolled onto his back and stared at the ceiling. 'To be perfectly honest, I've had a rough few weeks. I did some intense therapy as soon as I landed back in Detroit.'

His discomfort was evident, even though he'd mentioned his therapist when they were in Scotland.

'I'd never had an anxiety attack before,' Jordan said. 'It was one of the most terrifying things I've ever been through.'

That was saying a lot. Pearl had seen the video of Jordan's crash with Luca, along with a few others throughout his driving career that she'd found online.

'But even more than that, I knew I'd hurt you, and I thought I was done hurting the people I care about.' He turned his head, his gaze to her. 'I want to be done.'

Her heart ached at that admission – and also leapt. He had cared about her, just as she had him. 'I tried to convince myself that I'd made what happened between us into more than it actually was. We never talked about what might happen after Scotland, and then you were gone.'

'For the record, I planned on talking to you on the drive back,' Jordan said. 'I wasn't ready for it to end, Pearl. I'm still not.'

Pearl had a sudden urge to touch him, to feel his warm skin with her fingertips. But as she was about to shift over and lay her head on his chest, her phone buzzed. At least, she thought it was her phone – as she dug it out of her pocket, she noticed Jordan doing the same.

'It's been a while, so I'm sure either Di is ready to go, or Barb is ready for her to go.' As soon as Pearl looked at the screen, she rolled her eyes. 'It's a group chat.'

'God help us,' Jordan laughed.

Among the four phone numbers were hers and Di's. The other two belonged to Jordan and she assumed Barb, who wanted to let them know that everyone was turning in for the night.

Di sent a message right after to Pearl alone, letting her know she'd be camping out in a nearby guest room if Pearl needed anything. She typed back a quick reply to let her know she was fine and then saw that Jordan had given Barb's message a thumbs up. He handed her his phone, and she put it, along with hers, on the nightstand.

Jordan laid back down, and within seconds, her head and hand found what they needed on his body.

'For the record,' Pearl said. 'I didn't want it to end either.'

Chapter 28

The next morning, Jordan reached for Pearl before he opened his eyes, only his hands found nothing but a sheet. He sat up and scanned the room for any sign of her as the door to the en suite opened, and Pearl emerged in the clothes he'd given her to sleep in.

They hadn't done more than kiss before falling asleep. He told himself it was because they were both emotionally spent after talking past midnight, and there was no need to rush things. But the truth was, he needed to know she truly trusted him again before making love to her. Because for him, that's what it would be.

That was going to be tough, especially considering how cute she looked in his boxers and old Detroit Red Wings T-shirt, and how randy he was in the morning.

'I thought maybe you needed to head back for work,' Jordan said.

With a quick shake of her head, she climbed back into bed smelling like soap and mouthwash.

'Are you still on bereavement leave?'

'No,' she said. 'Actually, I'm no longer the Pearl of Wisdom.'

Considering everything they'd shared the night before, Jordan couldn't believe she hadn't told him about losing her job. Not that he'd mentioned his offer with Clark Motorsport.

'What happened?'

Pearl cringed. 'My editor found the sheep video.'

How ironic that saving a sheep's life had derailed Pearl's. By the time she'd finished, he was even more grateful that Barb had packed up his office when his days at Rubie Racing were over. He wanted to find this Madeline woman and make her pay for making Pearl march through the office with security guards.

'Madeline was unhappy from the moment I sprung going to Wales on her,' she said. 'Actually, before that even. She always made me feel like I owed her for my career, which is ridiculous.'

When Jordan found out how close Pearl had come to not seeing his letter, he was almost sick to his stomach. Although considering the role fate had played, it would've found another way to bring them back together.

'I'm sorry,' he said. 'Any thoughts on what's next?'

Boy, did he have a few ideas if she didn't.

'Besides finding an attorney to look over my separation agreement?' she asked. 'Not a clue.'

'Well, I can help you there,' he said. 'Cliff's a lawyer, and considering Barb is about to become his blushing bride, he owes you one.'

Knowing that Pearl didn't need to rush back to Chicago made Jordan happier than it should have, given the reason. He wasn't ready to say goodbye.

'Think I can persuade you to stay for a few days and help me with a project?' he asked. 'I could use an extra set of hands.'

'Well, you know what they say – idle hands are the devil's workshop,' she said, holding up hers. 'I'm not sure what good they'll do you, but sure. They're yours.'

He liked the sound of that, especially if the rest of her came with them.

Jordan left Pearl to get ready while he searched out Cliff. He found him in the study. At a different point in time, seeing Cliff so comfortable at his dad's mahogany desk would've been too much for Jordan to bear. But once he'd gotten used to the situation, Jordan was grateful Barb had chosen Cliff over someone he and Mia didn't know.

'We were wondering when the two of you would surface,' Cliff said. 'All okay?'

'So far, so good,' Jordan said, taking a seat in a nearby chair. 'Where is everyone?'

He'd stopped in the kitchen to grab a cup of coffee, expecting to find Barb and Di at least. But there was only a fresh pot of coffee, a note from Barb about a quiche in the refrigerator, and Top.

Unsurprisingly, Mia, Luca, Brian, and Star were already at the Rubie Racing complex. A day off during the Apex season

221

was rare, and the cars were probably just getting back from Baku. Engineers would spend the next week making sure they were in top form for the next race in Singapore.

But learning that Di had tagged along on errands with Barb was somewhat of a shock. Jordan couldn't think of people more different than those two.

'Can you do me a favor?' he asked Cliff.

Jordan could tell Cliff's interest was piqued. He wasn't one to ask for favors, or help, although he'd been working on the latter.

'Sure, buddy,' Cliff said. 'What's up?'

He shared about Pearl losing her job and the separation agreement her editor had expected her to sign on the spot. Cliff shook his head at that and offered to review it before Jordan even asked.

'Just have her leave it on the desk,' Cliff said. 'I'll make sure they're not putting the screws on her.'

Jordan had no doubt about that.

When Pearl found him in the kitchen, he was sitting at the island with a cup of coffee, the newspaper, and Top. Last night's wine glass had been exchanged for a coffee cup featuring a cartoon bluebird with the words 'of happiness' underneath.

'They've scattered to the wind,' Jordan said, pointing to the mug cabinet.

Pearl looked at the urn. 'She stayed behind?'

Odd phrasing. 'Yes. Why wouldn't she?'

Apparently, it was the first time Di had been more than

50 feet from her sister in three weeks, aside from leaving her in the car for a few minutes at Rubie Racing.

When he refilled his mug before heading up to shower, he noticed she was wearing another of his old T-shirts. He'd practically lived in that shirt for Rush when he was 14, after his dad and Cliff had taken him and Mia to Toronto to see the band at the famed Massey Hall.

He hadn't thought he could love that T-shirt, or band, any more. 'Pearl, have you been going through my drawers?'

'Fair is fair. I mean, you did go through mine a couple of times.' She laughed. 'Hey, speaking of drawers, do you have my clothes?'

Of course, he did. Sorting through the contents of their suitcases, then washing, folding, and repacking Pearl's clothes had been an excruciating task. He'd had to shut her suitcase in a guest room to make himself stop staring at it.

He grimaced. 'I do. Did I apologise for that yet? Because I'm sorry. Wow, look at that. I'm just whipping these apologies out left and right these days.'

'Yes, you've become a real pro,' she said. 'Speaking of ...'

Pearl pulled him to her with a pinch to the front of his shirt. If she was implying that he was a pro-level kisser, he was determined to deliver. Within seconds, his lips found hers, and his mind and body found the peace they had been searching for but had nearly given up hope of finding.

Chapter 29

'So, are we going to talk about Di?' Jordan asked later that afternoon as he rolled Cake Batter yellow onto the kitchen wall.

Pearl paused from cutting in the paint where the wall met the woodwork. 'You're going to have to help me out a little, Jordan.'

'The makeup, or rather, the lack thereof,' he said. 'I did a double take when I first saw her.'

'It came off little by little when Top took a turn for the worse and still hasn't fully returned,' Pearl said.

'Don't want to jinx it?'

'Maybe. Or spook her. The first few days after we lost Top were pretty awful. We just hung out at her house, waiting for her urn of ashes to arrive.'

During those three long days, Pearl had spent most of her time sitting next to a Di-shaped lump under the mound of blankets on Top's bed. A lump that hardly moved, responded, or ate.

Pearl looked up to find Jordan watching her brush the paint on the wall with the precision of a professional. She and Di had painted the rooms in their house so many times as she was growing up that Pearl didn't have to use painter's tape to get a perfectly straight line.

'That's one weird superpower,' Jordan said. 'I'm low-key impressed.'

'It's as much about having a good paintbrush and loading the right amount of paint as having a steady hand.' She demonstrated by drawing the line with the first sweep of the brush and then broadening the line a couple more inches with another swipe. 'That should be enough so you can roll without having to get near the trim.'

She'd already noticed that Jordan painted like someone who'd spent more time watching online videos of people painting than actually doing it. His routine didn't deviate: He rolled a W on the wall and then filled it in. He was careful – she couldn't spot a single errant drip – but he wasn't fast.

No wonder he'd asked for help.

When they'd left Barb's, the last place she'd expected to go was a paint store to help him pick the color for his kitchen. Pearl wasn't sure what it was about Jordan choosing a cheery yellow paint called Cake Batter, but her world had turned slightly on its axis and had yet to right itself. Considering how many times she'd caught herself staring at Jordan's well-defined abs when his T-shirt lifted as he rolled high on the wall or at his forearms as they gripped the paint roller pole, her steady hand was a miracle.

When they'd pulled into Jordan's driveway, and she saw it was a mansion, she couldn't imagine why he needed to paint. Then she'd walked in and had been blinded by the white.

Everything about the house made her wonder if she knew this person at all. Until Jordan had turned to her with his hands on his hips and the most adorably serious look on his face that she'd ever seen.

'No need to say it, I already know,' he'd said. 'It's horrible. I can't take it anymore.'

The quick tour he'd given her revealed more of the same, with only a couple of exceptions – his office and bedroom. A couple of coats of Cake Batter wouldn't fix everything, but it was a start.

She was glad he'd decided to tackle the kitchen first. Painting the immense living room would require scaffolding, even with the wall of windows facing the lake. Even though the kitchen was large, there were a lot of cabinets. Since he'd decided to leave them white and only replace the knobs and pulls, they'd covered them, the marble countertops, and the massive island with plastic tarps.

For the next few hours, they were like a well-oiled machine. She worked her way around the cabinets, doorways, and windows while Jordan focused on the walls. He was getting quicker, but Di would've rolled circles around him.

Out of nowhere, Jordan asked her, 'Tell me something about you I don't know.'

'Well, this could take a while,' she laughed.

'I'm serious,' he said. 'I'll start. I don't like bananas.'

'I thought everybody liked bananas.' Pearl arched an eyebrow. 'What about banana bread? Splits? Pudding?'

'No, no, and definitely no,' he said. 'According to my baby book, it's the one thing I wouldn't eat.'

They took turns revealing those idiosyncrasies that typically take eons to discover about someone. She told him about her aversion to spicy food, but not horseradish or wasabi; how she'd been obsessed with sloths before they were cool; and that her bucket list trip was to St John in the US Virgin Islands.

Pearl learned that Jordan always wanted a dog but had never been home long enough for one, and was obsessed with home renovation shows as well as baking shows of the British variety.

Before they knew it, the first coat was done, and together, they assessed their work. It was a new experience for Pearl, ending a painting project on speaking terms. She and Di never had.

'What do you think?' Jordan asked.

Pearl got within a nose of the wall and squinted. 'I like it, but it's going to need a second coat.'

'But it's one-coat paint,' he said, pointing to the can. 'It says so right there.'

'The can always lies, Jordan.' Pearl pointed at a section where white peeked through the yellow. 'The good news is, the second coat goes much quicker, and I won't need to cut in again.'

She'd purposely loaded her paintbrush to be sure she'd be one and done, not realizing that also meant she'd be done coming to Jordan's, too. Talk about your best-laid plans.

'I bet it will go even faster with two of us rolling.'

Jordan draped an arm over her shoulders and leaned his head conspiratorially toward hers. 'We might even be able to squeeze in a trip to pick out tiles for the backsplash if we start earlier tomorrow.'

Tomorrow.

'And watch videos on how to install a tile backsplash? I've never done that before.' Her arm snaked around his waist. 'I'm in, but you'll need to hire a professional painter to do the living room, or I'll be here until Christmas.'

'Well, that's tempting,' he said, giving her a kiss that proved it. 'But I have a decision to make. Let's go outside.'

He ducked under a tarp and grabbed each of them a can of sparkling water from an industrial-sized refrigerator, then led her through the sliding glass door down to the lake.

It was one of those early September days that still felt like summer, even though there was a hint of fall in the breeze. The pine trees surrounding them had yet to drop their needles, and the maples and oaks were still green. With no other houses in sight, Pearl could only imagine how pretty it looked when they were ablaze in red, orange, and yellow.

After they'd settled in two Adirondack chairs at the end of his dock, Jordan told her about his unexpected offer to drive in the Pinnacle series. Now she understood his surprise at her not sharing about losing her job, but she could hardly blame him. Her news had been bad while his, at least she assumed, was good.

'I just have one question – what's Pinnacle?' she asked.

He grabbed her hand, his fingers playing with hers as he explained how Pinnacle differed from Apex. The cars looked similar but were smaller and less powerful.

'So driving them will be easier?' Pearl asked, kicking off her shoes and tucking her legs under her.

'Yes and no,' he said. 'Although more drivers successfully shift from Apex to Pinnacle than the other way around.'

'And you've never driven one of those cars?' Pearl asked.

'Nope.' There was a touch of anxiety in his voice.

'Has Mia?'

He shook his head.

'Do you miss racing?'

Jordan was quiet for a minute. 'It's all I've ever done, so it feels like something's missing. But the last time I was in a race car was when I crashed into Luca.'

'Was that your first crash?'

'God, no.' He laughed. 'But it is the first time I crashed and didn't have to get right back in the car. It's been over a year, and I haven't even been near a simulator.'

Pearl nodded like she knew what a simulator was and made a mental note to google it later. 'When do you have to tell him?'

'Sooner than later?'

'Ah,' she said. 'So, sooner.'

'Exactly.'

They sat in silence for a few minutes, staring at the water. She couldn't help but wonder what this meant for the two of them, even if Pinnacle mainly stuck to tracks in North America. Or if there even was a two of them.

After a few minutes, Jordan shifted in his chair so their clasped hands matched how they'd been bound together in Gretna Green.

'My dad had a saying, "You're in it to win or you stay the hell out of the way,"' he said. 'I haven't always embraced that as much as Mia. More often than not, the only person who's gotten in my way has been me.'

He reached into the pocket of his paint-splattered joggers and pulled out the length of tartan. Her heart skipped a beat as he slowly wrapped it around their enjoined hands. When he couldn't tie a knot with the two ends, Pearl helped him.

'I know it doesn't make any sense because we hardly know each other, but I've missed you,' he said. 'So much.'

She swallowed the emotion that bubbled up. 'I tried to convince myself that I'd imagined this. I mean, it doesn't make any sense to feel this way about someone you spent only a few days with.'

'Except it makes perfect sense,' he said, tugging her over to sit on his lap, 'when we're together.'

The second his lips found hers, every feeling she'd tried to dismiss, every memory she'd tried to bury, came rushing back. Mind, body, and soul, she leaned into this moment, wondering only how long they could make this kiss last.

Jordan broke it off too soon, his forehead resting on hers, and he caught his breath. 'I'm in it to win it if you are, Pearl.'

'Well,' she said, 'I'm certainly not getting the hell out of the way.'

Chapter 30

It wasn't until they came up for air a second time that Jordan realised he and Pearl needed a better place to do this than an Adirondack chair on a narrow dock. Wanting her closer, needing her closer, he lifted them both up off the chair and carried her onto the pontoon boat. They might be lucky to make it ten feet from shore before he threw her onto the sun lounger.

'Any fear of boats? Before you say yes, know that we're not going far.'

When she shook her head, he set Pearl down and used his free hand to search for the spare key he'd hidden in the storage compartment. After making sure the engine turned over, he eyed the lines attaching the boat to the dock and then the tartan connecting him to Pearl.

'I'm so glad this made it home with you,' she said before undoing the knot and unfastening their hands. 'But with or without it, I'm bound to you.'

At that declaration, Jordan couldn't launch the pontoon

fast enough. 'Ready?' he asked when he was in the captain's chair.

Pearl sat down on his lap and leaned into him. 'Hit it.'

The 200-horsepower engine was overkill for a body of water this size but he had zero regrets when they dropped anchor in the middle of the lake minutes later. Once Pearl was off his lap, he made quick work of transforming the sofa in the back of the boat into something more suitable for their current needs.

She arched an eyebrow at him. 'You have a bed on a pontoon?'

'Technically, it's a sun lounger,' Jordan said, suddenly nervous about how it looked. 'I swear, I just got this boat, and nothing even remotely as exciting as this has happened on it. Actually, scratch that. Nothing has happened on it, aside from a few loops around the lake with Barb and Cliff and a little fishing.'

Pearl wrapped her arms around his neck and pulled his face down to hers. 'As cool as this pontoon is, in no way was I implying that you've been using it to cruise for chicks.'

And then she kissed him. Long and hard, leaving zero doubt that she wanted this to happen as much as he did.

He must've imagined being with Pearl again a thousand times. Thoughts about what it would be like to kiss every inch of her, savor every taste of her. But he'd never pictured the two of them tearing each other's clothes off on a pontoon boat in between frantic kisses.

It was a feeding frenzy.

'Tell me what you want, Pearl.'

'I want you,' she gasped.

'To do what?' His hands slid down her bare body, finally landing on her waist and pulling her closer.

Pearl gazed up at him. 'To make love to me.'

His heart pounding, he lifted her into his arms for the second time that day and set her on the sun lounger. He kissed his way up her body, lingering longer in the places that made her whimper, until his body covered hers.

'Hey,' he smiled down at her. 'Did I mention that I missed you?'

Her hands framed his face. 'A few times. But I definitely think this is one of those cases where actions speak louder than words.'

He ground into her, and that first brush of his hardness against her softness would've brought him to his knees if he wasn't already there. Her legs wrapped around his waist.

'I don't think I can last much longer,' he growled. 'Please tell me you're close, too, so I don't have to throw myself overboard in embarrassment when we're finished.'

She silenced him with her mouth and lifted her hips. By the time he'd thrust himself to her limit, they were both shaking. Waves rocked the boat, the slight motion making them both moan. Jordan reached between them to the spot he knew would take her over the edge.

Once her cries echoed across the water, he followed her. Because in truth, he would follow this woman anywhere.

*

They watched the sunset wrapped up in nothing but each other. When they finally putzed back, a far more relaxed Pearl was on his lap.

As they neared shore, she leaned forward. 'Someone's waiting for us.'

It was Cliff, sitting in what Jordan would now always think of as his and Pearl's spots on the dock.

'Ahoy there!' he yelled when they were within earshot, then jumped up and caught the pontoon before it knocked into the dock.

Jordan turned off the engine. 'Ahoy there, yourself.'

After giving the two of them a knowing smile, Cliff helped tie the boat to the dock. 'Certain people were getting worried. For the record, I wasn't one of them.'

'Yet here you are,' Jordan said.

He was impressed that Cliff managed to keep everyone else at bay. It couldn't have been easy, and arriving back at the dock to a welcoming party would've put a damper on what had been a spectacular boat ride.

As they walked up to the house with Cliff, Jordan couldn't help but shift side to side.

'Is there a problem, Jordan?' Pearl whispered.

'I think you know full well what the problem is.'

He was going commando. When they'd finally put their clothes back on, his boxer briefs were nowhere to be found. Apparently, in their enthusiasm to get each other's clothes off, they'd gone overboard.

His hand took hold of hers. 'They were special.'

After being stalked by internet ads for a surprising number of products in the world featuring sheep, he'd finally caved when he saw the green boxer briefs adorned with a flock of dancing sheep.

She squeezed his hand. 'I'll buy you a new pair.'

Once they showed off their progress in the kitchen, Cliff pointed toward the refrigerator, where Jordan found an entire dinner. Trademark Barb. He warmed up the containers of pulled pork and scalloped potatoes, and then he and Pearl ate standing up at the island while Cliff filled them in on the goings-on of Barb and Di. The two had become BFFs and were having the time of their life.

'I can't believe Di hasn't mentioned going home,' Pearl said between bites. 'It's been forever since she's slept in her own bed.'

'She has, but Barb keeps plying her with food and wine,' Cliff said.

'Well, I hope she knows what she's getting herself into,' Pearl laughed. 'Squatter's rights and all.'

Her smile faded when Cliff grabbed a file folder from the counter and handed it to her. While she flipped through the pages, which were marked up with scribbled notes and several crossed-out sections, Cliff summarised his thoughts. They were a mixed bag.

'This isn't my specialty, so I called in a favor from an old law school friend,' he said. 'Her main question was about the name of the column.'

'What about it?' she asked. 'I'll be honest, in the craziness of the last few days, I didn't do more than skim the first few pages. And that was as I was being fired.'

Cliff glanced at Jordan. 'They say it's theirs.'

Pearl's mouth dropped open. 'I think not. When I was promoted to advice columnist, I suggested Pearl of Wisdom because it was the name of my advice column in my high school newspaper.'

The thought of someone else using the name – Pearl's name – had Jordan practically foaming at the mouth. It already killed him that she was no longer the Pearl of Wisdom, and that it was partially because of him.

'In that case, let me do a little more digging,' Cliff said. 'Also, I'm not sure you violated their ethics and standards as they stated. I could find an attorney in Illinois to help you fight it and get your job back if you'd like.'

To Jordan's surprise, Pearl shook her head. 'No, thank you, but I don't think I'm interested.'

'Really?' he asked, amazed at how sure she sounded.

She smiled at him – really smiled. 'Absolutely. I know it sounds crazy, but there's no way I can go back there now. It would be a hostile work environment, and I'm not sure who would be more hostile at this point. I have savings and an inheritance from Top to see me through while I figure things out.'

She turned to Cliff and asked, 'So, what do I do now?'

'I have some other recommendations for changes to make. But it might be best to sit down somewhere.'

Jordan led them to his office. Even though he was tempted to hover as they reviewed the document, he knew Cliff would see that Pearl was taken care of. The man was a genius – after all, he'd helped his best friend create a will so ironclad that the son who was cut out of the family business couldn't do anything about it. Thank God. He shuddered to think what his life would be like now if he'd managed to wrest Rubie Racing away from Mia – against the wishes of his father.

In need of a distraction, Jordan started the second coat. His brain was spinning, thinking about how Pearl had told Cliff no with such confidence while he couldn't bring himself to say yes to taking the leap to Pinnacle. But with each methodical roll of yellow, his mind emptied in a way it never managed to through meditation. He was in such a zone that he didn't notice Pearl had come back into the kitchen until her hand rested on his shoulder.

'I'm tapping you out,' she said when he jumped, taking the roller out of his hands and coating it with fresh paint.

Jordan hopped to sit on the island and watched as she worked with equal precision but at twice his speed. He was glad for the break; his arms were sore from the hours of painting this morning. He hadn't been working out enough – that would need to change in a major way if he was going to drive again next season.

'Did Cliff leave?'

'Yes. He yelled goodbye.' She used up the paint on the roller and turned toward him to reload. 'I told him I'd be back later.'

Stay here.

The paint roller went slowly back and forth in the tray, gathering more of the bright yellow. Only when it was fully reloaded did Pearl look up.

'Or maybe I'll stay here,' she said.

'Stay here,' he said.

With a smile, Pearl began making quick work of the next wall, too. 'I told you the second coat would go faster.'

'Only since you took over. You should know that at one point in my life, I would've figured out a way to out-roll you. Even if it meant staying up all night and painting the whole living room to prove it.'

The roller came to a screeching halt mid-wall. 'Well, I'm glad that bit of insane competitiveness is in the past because I can think of far better things for you to do tonight,' she said.

'Second place it is,' Jordan said, leaning back on his elbows. 'I'm enjoying the view anyway.'

Chapter 31

They stayed in bed through the next afternoon, trying various positions – both of the active and passive kind. Her spooning him had somehow led to her drawing pictures on his back with her finger. He'd guessed every one wrong.

'A horse and buggy?'

'Why on earth would I draw a horse and buggy?' she asked.

Her palm rubbed back and forth across the area of bare skin she'd been drawing on.

'I'm not sure how to answer that.' Jordan rolled onto his back. 'Also, are you erasing invisible pictures? Because that may be the cutest thing you've ever done.'

'*May* be? And for the record, it was a race car. That was supposed to be a gimme.'

He coaxed Pearl on top of him so his hands could wander down her body. He'd discovered two especially ticklish areas in his quest to reacquaint himself with every part of her.

'What are you smiling about?' Pearl asked.

'Everything.'

Pearl moved her head to his chest, kissing his clavicle on the way, and hummed. 'How long do you think we can stay here like this?'

He kissed the top of her head. 'Not sure, but I'm willing to find out if you are.'

When they woke up again, it was getting dark. Starving, they reluctantly dragged themselves out of bed to see what they could scrounge. While he pulled down the tarps, Pearl wandered the parameters of the kitchen in one of his Rubie Racing T-shirts and nothing else, looking closely at the walls.

'I can't find a single drip. If all else fails, we could start our own painting company.'

He came up behind her. 'I'm not sure how much work I'd get done, especially if you walked around in that.'

The sudden huskiness of his voice tipping her off, she swatted away his hands as they cupped her butt cheeks. 'No more of that until we eat something.'

He'd taken to having meal kits delivered while he'd been recovering from his injury, and one had arrived the same day as Pearl. He handed her the cards for the three options he'd ordered and told her to choose.

'This is how I've been teaching myself to cook,' Jordan said.

She handed him the card with the quickest cooking time. 'Let me guess, travel and Barb?'

'Bingo,' he smiled.

Together, they chopped vegetables and herbs, and then

he manned the stove as Pearl guided him through the cooking steps. Less than an hour later, they were back in his king-size bed with a bottle of red wine and plates filled with chicken, orzo, and roasted vegetables. They focused on their food first, practically inhaling their meals within minutes.

Pearl leaned back, rested her hand on her stomach, and took a sip of the wine. 'Hey, Jordan. Tell me something about you I don't know.'

He liked that she was turning his fun getting-to-know-you game from painting into a running Q&A. 'Haven't you learned enough?'

'Absolutely not.'

He swirled the wine around in his glass while considering what to say, having covered the easy stuff during their first round the day before. After a quick swallow, he set the glass on his nightstand.

'My dad wrote letters to Mia and me, and Cliff and Barb, to be given to us after he died.'

Pearl's eyes widened. 'And?'

'I still haven't read mine.' He opened the drawer to his nightstand and pulled out the envelope he'd received a year and a half ago at the reading of his dad's will. 'Things had been a little awkward between us since he'd brought Luca back to the team the season before. I didn't handle it well.'

She arched an eyebrow at him.

'OK, I was a total asshole.' He took a deep breath. 'It wasn't because Luca was a better driver. I mean, that goes without saying. The guy's the current world champion for a reason. They were almost like two peas in a pod, and it burned me.' He paused. What he was about to say next, he hadn't even shared with Adam. 'And then the night before Dad died—'

Her hand took his.

'I overheard them in Dad's office, talking about Luca's car. We were both getting our cars ready for the season, and Luca's was finished first. I'd lingered in the French Riviera for a while when the season ended.'

'With your racing friends?' she said hesitantly.

Even though the 'who' was neither here nor there in this story, Jordan decided he may as well be 100 per cent honest.

'Yes, but also with Julia Sullivan,' he said. 'She and Luca had just gone their separate ways, and she invited herself.'

And so began one of the biggest mistakes of his life. Too bad he hadn't realised sooner that not all supermodels were as attractive on the inside as they were on the outside, like his mother. If only he'd known that one day, he'd meet someone who truly was.

That person was squeezing his hand. 'So, that night?'

'It shouldn't have been anything. They were both just so excited about Luca's car being finished, and I was about to walk in and give my report, but then I heard Dad call him "son." And it hit me. I wasn't the number one driver, I wasn't the number one kid – that was always Mia, even during the years she and Dad weren't getting along—'

'And you weren't even the number one son.'

He gulped air. 'That one should've been a lock, at least. I mean, I was his only son.'

He set the letter between them on the bed, grabbed his wine glass, and talked. Once he started, the words wouldn't stop. He'd sprung a leak, and every feeling, every emotion that he'd ever bottled up poured from his mouth. Sorrow. Embarrassment. Shame. Fear. Emotions he'd let a chosen few – anger, hatred, jealousy – overpower. With those three taking the backseat, finally, the others were eager for their turns sitting up front.

After years of training his mind to focus on only the task at hand, he should've been able to shove these emotions into the passenger seat and tune them out. But they wouldn't leave his line of sight. Some days, it felt like he was clinging to the rear bumper instead of sitting in the driver's seat.

'Is that why you haven't said yes to driving for Pinnacle?' Pearl asked.

'That's part of it. People will think I'm still that same asshole and that I'll end up proving them right. I'm scared that what drove me the day of the crash is still deep inside of me, and what drove me during every other race isn't. I don't want to make a fool out of myself.'

She squeezed his hand. 'Tell me, Jordan, why did the chicken cross the road?'

That wasn't the question he expected after sharing his inner demons. 'Excuse me?'

She smiled. 'Just answer the question.'

He shrugged. 'To get to the other side.'

'Why else? I mean, where was he going?'

What the hell was she getting at? 'That's the punchline, Pearl. That's all she wrote. Does it matter?'

'Maybe not, but I like to think that we don't know any more than that because it's none of our business. The chicken doesn't owe us an explanation about why it wants to be on the other side of the road.'

Jordan looked at the ceiling. He needed to add humiliation to his emotional pity party invitation list because he felt a little dumb. 'Pearl, I need some guidance finding your point.'

'Do what you want to do, Jordan. It doesn't matter what anyone else thinks.'

'So, I'm the chicken in the story?' If she was trying to convince him to race again, she might have chosen a more streamlined bird.

'Yes, but please don't focus on that,' she said. 'What do you want to do?'

His heart was pounding in his chest. Jordan picked up the envelope and looked at his dad's handwriting. 'Will you open it for me?'

Pearl nodded and, with her nail, unsealed the flap and handed him the envelope.

Jordan shook his head. 'Read it to me.'

He watched as she pulled out the card and took a couple of deep breaths. 'I love you.'

'I love you, too.' The words came out like he said them to people every day instead of hardly ever. But they were real. They were true.

Pearl turned the card around. In the center, his father had written those three words: *I love you.*

Oh.

With a watery smile, she handed him the card and then inched closer. 'But just so you know, I love you, too.'

Chapter 32

Pearl couldn't believe Rubie Racing couldn't let Jordan drive one of their race cars around a track somewhere for a while. But according to Mia and Luca, Apex was strict about where cars could run and when.

The cars at the complex being readied for the next race had to stay put.

Jordan had invited everyone over for a barbecue and to show off his cheery new kitchen. As soon as they'd arrived, Pearl had sent Cliff and Jordan out for a few things she'd purposely forgotten to pick up at the store that morning.

'But it's *your* car. And really, who would know? You're the only team this side of the Atlantic.'

At that, Di couldn't stay quiet. 'I can't believe Little Miss Ethics is telling someone to break the rules. I never thought I'd see the day.'

After hate-reading the last few Pearl of Wisdom columns, Pearl could honestly say she was glad that day had come.

Mia shook her head. 'The best we could do is to get him

in one of the testing seats in Spain next February. I can make some calls – it doesn't have to be an Apex car; any race car on any racetrack would do.'

At that, Pearl's head jerked up at the same time as Di's, and a similar grin spread across each of their faces. Even if they weren't mother and daughter, they shared a wavelength developed from years of living as if they were.

'You think?' Pearl asked.

Di bit her bottom lip – a telltale sign she was considering doing something she wasn't entirely comfortable with. 'The season's not over—'

'Can you? Do you still have his—'

'Yep.' Di picked her phone up off the counter and stared at it. Never revisiting old flings was one of her few hard and fast rules. 'What the hell. Why not.'

Di sauntered out of the room. Barb and Mia, who'd been watching them volley incomplete thoughts back and forth and answer each other's unspoken sentences, turned their attention to Pearl.

'I, for one, am going to need a few more words to know what's happening here,' Mia said.

But Pearl wasn't ready to divulge, at least not until she knew if it was an option or, better yet, doable.

'We're in luck,' Di said. 'But … only if we can get up there tomorrow because it's their off day. And we'll need to bring our own cars, so I don't know if that's even possible.'

'Oh, it's more than possible,' Pearl said. 'It's happening.'

Pearl picked up her phone and searched the dirt track Di's

long-ago summer fling raced on and, presumably, now owned. When she faced the screen to Luca and Mia, it was snatched out of her hand in seconds.

'Do you have any race cars like these?' Pearl asked.

Before Luca finished shaking his head, Mia was tapping out a text message. 'Not yet. But we will.'

Mia put Star and Brian to work tracking down the cars, whatever the cost, while everyone else acted as if they weren't driving two hours north the next day. Knowing what was in store for Jordan upped their enthusiasm for the bright yellow paint to a weird level, and they wouldn't stop asking what he planned to do next.

When they left, Jordan led Pearl to the conversation area, where they sat in the ridiculous-looking and not-at-all-comfortable chairs. She could see why he couldn't wait to be rid of them.

He looked around the space tucked away from the living room. 'What do you think about blue paint, a cool desk made from reclaimed wood, and a weathered leather lounge chair?' he asked.

'But you already have an office,' Pearl said.

She and Cliff had used it the other day to go over her separation agreement, and next to Jordan's bedroom, it was her favorite room in the house. Jordan had told her that even the decorator hadn't had the heart to tear out the rich mahogany wall panels and built-in bookcases, which he'd filled with photos and trophies from his career as a race car driver.

He shrugged. 'But you don't.'

She knew what he was suggesting — moving in together after only a couple of weeks. Granted, during that time, they'd been together almost 24/7. But the old Pearl of Wisdom would've had a field day with a reader who served up that scenario.

This Pearl of Wisdom? Her heart raced.

'I know we both have a lot to figure out, but I meant what I said, Pearl. I'm in it to win it. You don't have to move in tomorrow, but I would be okay if you did today. The days we were apart were some of the longest in my life. I'd rather not repeat even a second of them.'

Of all the uncertainties in her life right now, Pearl realised that this — what she and Jordan had — wasn't one of them. She climbed into his lap and kissed him.

'We'll figure it out together,' she said when they came up for air.

'I think we already are,' Jordan said.

As soon as they woke up the next morning, Pearl told Jordan to get ready for a surprise. That was a mistake. His excitement over what he thought she'd meant delayed them for nearly an hour.

Not that it wasn't worth it, except when she clarified afterward that she'd had a different surprise in mind — well, that pushed their departure time out another half hour.

It was a miracle they ever got on the road.

Out of extreme paranoia that Jordan would somehow figure

out they were headed to an out-of-the-way dirt racetrack he'd likely never heard of, Pearl was behind the wheel of his Porsche SUV. She'd never driven anything this fancy, which on its own was nerve-racking.

'You know it's a big deal for a race car driver to let someone else drive his vehicle, let alone one as nervous as you,' Jordan said as they headed north through the center of the state.

As if he was the poster boy for calm and collected. They were only a half-hour into the two-hour drive, and his restlessness was more than apparent.

'I'm more out of practice than anything,' Pearl said. She hadn't needed a car in college or grad school and, after moving into the city from Evanston, had easily adjusted to either walking or taking public transportation. Although plenty of Chicagoans own cars, her building had been built just after the Great Chicago Fire in 1871, in the time of horses and buggies. Given the hassle of street parking, she rented a car when necessary, mostly to head back to see Di, or took Amtrak.

But staying in Michigan meant she'd need to get used to driving again. Even if Jordan didn't live in the boonies, being carless in a state known for the automobile industry was practically impossible.

'I may know someone who could help with that,' he winked, then went back to manually adjusting each one of the sound system's 21 speakers.

Considering how fidgety he was as a passenger and how her body reacted whenever he was close to her, Pearl had her doubts. 'Let me get my own car first, and then we'll talk,' she said.

'Don't let Mia hear you say that,' Jordan said. 'She'll try and unload that sorry excuse for a car she abandoned in Barb's driveway last year on you.'

Her eyes darted from the road to Jordan because he had to have been kidding. There was no way that plain-in-every-way sedan belonged to the woman currently vying for the Apex world championship.

Only Jordan was nodding. 'It's true. Apparently, it was a measure of self-punishment for Scott's crash during that 24-hour race. A little extreme if you ask me.'

As they passed acres of farm fields, Pearl wished they'd had time to take a more scenic route, but the highway was the most efficient way to get where they were going. This road trip was about the destination, about ending a journey.

'Potentially sensitive question ahead,' Jordan said, 'but what are you going to do with Top's ashes?'

The urn hadn't left Barb's house since they'd arrived, whereas Di had been out and about without her sister in tow. Pearl made a mental note to corner Barb and find out exactly what was going on with the woman who'd raised her and why she was still camped out in one of her guest rooms.

'We haven't even talked about it,' she said. 'Is it weird having your parents in your lake?'

'Mia says she'll never swim there, but I like knowing they're nearby and together,' he said. 'Sometimes, when I'm out on my standup paddleboard, I feel them with me. It's nice.'

Pearl couldn't imagine a place where Di would feel comfortable leaving her sister. The earl had been buried with the first love of his life in the family plot, and Top hadn't been invited to that afterlife party. But then, she'd never been particularly close with his son. Not only had he been grown when the two of them had met and fallen in love, but he hadn't been fond of the eccentricities Top encouraged in his father.

She and Di should do something to mark Top's passing, perhaps a small memorial service.

After another half hour ticked by, Jordan was practically squirming in his seat. 'You're not even going to give me a hint?' he asked.

'Fine,' she said. 'It has both something and nothing to do with your at-bat song.'

After fiddling with his phone, Iggy Pop filled the interior of the SUV. After the sixth time 'Dirt' played, she told him it was time to give it up.

'Fine,' he said. 'Tell me something about you I don't know.'

Pearl shifted in her seat. 'I'm really bummed that I haven't heard back from Harrison Carter.'

She couldn't bring herself to call a man she didn't know her father or dad. They rolled off her tongue even more awkwardly than 'mom' did.

Jordan messed with the passenger seat controls as if discovering them for the first time. 'I can't pretend to know how you feel, but I'd say there's no harm in reaching out to him again. If he still doesn't reply, we could hire a private investigator, or you could do one of those DNA tests. Who knows, you might have siblings.'

In the craziness of the past month, Pearl hadn't considered that she could have brothers and sisters, aunts and uncles, or even grandparents who were still alive. It had just been her, Di, and Top for so long that she had a hard time grasping the concept of what it meant to have more than just a small handful of people to call hers.

'What do you think I should do?' she asked.

'Keep thinking about it,' Jordan said. 'There's no rush. Whatever you decide you want to do, we'll do.'

We.

'I like that,' she said. 'We.'

'Me, too,' he smiled, then turned up Iggy once more.

The dirt track was just as Pearl remembered it. And so was Greg, who seemed as excited to be around Di again as about meeting Apex royalty.

She and Jordan were the last ones to arrive, and everyone stared at Jordan as he looked, in equal parts awe and confusion, at the tiny oval and the lone car waiting for him at the start line.

How Star and Brian had managed to find a 'dirt car' – the technical term, Pearl had learned – in a matter of hours, she'd never know. But apparently, the guy agreed to rent it to them as long as they repaired any damage. After taking one look at it, Pearl wasn't sure how he'd be able to tell any new damage from the old. It was a bigger beater than the hand-me-down car she'd driven in high school, which was saying a lot.

'What is happening right now?' Jordan asked.

'Dirt!' Pearl said. 'I can't believe you didn't figure it out. I thought for sure I'd given it away.'

At that, he howled. 'Seriously?'

'What do you think?' Mia's question came out as a squeal, and she clapped her hands and danced around like a kid about to get her first balloon. 'Pearl arranged it.'

When Jordan didn't answer right away, Pearl's heart sank. Had she managed to cross a line mere days into their relationship? That had to be some sort of a record. Maybe she should see if the concession stand was open and drown her sorrows in snow cones and cotton candy.

But then, Jordan tugged her to him. He used a single finger to lift her chin until their eyes met. His glistened with emotion.

'You did this?' His voice cracked. 'For me?'

She was suddenly a little teary, too. 'You said it had been too long since you were behind the wheel of a race car. I wanted to help.'

'We all did,' Barb said, coming up behind him and resting a hand on his shoulder.

Jordan looked around the circle of people as if he couldn't believe they were all there for him. Then he picked up Pearl and swung her around.

'The best day of my life was when you fell head over heels for me on that beach,' he whispered in her ear.

'Spoiler alert,' Pearl whispered back, 'I'm still falling.'

Chapter 33

Luca leaned his head in through the passenger side window of Jordan's car. 'Is it your foot? Is your ankle bothering you?'

Jordan wished it were as simple as that. He tapped his head. 'No, it's up here. Do you have a screwdriver? I think something's loose.'

He was, in a nutshell, overwhelmed. He couldn't believe Pearl had instigated this, and that everyone in his life had helped her. He was equal parts afraid of letting her, them, and himself down.

'Nonsense,' said Mia, who'd also squeezed her head through the space. 'There's nothing up there.'

'You're not helping, love.' Luca kissed his wife on the cheek, then whispered in her ear. Whatever he said, worked, because Mia's head disappeared along with the rest of her.

'But seriously, mate, it's all connected,' his brother-in-law said. 'They wrote a song about it and everything. The leg bone's connected to the … whatever bone.'

Jordan shook his head. 'That's about bones, not organs. The brain is an organ.'

Pearl's head popped through the driver's side window at exactly the wrong part of that conversation. 'What's an organ?'

Before Luca could open his mouth to give her what was likely to be a highly inappropriate answer, Jordan waved him away, then slumped back in the seat. The doubt that washed over her face eclipsed his own feelings of the same emotion.

'What's wrong?' She nibbled on her bottom lip. 'Is the car not okay?'

In truth, the stock car was the biggest piece of shit he'd ever sat behind the wheel of, but he wasn't about to tell her that. Apex cars were pieces of art, whereas this thing was being held together with duct tape, coat hangers, and probably some well-chewed gum. His first kart had been higher tech.

But hands down, this POS was the nicest thing anyone had ever done for him. If it had a backseat, he'd drag her into it and spend a good long while kissing the doubt right off her face.

'It's perfect, but I' – a cloud of dust appeared in his rearview mirror, and from it, another beater emerged and came to a stop next to him – 'what the hell?'

Its fresh coat of pink paint – multiple shades, as if someone had bought every can of pink spray paint in the vicinity – matched his sister's driving suit and helmet.

'What do you say, hot shot?' she yelled through the open

window, just like she used to from her pink kart, and revved the engine. It stalled.

Jordan took the opportunity to pull Pearl's face through the window. His hand in her hair, he brushed his lips lightly across hers. But before he full-on kissed her, he whispered the three words he hadn't been able to stop saying out loud.

Instead of saying them back, she put her forehead to his. 'All right, Jordan, go be a chicken.'

By God, he really did love this woman. He laughed and kissed Pearl again, deeper than before, only breaking when Mia leaned on her horn.

He'd never driven on a dirt track, which he knew technically was clay. It had to have been at least 15 years since he'd driven on an oval track of any kind and never on one only a quarter-mile around. He foresaw a lot of left-hand turns in his immediate future.

Jordan started slow and did a quick run-through of the car. There was nary a bell or a whistle to be found, but the brakes worked, and the speedometer did, too. Mia, her car finally moving, was doing the same as they took a practice lap.

He turned his focus to driving the car and how to milk the most out of it. A professional milking machine wouldn't have had much luck, but he motored along, creating a wall of dust that rolled over the bleachers when he went by. He laughed out loud when he noticed Pearl, Barb, Cliff, Star, Brian, and Luca were wearing matching oversized sunglasses of the gas station variety to keep the dirt out of their eyes.

When Di appeared out of nowhere with a red flag, Jordan stopped on his next lap, pulling up next to Mia. She looked over at him, her face covered in dirt, their dad's grin wide on her face. He returned the pout that had put his mom on the cover of every fashion magazine in existence.

'Nice driving, Pinky Tuscadero,' he said, using her childhood nickname for the first time in 20 years. He'd given it to her when they'd spent two weeks in northern Michigan with nothing to do at night but watch VHS copies of old 'Happy Days' episodes. Mia had a girl crush on a character named Leather Tuscadero, a leather-clad singer in a high school band, but Jordan mercilessly teased her by calling her the name of Leather's not-as-cool older sister.

It still made more sense to him since Mia and the aptly named Pinky both had pink vehicles and outfits. But that's not why he did it. He'd wanted to get under her skin. Since it worked, he hadn't let it go for the entire summer, until their dad had warned him that if he didn't stop tormenting his sister that they'd both have pink karts.

He glanced over to find his Mia's eyes narrowed. She laughed and flipped him off.

'It's Leather, you asshole,' she yelled.

The green flag appeared. Only this time, it was in Luca's hand. He looked a little anxious, but he probably had reason to be. The last time he'd been on a track with Jordan, he'd ended up in the hospital. He gripped the fabric flag to its stick, using it to point from sister to brother and back again, mouthing, 'Be nice.'

Jordan didn't know how his sister was reacting to the silent lecture – probably not well, he guessed. But he met the eye of the man he'd nearly killed, who was now his brother in every sense of the word, and gave him a quick nod.

When Luca finally held the flag away from him over the track and waved it, Jordan hit the gas. He heard an excited whoop from Mia's car and joined her without thinking twice. They took it easy for a couple of laps, and then Mia became Mia and drove the short straightaways a little faster, took the corners a little tighter. She passed him, but he hung with her, mimicking her style until he found his own.

It was the most fun he'd had driving a race car in years. Even though he could barely get the POS up to 80 miles per hour, he was inhaling more dust than air, and he passed his twin as many times as she passed him. Once more, in the end. Because when Pearl waved the checkered flag after the agreed-upon 35 laps, his sister was somewhere behind him in a cloud of dust.

He'd won, but then he already knew that.

Chapter 34

'You know what's weird?' Jordan asked. It had been a week since he'd bested his sister and, practically on the spot, decided to move to Pinnacle for the next two seasons.

Pearl lifted her head off his chest and arched an eyebrow. 'Is this a new game? Because I don't think it has the same vibe.'

Not to mention, there was a lot more she wanted to know about Jordan Rubie.

The night before, they'd finally celebrated Jordan accepting the contract with Clark Motorsport. Cliff and Barb had joined them, as well as Di, but Mia and Luca had already headed out back on the road. The Apex season was coming quickly to an end, and Jordan was taking her to the final race of the season in New York.

Not happy about missing a second celebration dinner at Mario's, Mia had insisted that it wasn't fair that Jordan was going to the Rubie family's favorite restaurant twice in one month. She and Luca had stopped by to say goodbye, and they'd taken a pontoon ride around the lake.

'Are we going to get into fair, little sister?' he'd said over the quiet hum of the motor.

From experience, Pearl knew that one twin throwing their weight around because they're a few minutes older rarely led anywhere good. 'We'll just have to go back to celebrate you winning the world championship,' she'd told the woman sitting beside her.

'Then he'll have gone three times,' Mia had said, loud enough for only Pearl to hear.

Seeing the two of them together, it was hard to believe they'd been rivals for so many years. But then death has a way of bringing people together. She and Di were further evidence of that, even if they still struggled to put a label on what their relationship was now.

'I love that game, and I plan to keep playing it for a very long time,' Jordan said, coaxing her to straddle him, which she'd quickly realised was his favorite position. 'No, what's weird is how right this feels.'

Pearl leaned forward, her hands landing on what had to be the two most perfect pecs in existence as she ground down into him. 'I couldn't agree more.'

Jordan groaned. 'Believe it or not, that's not what I was talking about. I meant us, all of this. But since you brought it up ...'

Pearl had never believed making love would be different than sex, how she could feel that connected to another person on every level. That having someone whisper 'I love you' over and over again could bring her to a level where she somehow exploded and imploded at the same time.

'I love you,' she said when she collapsed on top of him. 'And trust me, there's nothing weird about that.'

After Jordan forced himself out of bed to hit his home gym, claiming he had a lot of work to do to get back in shape before the Pinnacle season, Pearl contemplated her next step. Her days of being unemployed had slid into weeks, and she still had no idea what to do next.

The newspaper had backpedaled on retaining the Pearl of Wisdom once Cliff pointed out that the column name both pre-dated her employment and was synonymous with her. According to Millie, Madeline was pissed with a capital P.

But they did dig in about keeping an archive of her columns on the website. The letter of the law gave the copyright to the *Chicago Daily Times*, since she'd written them as an employee. That was irksome for one major reason – the strait-laced advice she'd doled out daily was no longer the wisdom she wanted associated with her name.

The desk Pearl had chosen had arrived the day before, and she sat down at it and made a list of everything she needed to take care of. She'd been making do clothes-wise with what had been in the suitcase Jordan had brought back from Wales, the few things she'd packed the morning Di sprang the trip back to Michigan on her, and Jordan's T-shirts and prized Silverstone sweatshirt. But now that the weather was finally turning, she should head back to Chicago and pack up her clothes. Maybe she'd finally take Millie up on her longstanding offer to brighten up her wardrobe.

Over a tear-filled video call, Pearl had told Millie she was moving in with Jordan. She knew her best friend was happy for her, but it was the end of an era. Who would've thought that 17 autumns ago, the two college freshmen who'd stood in front of a dorm room door and laughed at each other's old lady names would only now, at 34, be calling it quits as roommates?

Since the condo was as much Millie's home as hers, Pearl had decided to maintain status quo for the time being. Plus, with Jordan being on the Pinnacle circuit for months of the year during racing season, and Clark Motorsport based in Indianapolis, they were considering making a change themselves. Knowing she could go back to Chicago and have a familiar place to lay her head was helping to keep her sane during this unexpected season of change.

Before Pearl could finish her list, a message came in from Di:

I have something for you. Lunch?

When they returned from northern Michigan, Di had gone back to the brick ranch she'd inherited from her parents. But Pearl knew that no matter how many colors they'd painted the walls, Di had never felt like it was her home. So it was no surprise when Di announced she was selling it, over chips and guac at their go-to Mexican restaurant.

'Where will you go?' Pearl asked.

'I may get a condo in downtown Detroit,' Di said. 'I've been looking online at some of the old buildings they've renovated.'

In the years Pearl had been away, Detroit had become known as a 'comeback city.' Buildings that had sat empty for decades were being brought back to life, including the massive train depot in the Corktown neighborhood. Once a symbol of the city's demise, it was now a sign of its resurgence.

It was the perfect place for Di, with one exception. The mall where she'd worked for as long as Pearl could remember was only five minutes from the house. A daily commute from downtown Detroit would be a nightmare.

'What about your job?' Pearl asked. It was hard to imagine Di giving up running the makeup counter, not to mention the employee discount, even if Top had left her more than enough money to be comfortable for a long while.

'They said I could transfer to another store if I wanted, but I think it's time for a fresh start,' Di said. 'I'm going to apply to art school. I think it's time to explore painting something other than my face.'

Pearl was finally used to the no-makeup makeup look that Di had transitioned to over the past few weeks. But then it was a face she was more than familiar with – Top's.

Oh.

Di must've noticed the realization dawn on Pearl because she shrugged. 'I miss my sister. Now I see her every time I look in the mirror.'

She smiled. 'I miss her, too.'

And she did. Being with Jordan again had helped distract her from the pain, but grief washed over her in quiet moments. In some ways, it didn't seem real because Top had always lived away from them. Part of Pearl's brain wanted to imagine Top still in her clifftop mansion, playing the part of the women she wrote about in her novels.

'What about you?' Di said. 'Are you settling in at Jordan's?'

'For now,' Pearl said.

What she hadn't realised when she'd helped Jordan regain his confidence in the car was that race car drivers, for the most part, lived near where their teams were located. Although it wasn't required, Jordan was toying with a move to Indianapolis to work in person with the Clark Motorsport team and wanted Pearl to go with him.

She hadn't thought twice about it until now. 'Am I crazy? I never thought I'd be the kind of girl who follows a guy.'

'Child, stop,' Di said. 'You love him, and he loves you. If anyone in this world deserves that kind of love, it's the two of you. Besides, you've spent your life taking care of me, yourself, and everyone who wrote to you. It's okay to let someone take care of you, at least for a little while.'

They finished their meal talking about the logistics of everything Di was planning to do. Even though Pearl would've advised a reader to hold their horses on making major life changes after such a significant loss, she realised that advice might not apply to this situation. At nearly 50, Di was finally figuring out what and who she wanted to be when she grew up.

When the table had been cleared, Di handed Pearl a canvas

tote bag. Inside were what appeared to be journals along with a small handful of letters tied together with red ribbon, which she took out first.

'Top and I had a secret hiding spot in the basement,' she said. 'I'd forgotten all about it, but all of this was still there.'

It wasn't surprising that Top had kept the letters from the boy who'd stolen her heart. Pearl didn't plan ever to be parted with the one from the man who'd taken hers.

'I'm sure Mom and Dad burned any that arrived after our sojourn in the Upper Peninsula, but hopefully, there's enough there to satisfy your curiosity,' Di said.

The ten journals ranged from old-fashioned diaries with tiny locks to more sophisticated bound books with cloth covers and ribbon bookmarks. Top had always been an avid journaler and had gifted Pearl plenty of them over the years. To this day, they were mostly blank – she'd never developed a habit of writing down her most personal thoughts and feelings. As a child, she'd been too worried the woman sitting across the table would find and read them; as an adult, she'd had Millie, who was essentially a vault.

And, of course, she'd always had Top – as had Di.

'I don't know what we are to each other anymore,' Di said when they finally hugged goodbye. 'We're not mother-daughter or aunt-niece. But friends doesn't cover it either.'

'How about all of the above?' Pearl asked, tightening her hold on the woman who'd somehow managed to both selfishly and selflessly raise her.

*

The letters were what one might expect from a teenage Romeo who'd lost his virginity to his Juliet. Pearl read them aloud to Jordan as he made dinner that night. There were five in total, with the final letter in the stack filled with angst and declarations of undying love.

'I can't help but feel for the kid,' Jordan said. 'He had it bad for Top. I wonder if he thought she'd purposely not written him back.'

'Is that what you would've thought?' Pearl asked.

'Yes,' he said, 'but thankfully, I never have to.'

After dinner, Jordan went to set up the simulator he'd ordered to help prepare him for the tracks Pinnacle raced on, and Pearl tucked herself in his bed with Top's journals. The oldest was one of the diaries that locked, which thankfully wasn't. It had been a gift from Di for their 13th birthday, according to the note written inside the front cover:

Happy birthday to my little sister, Topaz.
  Love, Diamond
PS I promise never to read this unless you say I can.

Pearl couldn't imagine that had held true.

Wow, Di hadn't been kidding about Top having a flair for the dramatic. She'd been one angst-ridden teenage girl. No wonder Di'd had so little patience for drama when Pearl had been young.

For the next several hours, Pearl read as Top navigated feeling different than everyone else, even the person she was identical to. She envied how popular Di was, especially with boys. She resented being the favored daughter, but she was too anxious not to follow the rules and do as she was told.

The arts camp experience was almost exactly as Top had retold it to Pearl in Wales. To ensure she'd have a summer she'd remember forever – she'd certainly gotten that wish and then some – she'd gone by Topaz and recreated herself in Di's image.

After reading pages upon pages about Top and Harrison's first kiss, Pearl decided she didn't care to know the details about two 14-year-olds 'making love,' let alone her parents. Plus, if her father ever replied to her message, she didn't need to add that weirdness to the mix.

Apparently, Top had been three months pregnant when she'd begged Di to go to a pharmacy and buy a pregnancy test. Even though she'd taken the bus to the next suburb, the biggest gossip from their church had seen her – and nothing spreads faster than wildfire than a girl who has gotten herself in trouble. Especially when the girl is Diamond Carrington, who'd always been a bit too 'friendly' with the boys. When their parents caught wind, they'd refused to believe Di when she said the test was for a friend. There had been a horrible screaming match, which Top had stopped by telling them the truth. Not that it had mattered to Pearl's grandparents. It had been more plausible that their bad angel had fallen a little further than their good angel had taken a tumble.

Pearl found the photo in between the journal pages halfway through the family's time in the Upper Peninsula. A very pregnant Top, hands cradling her belly, smiling for the camera. Happy.

Our Pearl.

Setting the journals aside, Pearl went in search of Jordan. She found him in the finished bonus room over the garage, where he'd decided to set up the simulator to limit distractions. Sitting in the low chair with his feet on the pedals and his hands gripping a steering wheel, he reminded her of Wonder Woman in her Invisible Plane. Only the actual race car was missing from the getup.

He was so focused on the racetrack filling the three screens ahead of and around him that he didn't hear her come in.

'Can I interrupt?' she asked.

'Always.' He hit pause and rubbed his eyes. 'How's the journal reading going?'

When Pearl held out the photo she'd found, Jordan crooked his index finger to beckon her to him. Within seconds, he slid the seat back, and she found herself straddling him in the imaginary yet aptly named cockpit.

'Wow,' he said, looking at the photo. 'She's so young. She still looks like a kid.'

Pearl nodded. 'She was. I mean, I can't even imagine getting pregnant at 14 and having a baby at 15.'

'You okay?' he asked, pulling her in for a hug.

She nodded again. 'I never saw a picture of Di pregnant but didn't think much of it.'

Overall, there weren't many photos from her childhood or Top's and Di's. Her grandparents had only pulled their camera out for birthdays and holidays, and then months would pass before they developed the film.

After a kiss, Pearl climbed off his lap. 'Meet me in bed in 30 minutes?'

She watched as he set an alarm on his smartwatch, gave her thumbs up, and then started racing again.

Pearl went back to her desk and placed the photo of pregnant Top next to her open laptop. After only a few seconds of looking at the blank screen, she typed, 'The Pearl of Wisdom gets wise.'

Chapter 35

Mia's 911 flashed across Jordan's phone screen halfway through his neck workout.

The intense exercises he'd done religiously for years had been the first he'd ditched post-crash, given the low odds of him encountering G-forces off the racetrack – and the even lower odds of finding himself on one.

But he'd been wrong, and not only because of landing a drive with Pinnacle. Falling in love with Pearl had hit him at full force, too.

Jordan was pleasantly surprised by how quickly those muscles had regained strength in only a couple of weeks. When he was finished with what had become his standard Tuesday workout, he picked up his phone to find out what his sister's emergency was, only to have it start ringing in his hand.

'Calla's out for Watkins Glen,' Mia said. 'She's getting her appendix out as we speak.'

The season's final race was that weekend, when Mia would

officially bring a second world championship to Rubie Racing and be the first female world champion. He and Pearl, along with Barb and Cliff, were heading to New York for the crowning achievement.

'Put in your reserve driver,' Jordan said. 'I'm sure the kid's champing at the bit to get in the car for an entire race weekend.'

'No.' Mia was quiet for a few seconds. 'I want you.'

He couldn't have heard her correctly. 'I'm sorry, you're going to need to repeat that. It sounded like you want me in the car this weekend.'

The twins hadn't shared a racetrack in years, not counting the dirt track he was still washing out of his hair. If she hadn't left racing for 15 years, they still probably wouldn't have raced together in Apex. He'd always known his seat in Rubie Racing had been intended for her.

But in their youth and teens, they'd raced against each other regularly and had been borderline-crazy competitive.

'You heard me correctly,' Mia said. 'Will you race with me? I mean, you're going to be there anyway. Why not suit up in Apex one last time?'

Although he realised the gravity of her request, Jordan was too stunned to speak. Plus, he'd made peace with his Apex career and how it had ended.

'We had fun on the dirt track,' she added. 'Let's do it in real race cars.'

Jordan could almost feel his dad's hand on his shoulder and its familiar, reassuring squeeze. For too many years, he'd taken for granted the opportunity to work with and learn from his dad. Maybe this was Rob Rubie's final lesson.

Still, he couldn't believe he was going to do this.

'Are you still there, Jordan?'

He blew out a long breath. 'Fine, but if I beat you, you have to wear a replica of your pink dress to your celebration dinner at Mario's.'

Trish Rubie had been dead set against her only daughter getting a go-kart — although she'd lost that battle, her husband had pacified her some with the color. When eight-year-old Mia and her pink kart had soundly beaten every boy in a 50-mile radius, including Jordan, their mom had bought her a frilly dress for the end-of-season banquet. Mia had made peace with wearing it because it matched her kart, but he'd known, deep down, that she'd hated it.

'What if I beat you?' she asked.

He laughed. 'You still have to wear it.'

'You drive a hard bargain, hot shot,' she said. 'But you have a deal.'

When Mia clicked off, Jordan's brain swirled with all he needed to do before climbing into a race car in a matter of days. But first, he had someone to share this interesting new development with, which made it even sweeter.

Chapter 36

'To this weekend's race winner,' Pearl said, lifting her wine glass and waiting for Jordan to do the same – but he only rolled his baby blues. 'I said, to this week's race winner.'

They were sitting in their Adirondack chairs, which had become part of their daily routine. Pearl would miss these 'daily meetings,' as they called them, when the dock and the pontoon were pulled out in the coming weeks and stored for the winter. Until then, she was enjoying taking in the fall colors around the lake with the person sitting beside her.

'You're going to jinx me, you know,' Jordan said after he'd finally clinked his glass to hers, and they'd both taken a sip.

Jordan was leaving the next day for the racetrack, and she would fly out with Barb and Cliff closer to the end of the week. She'd learned that Apex drivers didn't just get in their cars on race day and hit the gas pedal. There were practice sessions and then qualifying, which determined the order of the drivers at the start line. Drivers also met with race engineers, strategists, and their team manager and principal – in

Rubie Racing's case, Brian and Luca. Although Mia owned the team, she'd handed off those duties so she could focus on her driving. Considering how the season was about to end, it had been a good call.

'How'd your reading and writing go today?' he asked.

Pearl had been splitting her days between reading Top's journals and creating her own. She'd started the night she cracked open the first diary. Since then, writing had become a way for her to deal with the many surfacing emotions.

'Let's see. Top is as excited to leave for Boston as she is sad about leaving me,' she said.

Even though Pearl had no memories from those first few years of her life, the words were painful to read. Because she already knew how that storyline ended – after Top had left for college, she'd never come back to live with them again.

When Jordan went into the house to grab the bottle, Pearl took out her phone and logged onto social media. After commenting on Millie's photos from a Chicago Cubs playoff game at Wrigley Field, she went to her messages and looked at the one she'd sent to Harrison Carter from Wales more than two months ago. She'd checked a few times a day for a while, convinced he'd message her back right away. But he'd never even looked at it.

Until today. There it was, the tiny photo of him next to the message. He'd seen it. And then, as she watched, a bubble appeared.

The bubble was still there when Jordan came back and refilled their glasses. She showed him her screen, and he sat down on the arm of her chair. Together, they watched as her father took his sweet time typing her a message.

'Even my dad typed faster than this,' Jordan said.

Finally, words popped on the screen:

> Yes, I remember Topaz. I would love to know how she's doing. Please feel free to pass along my phone number.

She looked up the area code. New York City.

'What do I do?'

Jordan leaned down and kissed her. 'Be a chicken, Pearl.'

With one hand in Jordan's, she pressed the number on the screen.

'Carter here,' a deep voice said.

Pearl swallowed. 'Hi. My name is Pearl Carrington, and I'm Topaz's daughter.' She took a deep breath. 'And apparently, yours, too.'

'Do you know what I don't understand? Travel-size dental floss. I mean, how small is your suitcase that you can't squeeze in a regular-size dental floss?' Pearl held both up to Jordan to demonstrate. 'There's like a quarter-inch difference between the two, if that.'

From across the bedroom, Jordan looked up from the stack of Rubie Racing gear he was neatly folding and placing just so into his suitcase.

'I mean, have you ever gotten to the airport and found

out your suitcase weighed too much and thought, "You know what, I'll ditch this dental floss. That should do it.'"

Pearl knew she was babbling, but she was nervous. And when she was nervous, she babbled.

Given the puzzled look on Jordan's face, it was a good thing she was rarely nervous.

'Don't get me started on the environmental impact of all of these plastic containers filling up our landfills, probably still full of dental floss because so many people also take a vacation from flossing their teeth.'

Jordan stopped what he was doing, walked over, and wrapped his arms around her. 'I promise I will always floss my teeth on vacation and that I will never, ever buy travel-size dental floss again. Also, and most importantly, he's going to love you.'

She was meeting her dad. Tomorrow. The night before, she'd spoken for nearly an hour to Harrison Carter, or rather, Carter Harrison. For his stage name, he'd swapped his first and last names, and it had stuck. He'd only created the account with his actual name so people from his past could find him. Since he thought that had already happened, he rarely checked it. It was a stroke of serendipity that he'd looked that day. But he had. At this point, she was half afraid her string of happy coincidences was tempting the hand of fate.

Carter may have babbled when he was nervous, too – not to mention, shocked. It's not every day that someone rings you up to say the teenage girl you lost your virginity to had borne your child – 34 years ago.

But overall, he seemed to take it in stride. Of course, he was a professional actor.

'Topaz wasn't only my first, but she was also my last,' Carter had told her. 'I found my own Romeo the next summer.'

Right out of college, he'd left the Midwest for New York City to find fame and fortune. He hadn't found either, he laughed, but he did act full time. Although the stage had his heart, he'd been in just about everything at this point in his career. He'd even played the random guy who finds the dead body in the cold opening of her favorite crime series.

'I am sorry to hear about your mom,' Carter had said. 'I hope your memories bring you comfort.'

If he only knew the half of it – hell, even a quarter. But that was beyond what she'd been willing to share in their first phone call.

'If you're willing, I'd like to meet you in person,' he'd said. 'I'm not scheduled to be back in Michigan until the holidays, but perhaps I can squeeze in a trip before then.'

'Coincidentally, I'll be in New York this weekend, but nowhere near the city,' Pearl had said.

From the arm of the chair, a wide-eyed Jordan had nudged her and mouthed, 'We can go.'

So what if meeting up wasn't convenient? Not knowing she'd had a dad for 34 years wasn't ideal either.

'I suppose I can do a side trip before or after if you're available,' she'd said.

279

They'd decided on before, and since Carter was free the next day, Jordan delayed his arrival at the track by one day. Mia wasn't happy, but Jordan refused not to be there for Pearl. Depending on how the visit went, Pearl would either leave with Jordan or stay a day or two on her own.

Even though Carter had sounded excited during their phone call, Pearl couldn't help but have her doubts about meeting him face to face. It was a lot of pressure for both of them. She wanted to believe that Jordan was right and that Carter might embrace the unexpected role and love his long-lost daughter.

'How can you know that?' she said into Jordan's chest.

'Because I don't think it's possible to know you and not love you,' he said.

'But what if he doesn't even like me?' Pearl asked. 'What if he's some sort of a weirdo?'

'On the very off chance that one of those two things is true, you're welcome to hang out at the track for the rest of the week,' Jordan said. 'Lots of girlfriends do.'

Girlfriend.

They'd never used those terms before or had the girl-friend-boyfriend conversation – but exclusivity had been implied when they'd decided they were in it to win it that day on the dock.

Still, she couldn't help but ask, 'So, I'm your girlfriend?'

He kissed her in a way that told Pearl everything she needed to know and more. 'For now.'

*

The next morning, Pearl wasn't sure what she should do when her dad walked into the coffee shop they'd agreed to meet at. Should she stand up? Hug him? Wave hi?

'Stop worrying, Pearl,' Jordan said. 'Not only is it unnecessary, but you nip at your bottom lip when you worry, and it drives me wild.'

She made a mental note to do that more often, preferably when they were alone. By the way Jordan nudged her, he must've been thinking the same thing. Pearl turned to give him a knowing wink to find his eyes as wide as saucers.

'Wow, do you look like my sister.'

Two men had appeared at their tableside without her noticing. Without a doubt, the one with gray eyes swimming with emotion was Carter Harrison.

Jordan was on his feet within seconds, shaking their hands.

'Hi,' Pearl said, her voice cracking as she stood up, too. 'This is my boyfriend, Jordan, and I'm Pearl. Of course.'

Before she could contemplate what to do next, Carter asked, 'Would it be okay if I gave you a hug?'

A half of a second after she nodded, Pearl was engulfed in a bear hug that she didn't want to end. Judging by how long it lasted, he must've felt the same way. When they both stepped back, there wasn't a dry eye among the four of them.

As soon as they all sat down, Jordan grabbed her hand under the table and gave it a squeeze.

Carter introduced them to his partner, Blake, who volunteered to get everyone's drinks. Jordan joined him, saying he'd need help carrying everything.

Alone at the table, Carter and Pearl stared at each other.

'There's certainly no need for a paternity test,' he finally said. 'You're the spitting image of my sister, Kate.'

He took out his phone and, after a few seconds, turned the screen toward her. The smiling woman could've been her mother instead of her aunt. Not only did she have the same gray eyes and heart-shaped face, but her hair was the same intense shade of brown.

He flipped through a few more photos. His parents, like Kate, lived in West Michigan, along with Kate's husband and two kids. They were a close family, and he'd told them all about her. They were eager to meet her when she was ready.

'I have to ask,' he finally said. 'How could Topaz not have told you who I was?'

'Well, that's a whole thing in and of itself,' Pearl said as Jordan and Blake rejoined them with a plate of pastries and four mugs of coffee. Only crumbs were left by the time she finished sharing the whole story of how Top and Di had swapped places and that she'd only found out the day before she'd messaged him.

'You had quite the life-changing summer,' Carter said.

'That would be the understatement of the century,' Pearl said, smiling at Jordan.

Afterward, they walked through Central Park, their partners lingering behind. Father and daughter fell into an easy conversation about likes and dislikes, looking for commonality in everything from politics to favorite ice cream flavors, and found more than a few.

When they reached a statue of a dog on top of a rocky outcrop, Carter stopped. He explained that the husky, Balto, had long ago been the lead sled dog during a mission to deliver life-saving vaccines to an Alaskan town enduring a diphtheria outbreak.

'Every time I walk here, I see kids climbing all over him,' he said. 'I get it – I was fascinated with Balto as a boy. The few times I've wondered what it would be like to be a dad, I was standing right here.'

Pearl shrugged. 'Well, I'm not exactly a kid anymore, but I'd be willing to give it a go.'

'Do it!' said Jordan, taking her handbag.

And so she scaled the rock with Carter right behind her. At the top, they posed on either side of the bronzed, brave dog as Jordan and Blake took photos with their phones.

Before they made their way down, he stopped her. For a second, he simply looked at her in disbelief.

'I want you to know that when you called, I was shocked, obviously, but also so happy,' Carter said. 'I still can't believe I have a daughter. I've missed too much, Pearl. I'd like to be there going forward.'

In the journal entry Pearl had read on the flight, college freshman Top had written that being away was easier than being near the daughter she couldn't acknowledge as her own. But the guy before her hadn't made that choice – he hadn't been given any choice in the matter.

She grabbed the hand of the man who'd provided half of her DNA. 'I'd like that, too.'

Chapter 37

'You should know that race car drivers have weird routines, and they're pretty superstitious about breaking them,' Jordan told Pearl the morning of the race.

They'd spent the night at the track in a caravan so that she could get the full race weekend experience. It had been years since he'd camped out before a race, but it felt right for this unexpected last Apex hurrah.

As excited as Jordan was to get to the start line, he wished they could lounge in bed all morning. Pearl had stayed two extra days in New York to spend more time with her father and had flown to the Finger Lakes region the morning before, arriving just in time to watch Jordan qualify in fifth. While he was glad Pearl and Carter had hit it off so well, Jordan had missed her. If someone had told him four months ago that he was about to meet the person who would change him and his life forever, he wouldn't have believed them.

And even if he had, Jordan never could've imagined love could be like this.

But he did have a race to get to and a superstition he was very much looking forward to getting out of the way.

Pearl arched an eyebrow. 'You don't say. What's your weird thing?'

'You mean our weird thing.' He grinned. 'You inadvertently set it in stone the morning I raced Mia on the dirt track.'

He could see the wheels spinning in her brain as she tried to remember – to be fair, they'd made love dozens of times since then. At this point, it would be hard to determine who was more insatiable in that department, but for once, he was more than happy to take a tie.

The second Pearl remembered, she put her hands over her face and groaned. 'I did that to be funny.'

And it had been – along with amazing.

'I'm sorry, Pearl, but I can't break a streak.' Jordan slid off his boxer shorts. 'And I know how horrible you would feel if I lost today, and it was all your fault.'

That did the trick. Pearl sat up, pulled his old Red Wings T-shirt over her head, and crawled onto his lap. 'You're lucky I love you,' she said.

'You've got that right,' he said. 'Now turn it around, cowgirl.'

JOSEPH LINWOOD: I'm Joseph Linwood, here with Nigel Rose for Horizon Sports, at the final race of the season for the World Apex Grand Prix Motorsport Series.

NIGEL ROSE: And what a season it's been. How fitting that

for the first time in years, we're closing out the season in Watkins Glen, New York, as we'll officially crown our first American world champion. That is, of course, Mia Rubie, who also happens to be Apex's first female world champion.

NIGEL ROSE: And there's more big news from Rubie Racing this week. Mia Rubie's twin brother, Jordan, will be back on the track with her, taking the place of Calla Tremblay, who had an emergency appendectomy earlier this week so wasn't medically cleared to race.

JOSEPH LINWOOD: I'm sure we all wish Tremblay a speedy recovery. As a rookie, she's had a remarkable season.

NIGEL ROSE: Definitely. I can't wait to see what the young Canadian does in the future. But Joseph, I'll admit that I'm surprised to see Jordan Rubie back in the car for his family team after last year's crash in Hungary.

JOSEPH LINWOOD: You're not the only one. Equally surprising is how the team seems to be taking it all in stride. If there's any bad blood, I've not seen it.

NIGEL ROSE: One last thing since they're lining up for the start. For a guy who's been out of the car for over a year and underwent multiple surgeries, I don't know that I've ever seen Jordan Rubie drive the way he has the past few days in practice and qualifying.

JOSEPH LINWOOD: I agree. If he keeps it up, we may have two Rubies on the podium this afternoon.

NIGEL ROSE: Somewhere, Joseph, Rob Rubie is smiling. But then he always was.

*

Brian had been in his ear since the light turned green.

'How are the tires feeling?' his team manager asked.

'Great,' Jordan said. 'The rest of the car, too.'

It was almost as if the tweaks the Rubie Racing team had made for this season to the RR1 – now the RR2 – had been meant for him. He'd never had a car handle so intuitively, but that could also be because he'd never been so relaxed behind the wheel.

He'd passed two cars on the first turn and maintained third place throughout the race. If he could keep it up for 20 more laps, he'd be standing on the podium for the first time in more years than he cared to count.

Oh, the irony.

And if he could get within a second of Henri Aveline on one of the track's straightaways, he'd be able to boost his speed. But another lap passed without him being able to activate the system that adjusted the rear wing. And then another few ticked by without that aerodynamic assist.

But with 15 laps to go, the light flashed on his dash, and he pushed the magic blue button.

The Frenchman and three-time world champion wasn't about to play nice. Perhaps because Luca had robbed him of the drivers' championship last year, and now it was Mia's turn.

In truth, Jordan had never had a problem with Henri, but he'd always been Luca's nemesis and had become Mia's upon marriage. By default, he was Jordan's, too, now that Luca was family – and he was done letting his family down.

'Damn it,' Jordan said when Henri positioned his red car so perfectly on the track, making the pass too difficult.

'Next time,' Brian replied. 'You're gaining speed. Keep doing it, man.'

Jordan didn't think he could stop if he tried. He'd never been so hyper-focused; he swore he spotted Pearl in the back of the garage during his last pit stop, wearing the pale blue Silverstone sweatshirt he was never getting back. Thank God. Once she'd found out how much that particular item of clothing meant to him, she'd taken to wearing it as lingerie. Now, he loved it even more.

Plus, after this race, he'd need one of those 'I heart New York' sweatshirts. Maybe he'd get Mia one, too, given that they'd be standing next to each other on the podium – him to her right if he could get past Henri and take P2.

But when the next lap led to another missed opportunity, and Jordan neared the pit entrance, he asked Brian, 'Where will I be if I come in for soft tires?'

'You might lose one position, but you should be able to make it up.' He paused. 'It's a long shot but it could be worth it.'

As far as Jordan was concerned, if he was going to be on the podium either way, what did he have to lose?

Brian must've come to the same realization. 'Bring her in. Let's do this.'

When Jordan pulled back onto the racetrack less than 20 seconds later, he knew his pit crew would pick up the prize for the fastest pitstop. He was within spitting distance of the fourth-place car, and his fresher and grippier tires had him back up to third in half a lap.

'Aveline's heading in for softs, too,' Brian said.

Jordan hadn't expected such a ballsy move from Henri with only a few laps to go.

'No pressure, but Aveline's teammate is having a bad day,' Brian said. 'They're in danger of losing the team championship.'

If Jordan got his way, everyone on the storied red team was about to have a horrible day. Because what his team manager hadn't needed to say was that Rubie Racing would be the one taking the other championship of the season away from them.

'Got it,' Jordan said.

Judging by where Henri exited the pits, right behind Jordan, his crew was losing the fastest pit stop prize, too.

Whereas Henri now had the advantage of newer tires, Jordan's were only slightly older and already warmed up. As they hit the next straightaway, it was his turn to make sure Henri couldn't get by. And at the next braking point, Jordan positioned his car perfectly, not moving and denying Henri another chance.

'Five laps,' Brian said.

The next voice Jordan heard wasn't in his ear, but his dad still came through loud and clear: 'I didn't stick you in a Rubie Racing car just because you're my son. I did it because this is what you were always capable of.'

If only Jordan had listened to the late great Rob Rubie

when he'd been alive, the man wouldn't have had to leave a note to make sure his son knew how much he loved him. Instead, Jordan had wasted so much time stewing on what was behind him that he'd lost focus on what was possible ahead of him.

Until now, when his head and his heart were in the right place.

Love. Light. Pearl.

But first, it was up to him to make his father's dying wish come true and bring the team championship to Detroit for the first time.

With only a few laps to go, Jordan and Henri had fought their way up to Mia, who'd started first on the grid. But her tires were tired, and Jordan made it his job to keep Henri from getting near her.

His earpiece came to life again with Luca's voice. 'I have a message from your sister. She says she's in it to win it.'

'Well, she'd better not get the hell out of the way,' Jordan said. 'I'm serious, Luca.'

The radio went silent for a few seconds. 'Another message.' Luca. 'She said you'd better be in it to win it, too.' His brother-in-law paused. 'This is your race to lose, hot shot. Not hers.'

Because Mia was a winner either way. Unlike the team championship, Mia's world championship hadn't come down to just one more podium spot. She'd had it buttoned up for a couple of weeks.

Suddenly, he and Mia weren't in multimillion-dollar race

cars on one the most legendary tracks in the United States. They were in their karts on the track by their house, and their parents were cheering for both of them.

Even as a child, his sister had been one hell of a driver; a season and a half in Apex had fine-tuned those long-dormant skills. But Jordan had skills of his own, learned and earned from a decade of mid-pack battles.

As the final laps ticked down and Mia kept a perfect line, he bided his time, waiting for an opening while continuing to fight with Henri. With the checkered flag waving, Jordan made his move and squeezed by his sister – winning literally by a nose.

'Hell yeah,' he cried as Brian yelled in his ear, 'P1 baby.'

By the time Jordan parked the car in front of the sign for the race winner and tore off his helmet, he was all-out bawling. The tears were still flowing as he stood up and fist-pumped the sky, then climbed down from his car to have a crying Mia fling herself at him.

But there was only one person Jordan wanted to see – needed to see. His sister pulled him over to the waiting Rubie Racing team, and he dove into the crowd of orange.

It was only when his former teammate lifted him up that Jordan saw her.

Pearl, his Pearl, in the Silverstone sweatshirt with her hair tied back with that beautiful length of tartan.

Just as he had so many months before, Jordan reached out his hand. And the woman who not only made his heart race, but had also given him back his racing heart, grabbed it.

Chapter 38

Winning Watkins Glen had only proved to Jordan that he needed to move to Indianapolis full time to prepare for the racing season. It was the right call but a tough call, especially now that he had a house that felt like a home, and someone to share it with.

'Think of it this way,' that someone had said to him after they'd christened yet another freshly painted room. 'It's always going to be here, waiting for us. That's literally what home means.'

He liked that.

He loved her.

And since he was a multimillionaire who'd just signed another million-dollar contract, they weren't moving anything. Instead, right after Thanksgiving, he and Pearl had spent a long weekend in Indy looking for a place to live. Once they'd managed to convince their real estate agent that they weren't interested in a mini-mansion in a gated community, they'd fallen in love with an old neighbourhood in the city with towering century-old trees, a path alongside a canal for running, and restaurants they could walk to.

When they'd discovered the Arts and Crafts-era bungalow with the huge front porch and built-in bookcases that made Pearl moan with pleasure, they knew they'd found another home – even if it ended up just being a short-term one.

After all, at 34, he'd be one of the older guys in Pinnacle. It was no secret that his days on the track were numbered.

After celebrating Christmas with their families, they were starting the New Year in their new home. Pearl and Di were already there to put things in place and paint a few rooms. Even though they'd decided months ago that tiling was outside their comfort zone, regardless of how many YouTube videos they watched, her latest texts showed photos of the kitchen sans backsplash.

Jordan planned to join her just as soon as he did the thing he was dreading most – saying goodbye to his twin.

'You should've texted, and I would've let you in through the back,' Mia said when she found him sitting in the reception area of Rubie Racing, chatting with his former assistant.

'And allow me access to the state secrets? No way that was going to happen.'

After all, he was headed to another team. Even if Clark Motorsport wasn't in direct competition with Rubie Racing, their engineers would love to know what was being developed for the next Apex season behind the many locked doors in this building.

Mia's perma-grin faded slightly. 'Don't be silly. I trust you, Jordan.'

'I know.' He did believe her. The person he needed to work on trusting more was himself.

He'd expected to head right to her office, but instead, they wove through the building to the space holding their father's car collection.

Before Mia flipped on the light, she turned to him. 'I've added a couple of new cars.'

He went to the center of the space and looked around. His eye immediately found the 1969 Chevy Corvette L88, which was hands down his favorite car in the whole world.

'That one's yours whenever you want it,' she said.

He smiled. 'Nah, it belongs here. I've always suspected the Vette and your DeLorean get into all kinds of trouble when this place shuts down for the night.'

That's when he saw it, next to the R25 from his winningest year in Apex. The POS stock car in all its glory.

He groaned. 'My God, it looks even worse under fluorescent lights.'

Dust and dirt still coated what white paint wasn't covered with duct tape. But like every other car in the space, a small plaque had been placed at its nose. Before he could bend down to read it, Mia already had a hand over her mouth to try and contain her laughter.

'So immature,' he shook his head and read aloud: 'Inaugural Rob Rubie POS Champion – Jordan Rubie.'

'Inaugural?' He cocked an eyebrow, then reached his hand

out and rested it on the hood of the most unlikely car to ever change a driver's life, even more so, his. But it was fitting for it to spend its days side by side with an Apex car. They each represented a time when he was at his best, albeit in very different ways.

'When you win the 500, we'll bring that car here, too.' She winked as if she were joking, but he knew damn well she was 100 per cent serious.

He did a slow spin, taking in the space, stopping only when he faced his sister. 'I'm not sure how this is going to go. A lot of Apex drivers crash and burn in Pinnacle.'

'Not literally, I hope,' she said.

'I'm serious, Mia.'

'Me, too.' She sighed. 'Sure, not every Apex driver survives the transition, but plenty have done well.' She paused. 'Look, it's a risk, but you're going in with your eyes wide open. And if it doesn't work out, who cares? You can always come home to Rubie Racing.'

There was that word again. As much as it sucked to admit, this place was no longer home to him.

He shook his head. 'No, Mia. Dad made the right call when he left the team to you. I would've burned this place to the ground already. And that would've been after I terrorised almost everyone into quitting.' He ignored her attempts to interrupt him by literally placing a hand over her mouth, which she promptly bit. 'The team is yours for a reason, Mia.'

'I can dream,' she said. 'After all, you did play a pivotal role in bringing home the team championship.'

They spent an hour walking from car to car, reminiscing about their dad's career and laughing over some of the cars he'd put in the collection for purely sentimental reasons, like the cherry red 1967 Porsche 911 Mia had learned to drive in.

'Luca keeps threatening to pull her out of here and use it as our grocery getter,' she said. 'But it's not exactly car seat friendly.'

His eyes nearly bugged out his head. 'Holy shit. Are you pregnant, Mia?'

'No, but we're going to start trying after I win a second world championship. Or at the end of next season, whichever comes first.' She winked. 'For now, it's just one long practice session.'

Jordan stuck his fingers in his ears. 'Why would you think your brother would want to hear about that? No. Just no. And here I thought I was the one in the family who could never figure out where the line was. Not only did you cross it in record speed, but you beat me by a mile.'

'Well, I had to win at something against you this year,' she laughed.

They ended up in Mia's office in the inner sanctum of the team's headquarters. Even for the off-season, it was quiet. Too quiet.

'Star's working from Chicago,' Mia said, reading his mind. 'She'd missed one too many family Sunday dinners, so she's camped out at my place for a while.'

'Luca?' His brother-in-law was rarely more than an arm's

length from his wife. At least, that had been the case the entire time the three of them had worked together, when he and Luca were drivers and Mia was newly in charge. Sure, they were married now, but they were also newlyweds.

'Oh, thanks to you and your never-ending house reno, he was inspired to buy the floor beneath ours,' she said. 'He's currently meeting with a contractor about the best way to combine the two floors so they feel like they were always one space.'

He wasn't surprised that they'd decided to settle in downtown Detroit. Mia had loved her years living in Chicago, and Luca's loft was located in what was becoming a trendy neighborhood and had killer views of the Detroit River and Canada to boot.

'Brian?'

Suddenly interested in a stack of papers, she picked up the top one and set it down on the conference table they were sitting at. 'He's in Chicago, too. For a thing he had to do.'

Jordan raised an eyebrow – a trait he'd picked up within weeks of living with Pearl – but didn't say anything more.

He looked around. The office still managed to maintain their father's solid feel. Mia had only added a giant whiteboard, which had a column of names under the heading 'potential drivers for upcoming seasons.' An equal number of women and men were listed in various colors. He quickly spotted his name, which was the only one written in red. He didn't ask what the color coding meant. He wasn't sure he wanted to know.

Mia walked over to the closet and opened the safe in the wall inside. It was hard to believe that at one point, all of the plans and drawings for the team's strategy and cars were stored in there, not on a hard drive protected by multiple passwords changed almost daily. When she came back, she set a black velvet box in front of him on the table.

'You're sure?' Jordan asked.

She nodded. 'She's already one of us, so you might as well make it official. May God have mercy on her soul.'

The lid creaked when he opened it, revealing his mother's engagement ring on a rich red velvet pad. Somehow, after 20 years in the dark, the ruby was even more beautiful, richer, as if the stone had absorbed its inky black surroundings.

'Mom and Dad would've loved her,' Mia said.

He snapped the lid of the box closed. 'I think so, too.'

They chatted for a while longer – about Barb and Cliff's wedding, his and Pearl's. As far as he was concerned, it was just a formality. He'd been tied to her since the day their hands had been fastened together in Gretna Green.

When he finally got up to leave, Mia led him out of the office, stopping in front of the whiteboard. After an elbow nudge to his side, she leaned in and whispered, 'Red means you have a ride whenever you want it, hot shot.'

He put his hands on his sister's shoulders. 'I'm officially getting the hell out of the way, Pinky.'

Still, when he left her office and was almost out of earshot, he heard her say to herself, 'You'll be back, brother. You'll be back.'

He almost turned around and corrected her, but something in his bones kept him moving forward. In all honesty, he didn't have a clue what the future might hold. So, he walked away, leaving the feeling they both needed hanging in the air: Hope.

Pearl was in the kitchen, admiring her surprise for Jordan, when she heard the front door open. Seems she'd finished her project and shipped Di off for a spa weekend at a hotel downtown in the nick of time.

She'd fallen in love with the porcelain tiles at a local ceramics studio, especially when she found an entire run in their 'not perfect' room in a shade of mossy green. She'd spent an hour in the back room of the store, examining each piece, mostly guessing at the imperfections that had deemed it not fit for full price. It had been a waste of time because when she finished and saw the small stack of rejects, she felt bad leaving them behind and took them and their obvious flaws, too.

And then she didn't even banish them to the darkened corners of the room; she mixed the tiles back together and grabbed one after another. Because nothing's perfect, and this house – well, the old girl now played a role in a redemption story still in the making.

Demo had been far more difficult than she'd planned. But just as she'd been about to give up and wait three months for the professional installer to be available, the old tiles had begun to almost pop off the walls themselves, one right after another. Once she had a clean slate to work with, it had taken multiple trips to the local hardware store. More online videos and one pretty intense tile cutter later, she was in business.

But it had all been worth it.

'Surprise!' She turned toward Jordan, who was standing in the doorway. 'What do you think?'

'Beautiful.' Only instead of the backsplash, he was looking at her. 'So beautiful.'

Pearl's heart may have skipped a beat. 'Why are you looking at me like that?' she asked.

'Like what?' His voice was husky.

'Like you haven't seen me in a month.'

'It feels that way.' Jordan walked over to her and, after lightly pressing his lips to hers, whispered, 'I missed you,' before kissing her again. 'So much.'

Her heart definitely skipped a beat then.

'And I want to hear all about how this happened, when we clearly agreed that we weren't going to do any projects for a long time, and every hiccup you dealt with along the way.' He scooped her into his arms, 'but I have something I need to do first.'

'Whatever could that be?' she asked innocently when Jordan deposited her on the island and began closing all of the blinds in the room.

He paused in the front of the range, his eyes finally finding the reason she'd ended up in that local pottery to begin with. The handful of art tiles created a familiar scene. A field of

300

green. A few well-placed trees. Grazing sheep. And, front and center, a black sheep forever on its back.

He turned back to face her. 'I can't tell you how happy I am to see that it's managed to keep both of its eyes,' he said. 'Have I told you how much I love you today?'

'No, and I feel seriously neglected.' She patted the countertop next to her. 'Care to join me up here?'

She didn't have to ask twice.

'I wonder what happened to our sheep,' she wondered out loud an hour later. They were still lying on the island, spooning under a blanket Jordan had retrieved from the sofa. For granite, it was remarkably comfortable.

Pausing from lightly tracing an invisible path up and down her arm, Jordan nuzzled his face into her neck. 'Oh, I don't know. I like to think he realised he had been given a second chance and is living his best life. Maybe he channeled his inner chicken—'

'As one does,' Pearl interrupted. His smile was warm on her skin.

'As one does,' he said. 'Maybe there was a sheep he fancied and against all odds, they were able to make a go of it, settle down, get married, maybe have a few lambs in a couple of years.'

This sheep's life was getting very detailed. She'd honestly only expected to hear that it hadn't repeated whatever mistake had landed it on its back in the first place or maybe hadn't ended up as the main dish for someone's Sunday roast.

'I think a male sheep is a ram, actually,' she said absently.

Jordan grunted and shifted behind her before slipping off the island. Her body instantly missed his heat, but he was back and tucking her into his chest before she could ask where he'd gone.

'Sheep or ram, they've found their happily ever after,' he huffed, 'just like I have.'

Pearl rolled over so she could face him. 'Have you now?'

He hummed his answer when his lips pressed against hers. Under the blanket, his hand played with her left hand before sliding something on her ring finger.

Slowly, Pearl brought their hands from under the blanket to find the most beautiful ruby she'd ever seen, outside of the Rubie staring expectantly at her. The platinum band, lined in tiny diamonds, was a perfect fit. When her gaze finally shifted to Jordan, there were tears in his eyes.

After kissing her hand, he took a deep breath. 'Pearl, will you marry me and be mine?'

'Yes, Jordan,' she said, 'and I already am.'

Epilogue

Ten months later

The two pairs of eyes that looked up from their newspapers were filled with emotion – mostly pride and love. So much love.

'It's amazing,' said Jordan, his hand reaching across the table to grab Pearl's. 'I'm so proud of you.'

'Same here, kiddo,' echoed Carter. 'Same here.'

Even though they could've read her guest column online, Jordan had insisted they fly to New York City and get a copy of the newspaper 'hot off the presses.' So here they sat – a ragtag family Pearl couldn't have imagined 18 months ago – crammed into a booth at an all-night diner.

Only Di had read the piece before it was published. At first, like Jordan and Carter, she'd declined. But Pearl had been adamant that Di give her blessing – and Top's too – since the jewel sisters had starring roles in the piece she'd submitted on a whim to the renowned column about love and relationships. Although it was honest and Pearl's truth, it wasn't hers alone.

'What did I say?' Di asked from beside her. 'Not a thing to worry about.'

For a woman who'd worn a mask for years, she was taking the revealing of their long-held family secret with a remarkable amount of ease.

It had started with the stack of journals Di had given her at lunch that day. Reading through Top's teenage and college years had taken Pearl more than a month. Some days, she'd cried on already tear-stained pages; on others, she'd laughed at the absurdity of it all; always, she'd processed her feelings the same way the woman who'd given birth to her had.

Then, Di had gone to Wales and brought back all of the journals she could find stashed at the house in Abersoch, too. Those were another emotional minefield, especially the pages from the last months of Top's life. Pearl had read how Top had gone back and forth about telling Pearl the truth, weighing the pros and cons of unburdening herself in great detail. Apparently, her worst fear had been that Pearl would hate her – and, by default, Di – but one simple positive had far outweighed that and every other con.

'It's selfish, mayhaps,' Top had written. 'But I want my beautiful girl to know she's mine.'

When Pearl had turned the final page of Top's life, she realised what Jordan had told her so long ago in the beach hut rang true. Sometimes, there's no perfect way to set some things right.

Pearl had spent days contemplating how learning that Top

was her mother at another point in her life might've affected her. But each and every alternative led to the same conclusion – finding out about her past any other way, on any other day, would've changed her future.

This future.

With this man.

Pearl's thumb brushed the mother-of-pearl inlay on her husband's wedding band, as it had hundreds of times in the weeks since they'd purposely run off to Gretna Green. It had been just the two of them, which had caused quite a stir at the surprise wedding reception – until their family and friends had learned the reason behind their elopement.

Well, almost everyone had forgiven them.

'I can't believe you're having a baby before me,' Mia had said in the way one did when they'd lost some competition – as if she and Jordan had been in a weird race to produce the first Rubie Racing heir. But she'd quickly wiped away a few happy tears.

Getting pregnant absolutely had not been in the plan, but Pearl and Jordan had pushed the limits of modern contraception while traveling across the country to races on the Pinnacle circuit. Not to mention, they'd gotten a little lax as the season progressed and Jordan climbed the podium steps as he grew more skilled driving a different race car.

'You're going to be a great aunt,' Jordan had told his sister, his hands on her shoulders, 'and I'm sure my girls will have a cousin to play with in no time.'

'What'd you say, hot shot?' she'd sputtered.

His disclosure had earned him a punch in the arm and then a hug.

Yes, twins, two identical girls, who she and Jordan decidedly wouldn't be naming for jewels. They'd already be Rubies, just like their mother, who'd been unable to resist having a true gem as some part of her name.

At three months along, Pearl was more tired than anything else. So when she yawned, Jordan jumped up from the shiny wine vinyl booth seat.

'This was fun, but it's time to get my Pearl back to bed,' he said, grabbing the stack of newspapers he'd bought.

My Pearl. She liked that. Being his.

Di placed a hand on her arm. 'He's right. Disrupted sleep isn't good for you or the baby.'

Jordan nodded in agreement, as if they'd awoken from a deep sleep to meet the newspaper delivery truck. In reality, they'd been in bed but hadn't slept a wink. There was something else pregnancy was making her even more than tired.

Di got up, too, since she was staying at the same hotel, and Carter joined them after a last sip of his coffee. He gave Pearl a kiss on the forehead, followed by a long hug, which had become their parting routine.

'I'll see you for dinner at seven,' he said. 'Blake can't wait to celebrate.'

After never having a father, she'd somehow landed two and had grown to love them both.

'Can't wait,' she said, kissing him on the cheek. 'I'm so glad you're here, Dad.'

Carter smiled. 'Me, too.'

Once she and Jordan were back in their hotel room, Pearl collapsed into bed. Without a doubt, tiredness would win this round in the war of her wildly fluctuating hormones. Jordan climbed in after her.

'I love you,' he whispered, spooning her.

Pearl tucked her body deeper into his. 'You're okay with what I wrote about us?'

Although Jordan had given her carte blanche when it came to him and their relationship, she hadn't taken his trust in her lightly. But she'd revealed what was needed – from their chance meeting to his anxiety – to show how the Pearl of Wisdom had finally wised up.

'In case you haven't figured it out yet, Pearl Carrington Rubie, I love being part of your story,' he said, his hands going to her stomach. 'Considering all of the crashes I've been in over the years, I never once imagined I'd have an accident of the happy kind.'

'The happiest,' Pearl said, already dozing off – and dreaming about the next chapter they were writing, together.

A Note from the Author

Racing Heart is a work of fiction. Neither the World Apex Grand Prix Motorsport Series nor Pinnacle exists in the real world, so they don't follow real-world racing rules. If they did, many facets of this book wouldn't be possible. Likewise, racing teams are complex organizations with many more roles and dedicated people filling them than possible on these pages.

Acknowledgements

Behind every author are people who hear about little else than the fictional world their friend is creating for months on end. A huge thank you to Sandhya Krishan, Camille Pagán, Patti Smith, Jodi Helmer, Lauren Faulkenberry, Michele Leopold, Nicki Rought, and Jo Linwood-Barnes for being my village. You mean the world to me.

Thank you to developmental editor Jacquelin Cangro for helping shape the first draft of *Racing Heart*, and to Rebecca Weigler and Carolyn Mays at Bedford Square Publishers whose insightful editing carried it home. To cover designer and illustrator Mary Ann Smith, thank you for creating the cutest sheep on the planet.

And to my husband, Michael, thank you for inventing the 'Tell me something about you I don't know' game on our first date. I'm so grateful we're still playing 16 years later. I love you more.

ABOUT THE AUTHOR

Image Credit © Mark Bennington

Darci St. John grew up sneaking her mother's romance novels and reading them late into the night. Her love of motorsport began when she went to an IndyCar race with a new boyfriend – and then she fell in love with him, too. Now married, they travel to races together around the world. A longtime writer and editor, St. John lives in Michigan with her husband and rescue pup.

www.darcistjohn.com
🅞 **@darcistjohnwriter**

Bedford Square Publishers

Bedford Square Publishers is an independent publisher of fiction and non-fiction, founded in 2022 in the historic streets of Bedford Square London and the sea mist shrouded green of Bedford Square Brighton.

Our goal is to discover irresistible stories and voices that illuminate our world.

We are passionate about connecting our authors to readers across the globe and our independence allows us to do this in original and nimble ways.

The team at Bedford Square Publishers has years of experience and we aim to use that knowledge and creative insight, alongside evolving technology, to reach the right readers for our books. From the ones who read a lot, to the ones who don't consider themselves readers, we aim to find those who will love our books and talk about them as much as we do.

We are hunting for vital new voices from all backgrounds – with books that take the reader to new places and transform perceptions of the world we live in.

Follow us on social media for the latest Bedford Square Publishers news.

🐦 @bedsqpublishers
ⓕ facebook.com/bedfordsq.publishers/
🄾 @bedfordsq.publishers

https://bedfordsquarepublishers.co.uk/